MW00475233

PATCHWORK
QUILT
MURDER

Books by Leslie Meier

MISTLETOE MURDER
TIPPY TOE MURDER
TRICK OR TREAT MURDER
BACK TO SCHOOL MURDER
VALENTINE MURDER
CHRISTMAS COOKIE MURDER
TURKEY DAY MURDER
WEDDING DAY MURDER
BIRTHDAY PARTY MURDER
FATHER'S DAY MURDER
STAR SPANGLED MURDER
NEW YEAR'S EVE MURDER
BAKE SALE MURDER
CANDY CANE MURDER
ST. PATRICK'S DAY MURDER
MOTHER'S DAY MURDER
WICKED WITCH MURDER
GINGERBREAD COOKIE MURDER
ENGLISH TEA MURDER
CHOCOLATE COVERED MURDER
EASTER BUNNY MURDER
CHRISTMAS CAROL MURDER
FRENCH PASTRY MURDER
CANDY CORN MURDER
BRITISH MANOR MURDER
EGGNOG MURDER
TURKEY TROT MURDER
SILVER ANNIVERSARY MURDER
YULE LOG MURDER
HAUNTED HOUSE MURDER
INVITATION ONLY MURDER
CHRISTMAS SWEETS
CHRISTMAS CARD MURDER
IRISH PARADE MURDER
HALLOWEEN PARTY MURDER
EASTER BONNET MURDER
IRISH COFFEE MURDER
MOTHER OF THE BRIDE MURDER
EASTER BASKET MURDER
PATCHWORK QUILT MURDER

Published by Kensington Publishing Corp.

A Lucy Stone Mystery

PATCHWORK QUILT MURDER

LESLIE MEIER

Kensington Publishing Corp.
www.kensingtonbooks.com

KENSINGTON BOOKS are published by

Kensington Publishing Corp.
900 Third Ave.
New York, NY 10022

All Kensington titles, imprints, and distributed lines are available at special quantity discounts for bulk purchases for sales promotion, premiums, fund-raising, educational, or institutional use. Special book excerpts or customized printings can also be created to fit specific needs. For details, write or phone the office of the Kensington Special Sales Manager: Attn. Special Sales Department. Kensington Publishing Corp., 900 Third Avenue, New York, NY 10022. Phone: 1-800-221-2647.

KENSINGTON and the KENSINGTON COZIES teapot logo Reg. US Pat. & TM Off.

Library of Congress Control Number: 2023951837

ISBN: 978-1-4967-3379-5
First Kensington Hardcover Edition: May 2024

ISBN: 978-1-4967-3381-8 (ebook)

10 9 8 7 6 5 4 3 2 1

Printed in the United States of America

For Mommy
Who taught me to sew

Chapter One

"How is Tim doing?"

The question hung in the heavy air as a ruby-throated hummingbird zeroed in on a pot of red nasturtiums perched on Rachel Goodman's porch railing. Wings a blur, the tiny bird hovered momentarily above the flowers, sampled a few, and then zoomed away.

"They're miraculous, aren't they?" observed Lucy Stone, who was enjoying a morning off from her job as reporter and feature writer for the weekly *Courier* newspaper in Tinker's Cove, Maine.

"Where do they get the energy?" wondered Sue Finch, who was reclining on a brightly cushioned wicker chaise, her trim ankles neatly crossed. Sue adored everything French and was wearing a black-and-white-striped fisherman's jersey, Nantucket red shorts, and black espadrilles.

"Especially in this heat," offered Pam Stillings, fanning herself with today's issue of the *Courier*, the weekly paper that she owned with her husband Ted, who was editor, publisher, chief reporter, and Lucy's boss. Pam had been a cheerleader in high school and had retained her ponytail and her high spirits into adulthood, but lately she'd been worried about her adult son Tim, who had given her a terrible scare when he'd nearly died in what appeared to be a failed suicide attempt.

The four friends had gathered on Rachel's porch in lieu of their usual gathering spot, Jake's Donut Shack. The Shack, as it was known in Tinker's Cove, was not air-conditioned, so the friends had eagerly accepted Rachel's offer of iced coffee and blueberry muffins on her shady porch, which was filled with cushioned wicker furniture. Not that the shade really offered much relief from this August heat wave that had settled on the entire Northeast.

"Not even a sea breeze," complained Sue.

"We're getting off the track here," complained Rachel, who had majored in psychology and never got over it. "I want to know how Tim's recovery is going."

The four friends had been gathering for breakfast on Thursday mornings for years, ever since they realized how much they missed meeting each other at school and sporting events after their kids had all flown their nests. But now one of the fledglings had returned home. Pam's son, Tim, had seemed, like the other kids, to have a bright future when he graduated from Tinker's Cove High School. He majored in art history at the University of Maine, moved on to Yale for his master's, and snagged a great job as a junior curator at the Farnsworth Museum in Rockland, Maine. He was soon promoted to curator of special exhibits and seemed to be embarking on a brilliant career. And Rockland was a great little city for a young man starting out, with a vibrant arts scene, great shops and restaurants, and a bustling seaport.

But something had gone very wrong for Tim, who was found floating, unconscious and near death, off Rockland's big stone jetty on a cool June night. At first, it was thought he had slipped into the chilly water accidentally, but he later admitted to first responders that he had been deeply depressed and had attempted to drown himself. His parents, Pam and Ted, were notified and rushed to Rockland, where they discovered that mental-health facilities were sorely lacking. Tim was given medications to control his depression, but the hospital psychiatrist warned his parents that he should not be left alone. So Tim took a leave from his job at the museum and returned to Tinker's Cove, under the care of his parents. Pam spent days on the phone looking for treatment options but only managed to arrange weekly sessions with a therapist-led support group.

Tim had now been back home for almost two months, during which he had been a constant source of anxiety to his parents and their friends. So Rachel's question hung in the air as all three mothers waited to learn how Tim was doing.

Pam smiled. "I think we're finally making some progress," she said. "He's got a job."

"That's great!" enthused Lucy. Sue chimed right in, exclaiming, "Fabulous!" Even Rachel approved, saying, "That's a real sign of progress."

"It's not a great job," continued Pam. "It's part-time, at the new community center."

"Is he the new director?" asked Lucy, who covered the various committees that governed Tinker's Cove under the watchful eyes of the citizens. She knew the Personnel Committee had concluded their search and were about to announce their choice at tonight's meeting.

"He's not going to be the director," said Pam, shaking her head. "He's going to be the janitor."

There was a pause, as the women considered this unexpected turn of events, finally broken by Sue. "What happened to his job at the Farnsworth?" she asked.

"They said they couldn't hold it any longer," said Pam.

"And he didn't want it anymore, didn't want to go back. Didn't think he could handle it."

"Baby steps," said Lucy, in an encouraging tone. "He needs to go slow, feel his way. This is probably a good job for him now."

"Right," added Rachel. "It's an important step in his recovery. He'll gain confidence; he'll be working with other people; he'll even earn some money and become more independent."

Pam was having none of it. "He has a master's degree from Yale; he was a curator at a top museum; and now he's mopping floors and emptying the trash." She picked at her muffin. "I don't know, it's as if he thinks he doesn't deserve a better job, like he's punishing himself for . . ." She abandoned the muffin and waved her hand in a gesture of surrender. "I don't know what's going on in that head of his. I know he's suffering, and I don't know why." She raised her head. "But I do know that my son is too talented, too smart, to be a janitor."

Rachel reached out and patted her hand. "I think you have to let him decide what he needs."

"There's no shame in an honest job," said Sue, surprising them all. Sue, who only wore designer labels and treasured her status handbags, was all of a sudden defending the proletariat. "A job is what you make it, and I bet Tim will be a terrific, top-notch janitor!"

"Somehow I'm not finding that thought encouraging," said Pam. "Not at all."

A few days later, Lucy went to the brand-new community center to interview the woman who had got the job of director and to gather information so she could write a preview of the upcoming grand opening. The heat wave had continued unabated, and the spindly new baby trees didn't offer any shade in the oversized parking lot that surrounded the new building, a modernistic creation of steel and glass that glittered in the sun. The humidity was oppressive as she forged her way across the hot asphalt parking lot, and she felt like a steamed dumpling when she stepped inside, where she was greeted with a surge of refreshing cool air.

Feeling slightly guilty, aware that the air-conditioning, which offered relief from climbing temperatures, was actually contributing to global warming, she nevertheless enjoyed the cooling sensation. She could practically feel the perspiration evaporating from her skin as she took in the gleaming lobby, where a colorful mosaic mural greeted all who entered with the word WELCOME in various languages. A sign with extra-large, ADA-approved letters gave directions to the various facilities, which she knew included a gym, meeting rooms, and offices for the town's Council on Aging and its Recreation Department. There was no sign of Tim, but she was greeted enthusiastically by the director, Darleen Busby-Pratt, who had clearly been on the lookout for her arrival and came bustling into the lobby.

"Welcome! Welcome to our beautiful new community center!" exclaimed Darleen, who was a very tall and slightly plump middle-aged woman with rather obviously dyed hair and a carefully powdered face. She'd used lip liner with her lipstick, and it gave her mouth a rather harsh appearance, in line with the stenciled arches that served as her eyebrows. Lucy found her perfume a bit overwhelming but noted she had adopted the coastal-casual look favored in Tinker's Cove and was wearing blue-and-white-checked pedal pushers, tan boat shoes, and a light blue polo shirt. Plenty of heavy gold jewelry in the form of chains and bangles was a somewhat unusual addition, not quite appropriate to the sporty outfit. "You must be Lucy, from the paper! I've been expecting you!"

"Thanks for meeting with me," said Lucy, which was how she usually began interviews. "How are you finding Tinker's Cove?" she asked, opening her notebook. "Are you settling in?"

"Oh, it's a homecoming for me," said Darleen, with a big smile that revealed rather too perfect teeth. Implants or dentures? wondered Lucy. "I grew up here, you know. In fact, I applied for this job so I could be closer to my mother. She doesn't really need a great deal of care, not yet, but she's not getting any younger and . . ."

"Do I know her?" interrupted Lucy, raising her pen.

"Millicent Busby. She's in the old homestead over on Aunt Lydia's Path."

"Oh, yes. I think she's friends with Miss Tilley?"

"Ah, yes." Darleen was beaming. "They're quite close. My mother is actually allowed to call her by her first name."

Lucy was impressed. She knew that Miss Julia Ward Howe Tilley only allowed her nearest and dearest to use her first name. Lucy had enjoyed a long friendship with Miss Tilley and suspected she might be among that group but wasn't about to test the theory. She'd noticed that, even though Darleen had an impeccable pedigree as the daughter of a local notable, she hadn't claimed that special relationship with Miss Tilley. Somewhat ashamed that she found that thought comforting, Lucy suggested a tour of the new building, which she knew had been quite controversial. While the center had its supporters, not everyone in town saw the need for a community center, especially not one that cost millions of taxpayer dollars.

"Of course," agreed Darleen. "This is a building the community can be very proud of. It serves the needs of all age groups, from moms and babies' playgroups all the way on up to the lunch program for seniors."

"And it's air-conditioned," offered Lucy, "which is quite a relief considering this heat wave we're having."

"Exactly," agreed Darleen, leading the way down the hall to the gym. "I believe the Council on Aging is planning to open a cooling center so seniors can get some relief. It's a well-known fact that, as we age, our ability to regulate our temperature declines. Heat stroke is a real danger for seniors. But first," she pulled open one of a pair of heavy doors, "this is our gym!"

Lucy stepped inside and discovered that gyms hadn't changed much since her college days, being composed of cinder-block walls, wood floors, and retractable bleachers. "And what sort of activities will take place here?"

"Quite a variety. Basketball, yoga, Jazzercise, to mention a few. And the space can also be used for community events like art exhibits and antiques sales—all kinds of things. Community organizations only have to ask and we'll find space on the calendar, which is already filling up, I might add. In fact"—Darleen paused for emphasis— "we're going to have a quilt show in this very space as part of the grand opening."

"A quilt show..." Lucy was busily scribbling this down. "Sewn by local crafters?"

"Indeed. And it will feature a rare Civil War quilt actually sewn by Tinker's Cove women as part of a national effort to provide comfort for wounded Union soldiers. Imagine that! It's over a hundred and fifty years old!"

In spite of herself, Lucy was impressed. Darleen seemed to be starting off with a bang, and she was eager to hear what she had planned for the rest of the center. Apparently able to read her mind, Darleen led the way to the door. "But there's lots more to see," she said, continuing the tour.

Lucy followed along, viewing meeting rooms intended for various community groups, such as scouts and social clubs; a large multipurpose room set up with tables for the senior lunch program; the well-equipped commercial-grade kitchen that would serve the lunch program as well as fundraisers like Saturday night frank-and-bean dinners; and offices for town departments squeezed out of the crowded town hall. "This is my office," said Darleen, indicating an open door. Peeking inside, Lucy saw standard-issue office furniture, but no personal touches except a rather sad African violet on the windowsill.

Lucy gave her a knowing smile. "I see you have an open-door policy?"

"Absolutely!" declared Darleen. "You can write that in capital letters. I know this center is a big investment for the town, and I want everyone to know that they are welcome here. I hope everyone will come to the grand opening, and that they will continue to come and enjoy all the amazing programs our wonderful community center has to offer." She leaned forward. "Did you get all that down?"

Lucy chuckled. "I did. And I must say, I think you're off to a great start."

Darleen exhaled and spoke in a low voice. "I hope so. I know there's been controversy; not everyone is on board, but I'm going to do my best to win them over. This center is a good thing for Tinker's Cove."

"Well, thanks for your time," said Lucy, checking her watch and discovering she was late for a planning committee meeting. "I've got to run . . . is there a restroom I can use?"

"Of course. Just down the hall."

"Thanks again," said Lucy, wasting no time to deal with what had become a matter of urgency.

Accustomed as she was to the cramped and makeshift facilities in most town buildings—rust-stained sinks and toilets with handwritten signs that instructed users to jiggle the handle—Lucy was dazzled by the modern ladies' room. The light turned on automatically as she entered; she was greeted with a generous row of stalls, including one designated as handicapped, and was startled when she rose from the commode and it flushed automatically. The sinks on the opposing wall, arrayed beneath a huge mirror, all had soap dispensers and faucets that turned on with a wave of the hand, as did the paper-towel dispenser. She knew such restrooms existed, of course she did, but this was definitely a first for a municipal building in Tinker's Cove, and she couldn't help being impressed. As far as she was concerned, the restroom alone was well worth the million-dollar-plus price tag.

Enjoying the air-conditioning and reluctant to leave, she took a moment to pause at the glass doors, where she studied the heat waves shimmering above the asphalt in the parking lot. She decided she really needed to get a move on, and as she was pushing the exit bar on the door, a familiar voice caught her attention. It was Darleen, but her tone had definitely changed. Now she was speaking in a strident tone, scolding someone.

Lucy turned and was shocked to see that someone was Tim Stillings, dressed in a navy-blue uniform and equipped with a rolling bucket and a mop. She was about to greet him, but Darleen spoke first, waggling a finger in Tim's face.

"About time you showed up! You're late!"

"I wasn't late," mumbled Tim, taking a step backward. "I was on time, but I saw some litter in the parking lot and picked it up."

Darleen was waving a cardboard time card. "According to the time card, you're not here at all. You haven't even punched in."

Tim was studying the floor, which didn't seem in need of mopping. "Like I said, I picked up the papers and stuff in the parking lot."

"Well, you're not going to get paid for that, because you haven't clocked in."

Tim shrugged. "That's okay."

"It's not okay. First thing, when you get here, you clock in. That's how you get paid. Haven't you ever had a job?"

"Not one where I had to clock in," admitted Tim. "This is only my second day. I'll try to remember."

"You do that. And I expect to see this floor polished to a shine. We've got a grand opening coming up this weekend, you know."

"Uh, where exactly is this time clock punch-in thing?"

Exasperated, Darleen shook her head. "Didn't they show you when they hired you?"

Tim brushed his shaggy hair out of his eyes. "Nope."

"Well, follow me," she ordered, stomping off.

"*Sieg heil*," muttered Tim, which did not go unnoticed by Darleen. She whirled about, her face bright red, and screamed at him.

"You better watch your mouth! You can't talk to me like that! I'm in charge here, and I expect an apology!"

"Uh, sorry," said Tim, once again staring at the floor. "I didn't mean anything."

"You better watch your step, young man, or you won't be doing any stepping around here!" Darleen turned on her heel and marched off in the direction of her office, leaving Tim standing in the lobby. Noticing Lucy, he smiled at her. "Hi, Mrs. Stone."

"Hi, Tim. Everything okay?"

He shrugged. "I guess so. I still don't know where that time-clock thing is."

"Is there a break room or a locker room?"

He brightened. "Yeah."

"I bet it's there," said Lucy, who knew only too well she was running late herself. "I gotta go; I'm supposed to be covering a meeting." She gave him a smile. "Have a nice day."

"Sure," he said, ambling off. But as she watched him make his leisurely way across the lobby, she wondered if this job was going to work out. And he wasn't the only employee who didn't seem fit for the job. Darleen, it seemed, wasn't quite the polished professional her résumé indicated, nor the sensitive administrator the community center required if it was going to be a success.

Chapter Two

When the weekend rolled around, Lucy found herself joining the throng of townsfolk who had eagerly anticipated the grand opening of the community center. There was a happy buzz as arriving folks enjoyed the air-conditioning, which offered welcome relief from the continuing heat wave that was breaking records throughout the Northeast. They were met in the lobby by Darleen herself, smiling and encouraging everyone to fill out a name tag and take an information packet that included a diagram of the center and a calendar of upcoming events.

"Ah, Lucy," she cooed, "thank you for coming. And thank you for the terrific article in the paper." In honor of the occasion, she'd added more heavy gold jewelry, albeit of a nautical design featuring anchors, compass roses, and sailor's knots, to the white jeans and navy tee she'd topped with a sheer, flowing blue-and-white duster sort of garment.

"Just doing my job," said Lucy, looking around for Tim but failing to find him.

"Don't be modest," instructed Darleen, jangling those golden bangles. "I think you are largely responsible for this amazing turnout."

"I think you'll find that folks in Tinker's Cove are very interested in how their tax dollars are spent," said Lucy, who knew only too well that a small but vocal group of townsfolk were staunchly opposed to anything that would increase taxes, including the community center.

"Well, I plan to give them good value," promised Darleen. "Don't miss the quilt show."

"Wouldn't dream of it," said Lucy, spotting the sign pointing down the hall to the gym, where the exhibit was displayed. It was an impressive show, she realized, when she stepped inside and discovered a maze of temporary screens hung with a dazzling array of colorful quilts of all sizes. She was studying the first and oldest specimen, a red cotton coverlet worked entirely in tiny stitches that created a design of leaves and flowers. "It was made in 1725," said Pam, joining her. "It's amazing! It isn't even faded!"

"It's beautiful," said Lucy, awestruck by the complexity of the design and the thousands, maybe millions of stitches it contained. "Who made it? How ever did she find the time? And how did they keep it in such good condition for over three hundred years?"

"Doesn't say, just that it was passed down in the Hunsaker family, probably made by Felicity Warren Hunsaker," offered Pam, who was studying the label. "It's been dated and authenticated by the Smithsonian, however."

"Just look around at all these gorgeous works of art," urged Lucy, who was dazzled by the number and variety of quilts on display. "I can't even be bothered to replace a button," she admitted, guiltily.

Pam laughed. "We're not all needlewomen, that's for sure. Though I have done a bit of sewing in my time. I made clothes for my dolls when I was a kid, and I made a crib quilt for Tim when I was pregnant."

"Do you still have it?"

"Maybe," said Pam, with a shrug and a toss of her ponytail. "It's probably tucked away somewhere, saved for a possible grandchild." Her voice dropped. "Though that seems less likely now."

Lucy took her hand. "This is a hard time, I know, but someday you'll be looking back, and it will seem like a blip on the screen. A little hiccup."

"I hope you're right, Lucy," said Pam. "But right now it's"—she paused and blinked back tears—"it's really awfully hard."

Lucy gave Pam's shoulders a squeeze. "C'mon, let's find this famous Civil War quilt Darleen's been bragging about."

They continued past a number of quilts in various designs—traditional ones like log cabin, flying geese, and flower basket, as well as modern designs featuring large blocks of color, including a bold Gee's Bend quilt—then turned a corner and saw a rather drab and tired-looking specimen that most viewers were simply glancing at before moving on. But Lucy recognized the woman standing in front of it as Darleen's mother, Millicent Busby, who was trying to engage the uninterested observers in conversation. She was a small, round woman with a head of tightly curled white hair, shrewd eyes, and a disapproving frown, a frown that Lucy conceded might not be signaling disapproval as much as sagging skin. Lucy knew Miss Tilley tolerated no fools, and the fact that she and Millicent were good friends seemed to indicate that Millicent was sharper than her advanced age might lead one to expect.

"Hi," began Lucy, introducing herself and Pam. "I understand this is a very special quilt?"

"Oh, yes, Lucy," she said, brightening up. "You're our local girl reporter, aren't you?"

"Guilty," admitted Lucy. "So what can you tell me about this quilt?"

"Well, it's one of only fifteen quilts that have survived from the thousands that were made in the North and sent to Union hospitals."

Lucy gave the sad old specimen a second look. "Who made them?"

"All sorts of people. Church groups, sewing circles, families. The Sanitary Commission—that's the organization that ran the hospitals—sent out a call for the quilts. They were made to certain specifications, long and narrow to fit the hospital beds."

Studying the quilt, once white but now marred with brown stains, dotted here and there with faded patches of blue and red appliqués and remnants of embroidery, Lucy could imagine the folks left at home. They would be worrying about their sons and husbands as they stitched away and did what they could to aid the war effort and comfort the sick and wounded. They would hope that if their soldier brother, son, or husband became a casualty, he would be warmed, if not by their quilt, by one made by others.

"Only a few have survived," continued Millicent. "Some, as you can imagine, were soiled beyond saving, or even contaminated, and had to be burned. If a soldier was sent home with his quilt, chances are his womenfolk decided it was too shabby to keep. Maybe it was used for a dog bed, or a horse blanket, and was probably eventually ripped into rags."

"So how did this quilt survive?" asked Pam.

"It's quite a story," said Millicent, pleased as punch to share a bit of family history. "As you can see"—she pointed

to a faded bit of spidery handwriting on one of the squares—
"the women who made the quilt signed it. It's hard to see
now, but when it was new all the names were included, as
well as the town, Tinker's Cove. The people who made the
quilts did this a lot; they even included patriotic symbols
and encouraging words, to cheer the soldiers and let them
know they were not forgotten.

"And sometimes, the recovering soldiers actually wrote
letters of thanks to the people who made the quilts. That's
what happened with this quilt, when a wounded soldier
named George Busby whiled away his time in the hospital
writing letters. One of the quilt makers, Susan Hawkins,
responded, and the two struck up a correspondence, which
they continued throughout the war. When it ended, George
came to Tinker's Cove to meet Susan, and the two eventually married. And down through the generations, the family continued to treasure the quilt that brought the two
together."

"What a great story!" exclaimed Lucy.

"I think so," said Millicent. "And I know this quilt isn't
much to look at, but it's very dear to me." She paused. "As
are all the precious little bits and pieces that have come
down to me through my family. The Hawkinses were
among the first families that settled here in Tinker's Cove
over three hundred years ago!"

Lucy tucked that little bit of information away, thinking
Millicent might be a good subject for a feature story. But
first, it seemed, everyone was leaving the gym and gathering in the lobby for the official opening of the center. As
Lucy and Pam joined the throng, one quilt that they
passed caught Pam's eye. She grabbed Lucy's arm, and the
two paused to admire this portrait of a young black man
standing beside a bright red Ford Mustang. The entire

image was composed of hundreds of tiny cloth hexagons. The man's name was Darrel Anderson, and his story, about how the car was his pride and joy but had led to his death when he was shot by police during a traffic stop, was embroidered in the quilt's border. "Wow, that's a different sort of quilt," said Pam.

"A protest quilt," said Lucy.

Pam shook her head. "Imagine the love that went into it," she said, sadly. "It's really moving."

"So it is," agreed Lucy, somewhat impatiently. "We'd better get going; I've got to cover the official speeches."

When they joined the crowd in the lobby, Lucy immediately noticed that Franny Small, the select chairperson, had pulled out all the stops for the occasion and was wearing a floral shift dress and a pair of heels, if only low ones on a pair of sensible pumps. Franny was usually seen around town in comfy track suits, which gave no indication that she was actually the town's richest resident. Franny was a pioneer who had smashed the glass ceiling, not only as the first woman to head the town's board of selectpersons, but as an entrepreneur who had grown a little side hustle making jewelry out of bits and pieces of hardware into a highly successful corporation that she had recently sold for millions of dollars.

Taking her place at a podium, Franny tapped the mic, prompting the gathered townsfolk to stop chatting and pay attention. "We are gathered here today to celebrate a major achievement in our town," she began. "This beautiful building, this amazing community center, will provide much-needed space for our citizens to gather, to recreate, to create. So, first, I would like to thank the members of the Community-development Committee, who are responsible for turning what had long been a dream into reality.

Will you please come forward?" she said, inviting the committee members to join her.

Naming each person, she presented them with framed certificates of recognition, as well as small bouquets of flowers. She then called for a round of applause, which was generously offered, along with some grumbles from a few discontented citizens.

Franny ignored the dissenters and moved right along to introduce Darleen as the director of the community center, inviting her to deliver a few comments.

"Thank you, thank you, Madam Chairperson," Darleen began, after bustling up to the podium, her filmy topper an incongruous note in contrast to her substantial self. Somewhat surprisingly, Lucy noticed her open-toed wedgies revealed the flesh-colored Peds she was wearing underneath them.

Lucy found herself staring at those toes, wondering if those little mini-socks were even still available. Where would you find them? And why? Then, recalling herself to the matter at hand, she began scribbling down Darleen's comments in her reporter's notebook.

"This is a wonderful day for our town," proclaimed Darleen, "and it's just the beginning. I noticed how much you all seem to be enjoying the quilt show, and it is just the first of many exciting exhibits and other programs that will take place here in our beautiful, air-conditioned building . . ."

"Whadda we need air-conditioning for?" demanded a strident male voice. Lucy turned to see who was speaking and recognized a local character known as Wild Willy. Willy, who sported a long gray beard and thrift-shop clothes, was reputed to live somewhere out in the woods outside town, subsisting on a diet of foraged food. "It's a vicious cycle! Air-conditioning increases global warming, which requires more air-conditioning! Why not open the windows and let the fresh breezes blow in?"

This caused a varied reaction among the crowd. Some people chuckled indulgently, some shook their heads in disgust, and quite a goodly number nodded their heads in agreement.

"Uh, well," stammered Darleen, "getting back to the upcoming events, you will see that we are having a workshop on native plants that do not require fertilizer or watering and are therefore better for the environment . . ."

"We're gonna need more than pretty plants," declared Willy. "We've got a ticking time bomb here! The planet's heating up, and it's gonna go boom!"

Sensing that things were getting out of hand, Franny reclaimed the podium. "Thank you so much, Darleen, for that introduction. And now," she said, "I declare this community center officially open." She banged down her gavel and quickly added, "Refreshments will be served in the multipurpose room. Follow the signs."

A masterful stroke, thought Lucy, as the crowd surged down the hallway toward the promised refreshments. She looked about for Willy, hoping to interview him, but he was gone. She joined the crowd instead, chatting up people as she went and asking what they thought of the center.

"A long time coming, and much needed," said youth soccer coach Lori Cavanaugh. "Now we'll have a place for year-round training and practices."

"Waste of taxpayer dollars, if you ask me," grumbled Fred Gunderson, who always sported a plaid shirt and red suspenders. "Don't see what we need it for, and the upkeep, that's gonna cost a pretty penny."

"Right," agreed Mrs. Gunderson, a tiny bird of a woman who was quivering with indignation. "I've heard that Darleen woman is getting paid over a hundred thousand dollars a year! They say she wouldn't take the job for a penny less."

"I'll have to look into that," promised Lucy. "But don't you think the center will be a real asset to the town?"

Both Mr. and Mrs. Gunderson shook their heads, but Tony Marzetti, a selectman who also owned the local supermarket, was eager to express his approval. "This building is a real turning point for the town," he said. "It's going to give people a place to get together; it's going to provide services for seniors and kids, even for dogs and cats. I see a rabies clinic is scheduled for September. Imagine that! Shots for ten dollars, saves folks from those expensive vet visits. I tell you, the people who are grumbling loudest about the price of the center are going to be the first to sign up for the senior lunch program, and the yoga classes, and everything else. Mark my words."

Entering the multipurpose room, Lucy saw that Tony definitely had a point. The Gundersons, as well as everyone else, were eagerly helping themselves to cookies and lemonade, grabbing ice cream cups, and stuffing free tote bags with even more freebies like refrigerator magnets offered by the police and fire departments, reusable bottles from the Water Department, tree seedlings from the Natural Resources Department, and floating lobster key chains from the fishermen's cooperative.

The feeding frenzy finally subsided, and Lucy had decided to leave when she reconnected with Pam, who had the same idea. "I wish I could stay in here all day," said Pam, pausing at the door. "It's going to be hot, hot, hot out there."

"Me, too," said Lucy, with a nod. "But your husband wants me to post this story on the online edition ASAP, and I'm quoting him."

Pam laughed. "Sounds like Ted."

Together, they stepped outside, encountering a blast of overheated air. "You know, I'm getting sick of all this sunshine," complained Pam. "Remember fog?"

"Fondly," said Lucy. "Lovely, lovely fog. Cool and wet, sticking to your skin. It was great."

"No, it wasn't," laughed Pam. "Just goes to show we're never happy. We always want the opposite of what we've got."

The two women had reached the parking lot. "It's back to the office for me, but at least I've got Sunday off," said Lucy. "Unless there's breaking news."

"And home for me," said Pam, not very enthusiastic. "I never know what I'm walking into these days."

"How is Tim?" asked Lucy, who wanted to know but was hesitant to raise the subject.

Pam shrugged. "It's hard to tell. I think his recovery has kind of stalled. I'm not seeing much progress, but, unlike Rachel, I don't have a degree in psychology."

Lucy recalled how Darleen had scolded Tim and wondered if Tim had mentioned it to his mother. "How does he like his job?" she asked.

Pam gave a resigned shrug. "I wouldn't know. He doesn't really talk to me." She paused. "You know, that Darrel Anderson portrait quilt gave me an idea. I've been clearing out some closets, and I've found lots of Tim's outgrown clothes, even his Cub Scout uniform. There's old sports team and camp T-shirts, even a pair of favorite Star Wars pajamas. I could use them to make a quilt for him, a quilt that tells the story of his life. What do you think about that?"

"I think it's a good idea," said Lucy. "Maybe you could even involve him somehow?"

Pam's eyebrows shot up. "Sewing?"

"Probably not," admitted Lucy. "But in designing it, arranging the bits and pieces. A little trip down memory lane might bolster his sense of identity, boost his self-esteem, and get him to open up a bit."

Pam reached out and took her hand. "Lucy, I think you're on to something. A quilt is more than a quilt. It's a statement of self-expression."

"And comfort, even love. Like that Civil War quilt. A way of saying, you're important, you matter, I'm thinking of you."

Pam laughed. "A warm hug, to get him through the winter. If it ever comes."

Chapter Three

Ted had liked Lucy's suggestion that she follow up the community center story with a feature on the Civil War quilt, and she had made arrangements to interview Millicent Busby at her home on Aunt Lydia's Path. Millicent had eagerly agreed to the interview, promising to give Lucy an up-close look at the quilt as well as her many other treasures. She also informed Lucy that she was an early riser who was at her best in the morning, so Lucy had agreed to meet her at seven a.m., which turned out to be unwise. While Lucy was also an early riser, she was a slow starter, and she had barely finished her first cup of coffee when she checked the clock and discovered it was already a quarter to seven. Dashing back upstairs, she brushed her teeth, ran a comb through her hair, and tossed on yesterday's clothes, which she'd left, the night before, on the bedroom chair.

On her way to the door she checked the dog's water, which was fine, but also noticed the aged black Lab hadn't touched the breakfast Bill had given her. Glancing at Libby, she noticed she was lying with her chin on her paws and wasn't about to get to her feet to give Lucy her usual tail wag of a goodbye.

"Too hot for you, girl?" she asked.

Libby opened one eye and gave a big sigh.

"Not feeling great?"

Libby's eyes were both closed; she'd apparently gone to sleep.

Stepping out on the porch, Lucy decided she'd better check with the vet and called for an appointment as she hurried to the car. She was in luck and had booked an afternoon appointment before she backed out of the drive.

Millicent was every bit the morning person she had claimed to be, as Lucy discovered when she was enthusiastically welcomed into her home, which, quite surprisingly, was air-conditioned. Lucy wasn't about to question this modern convenience; she was happy to enjoy a brief respite from the heat that was building outside. This was one of the big old antique houses dating from the 1700s that were dotted through Tinker's Cove, although with many ells and additions added through the years. In the dining room, Millicent had coffee and freshly baked muffins, served on lovely blue-and-white Canton china, waiting. Lucy accepted the muffins gratefully since she'd skipped breakfast.

Lucy knew that antique Canton dinnerware, which had been brought from China in clipper ships in the days of sail, was rare and valuable. She admired its softly tinted, hand-painted scenes, which included a bridge, a pagoda, and a willow tree, and took careful sips as Millicent produced faded and fuzzy daguerreotype pictures of Susan Hawkins and George Busby. Susan had her hair smoothed back in a bun and was wearing a tightly bodiced dress with a huge hoopskirt; the crossed ends of a bit of ribbon around her neck were fastened with a cameo brooch. George, of course, was in his Union officer's uniform, complete with sword, sash, and waxed mustache.

"Quite a dashing fellow," observed Lucy, carefully replacing her cup on its saucer.

Millicent smiled. "Brave, too. He was wounded at Bull Run, leading a charge."

"Did they have many children?" asked Lucy.

"Eight, but only five survived, of which my great-great-grandfather was one." Out came another photograph, this one picturing a small boy in a Little Lord Fauntleroy suit, holding a hoop.

"Your great-great-grandfather?" cooed Lucy, amazed. She had no idea what any of her double-greats looked like and had seen only a few faded photos of two of her great-grandparents. "How did all these bits and pieces from the past survive?"

"Well, we never moved. There have been Hawkinses and Busbys in this house for hundreds of years, and the attic is quite large. They never threw anything out."

Lucy had a disturbing thought and posed her question carefully. "I hesitate to ask, but readers will wonder why your name is still Busby. Did you never marry?"

"Of course I was married; I had a child," offered Millicent, as if one had to be married in order to reproduce. "I married a cousin, so my maiden name and my married name are the same."

Lucy was still puzzled. "I didn't know cousins could marry."

"My late husband, Winslow, was a second cousin. There are lots and lots of Busbys. We used to have family reunions; hundreds would come, and that's how we met." She smiled fondly at the recollection. "Winnie was the most handsome of them all."

"Do you still have reunions?" asked Lucy, thinking of a possible future story.

"No." Millicent shook her head sadly. "The family's kind of dispersed, all over the country. People these days don't seem to value that sort of thing. Why, my own daughter, Darleen, always says that the Busby name and two bits will get you a ride on a streetcar." She leaned forward and smiled. "I know perfectly well that there aren't streetcars anymore, and if there were, the fare would likely be much higher than twenty-five cents."

"My daughter says it costs over two dollars to take the T in Boston," offered Lucy. "And Darleen is right—everyone who rides has to pay. Even the mayor."

"But I believe that knowing your ancestry does give a person a sense of pride because you know who you are and where you came from," said Millicent. She glanced around the dining room, which was filled with antiques. "That's why I treasure these lovely things I've inherited from my family." She popped up and trotted over to a corner cupboard that was filled with silver and more Canton china, opened the glazed door with a creak, and pulled out a silver teapot. "This is a Paul Revere teapot," she declared, proudly displaying it. "Imagine that."

"It's lovely," said Lucy, watching as Millicent carefully replaced it, then pointed to an old rifle that hung over the fireplace.

"That was George Busby's," she said. "He carried it all through the Civil War, and afterward, he used it to shoot a bear that was threatening Susan." She nodded. "She was hanging the wash."

"My goodness," said Lucy.

Millicent was on the other side of the room now, indicating a very ugly piece of heavily carved furniture, a sort of chest on chest, that Lucy had wondered about. It wasn't exactly a sideboard; she wasn't sure what it was, but Millicent quite obviously held it in high esteem. "This chest," she declared, with a flourish, "actually came over on the *Mayflower*. Come closer," she insisted, beckoning.

Lucy obeyed, and Millicent pointed out some numbers in the carving. "See here, 1618! It was made two years before the *Mayflower* sailed."

Lucy gazed at the chest, which was massive, and wondered how many chests the *Mayflower* could actually have contained. She'd seen a replica of the *Mayflower* on a family visit to Plymouth, Massachusetts, and remembered being somewhat surprised at the ship's small size. She'd wondered then how it could possibly have transported over a hundred Pilgrims, plus crew, not to mention all those chests that people claimed came with the Pilgrims. "It's, it's mind-boggling," admitted Lucy. "So old, and yet in such good condition."

"Beeswax," offered Millicent. "Nothing like it."

Lucy was beginning to feel things were getting a bit off track. She'd been interested in the quilt and the Susan Hawkin–George Busby love story, and now she was beginning to feel as if she were in an antiques shop. And Millicent wasn't done.

"See that basket up there," said Millicent, pointing to what Lucy recognized as a Nantucket lightship basket, perched atop a hanging wall shelf. "Can you reach it?"

Lucy stood on tiptoes and was just able, barely, to nudge the basket to the edge and grab it as it tipped over.

"Careful, there," warned Millicent. "There's quite a story behind that basket."

Lucy passed it to Millicent, who cradled it gently, caressing the tightly woven reeds and the wooden handle.

"This was actually made on a Nantucket lightship. Do you know of the lightships?"

Lucy did. She'd seen one at the South Street Seaport in New York City. It was a big red ship with NANTUCKET painted on the side in huge white letters, and it had once been moored off Nantucket island as a sort of floating lighthouse beaming a warning to mariners. "I've actually seen one," said Lucy.

"Well, that one in New York is one of the later lightships; there were several, you know. And my great-great-uncle Frank Busby, he married a Folger girl, from one of the island's very old families. Uncle Frank made this very basket as a gift for her while serving on the lightship."

"Another great story," said Lucy, as Millicent handed the basket over and asked her to replace it. Lucy made sure to handle it gently as she once again stood on tiptoe and pushed the basket back in place. Watching closely, in case it started to fall, she noticed a tiny gold oval sticker on the basket's bottom. She recognized the sticker, which was familiar, and included the words MADE IN CHINA.

"About that quilt," said Lucy, returning to the subject of the interview. "Could I get a few photos?"

"Of course, of course, my dear," said Millicent. "I'll just be a moment." And off she went, carrying her generously padded self on tiptoes, reminding Lucy of a fairy godmother in a Disney movie. In a moment, she was back with the quilt, which she spread out on the highly polished mahogany dining table. She stood behind it, smiling, as Lucy snapped a couple of photos.

The quilt, Lucy believed, was genuine. She had done a bit of research to prepare for the interview, and she'd seen photos of the other Civil War quilts. Millicent was correct, the US Sanitary Commission had requested the quilts, and it was estimated that over 100,000 had been made and sent to Union hospitals. Of those thousands, only fifteen were believed to have survived, and among them, she'd seen a picture of the very quilt she was now photographing. It was a remarkable survivor, outlasting all the soldiers who had fought in the war, all the people who had lived through that terrible time.

But, she thought, as she offered her thanks and made her farewell, she had doubts about that teapot and that chest. Honestly, how many teapots could Paul Revere have made, busy as he was riding through the countryside warning everybody that the British were coming? And wouldn't the *Mayflower* have sunk to the bottom of the sea, overloaded with all those chests people claimed it had contained? And as for the Nantucket lightship basket, she'd immediately recognized it as a cheap imitation. The basket's aged appearance was the result of a coat of hastily applied stain that had been slapped on over the sticker.

Climbing back in her car for the short drive to the *Courier* office on Main Street, she thought Darleen was right on the money. That basket and a valid Charlie card would get a person a ride on the Boston T. Luckily for her, Main Street was largely deserted this early in the morning, and she was able to park in front of the office, making a quick dash across the broiling sidewalk.

There was no relief when she stepped inside the steamy office, and no sign of Ted, either, but Phyllis was at the reception desk, where she had set up a small rotating electric fan. Even though the fan was blowing directly on her face and chest, Phyllis was suffering from the heat. She'd worn her coolest dress, a voluminous muumuu printed with colorful parrots and tropical foliage, but her face was red, and she was breathing heavily.

Lucy understood why, as soon as she stepped into the overheated office. "Gosh, it's hot in here," she said, grabbing a *Courier* from the stack on Phyllis's counter and fanning herself with it.

"It was shut up over the long weekend, and the heat built up," said Phyllis, with a nod at the thermometer that hung on the wall. "It's close to a hundred."

Lucy noticed that all the windows were open, but they offered no relief since there wasn't a breeze. Not a leaf stirred outside, and the wooden venetian blinds hung motionless.

"We need an air-conditioner," said Lucy.

"I tried. They're all sold out."

"We could close up here and go over to the Gilead office," suggested Lucy, collapsing onto her desk chair. The fact that the Gilead office was in a modern building equipped with air-conditioning had long rankled with Lucy and Phyllis, who Ted insisted remain in the inadequate antique building in Tinker's Cove.

"Power outage over there," said Phyllis, with a sigh.

Lucy could already feel the sweat dripping down her face and was considering mutiny when her phone rang. She'd take the call, she decided, and then insist that they both abandon ship. She lifted the receiver, saying "*Courier,* Lucy Stone speaking."

"Hi, Lucy, it's me, Natalie."

Lucy had been getting a lot of calls lately from Natalie Withers, a retired insurance executive who had become a self-appointed citizen watchdog. Natalie had decided it was her mission in life to make sure that every tax dollar collected in Tinker's Cove was wisely and appropriately spent. She'd recently questioned the high school soccer coach's purchase of Gatorade for the team, claimed the health inspector had inappropriately used a town-owned car for personal use, and failed to understand why the Parks Department was mowing the ball field every week instead of every other week.

"What's on your mind today, Natalie?" asked Lucy, figuring she'd seen Highway Department workers taking a break in the shade or even taking a quick dip in Blueberry Pond, which she'd occasionally seen them do, fully clothed with boots and all, in hot weather.

"Well," began Natalie, "I've been going through the town payroll . . ."

Lucy had heard similar complaints before and had little patience for them. "All the town employees' salaries are in line with other towns in the region," she said. "We offer competitive compensation and benefits in order to attract and keep quality employees. Salaries can vary based on an individual's experience and qualifications."

Natalie laughed. "Well, then, Darleen Busby-Pratt must be very highly qualified since she is now the town's highest-paid employee."

Lucy knew the Personnel Committee had had a difficult time filling the position at the new community center and had been pleased when Darleen, who had excellent qualifications and local ties to boot, had applied. But she did wonder if the job of community center director merited a higher rate of pay than the superintendent of schools, or the police and fire chiefs.

"Are you quite sure?" she asked.

"Oh, yes. Ms. Busby-Pratt is making over a hundred thousand a year . . ."

"But the school superintendent makes ninety-five," said Lucy, who knew a lot of people had thought that amount was excessive.

"About the same as Chief Kirwan and Chief Bresnahan," added Natalie. "But the big paycheck isn't all. It seems Ms. Busby-Pratt is leaving shortly on a two-week paid vacation!"

"That is odd," said Lucy, who knew that new hires generally had to work for a specified period of time, usually a year, before qualifying for paid vacation. She was suddenly thinking of her own meager paycheck, not to mention the complete lack of benefits, and the single week of paid vacation that Ted grudgingly allowed. "Are you sure about all this?"

"I am. I got it straight from Dot Kirwan."

Lucy knew that Dot, the cashier at the IGA whose numerous children and relations filled many town jobs, was an unimpeachable source. "Well, if Dot says it's so, it must be true."

"Exactly," agreed Natalie.

"Well, thanks for the tip. I will certainly look into it."

"I thought you'd be interested," said Natalie. "Stay cool."

"I'm trying," said Lucy, who suspected her temperature had risen, thanks in large part to Natalie's call.

"So what was that all about?" asked Phyllis, who had been listening in.

"Watchdog Natalie Withers says Darleen Busby-Pratt is the town's highest-paid employee, pulling in a cool hundred thou, and somehow she got the Personnel Committee to approve a paid vacation that's supposed to start any day now."

"But she just started the job . . ."

"Yeah." Lucy fanned herself. "I can't believe it. There's some mistake."

"Folks aren't that happy about the cost of the center; they're sure not gonna like this."

"And I think the cat's already out of the bag. Natalie says she got it straight from Dot."

"Dot talks to everybody."

"I'm going to call Darleen. I've got to get to the bottom of this."

Lucy placed the call to Darleen, who picked up promptly, sitting in her air-conditioned office. The very thought made Lucy sizzle with resentment. "Hi, Darleen, it's Lucy at the *Courier*. I've got a question for you."

"Anything," replied Darleen, pertly. "Anything at all."

"Well, it's kind of personal, but there's a rumor floating around town that concerns you."

"Oh, no," said Darleen, in mock horror.

"Oh, yes. It's about your pay. Rumor has it you're now the town's highest-paid employee."

"Well, I don't know about that. I do know that the Personnel Committee and I agreed on a figure that reflects my unique qualifications. They actually apologized for the amount, noting that I really deserved a higher figure, considering my extensive experience. I accepted their offer largely because my mother is getting older and I wanted to be close to her, here in Tinker's Cove. I told them I only had one tiny hesitation about accepting, and that was that I had already booked and paid for a two-week stay at a resort. Nonrefundable, no exceptions. They took it under advisement and eventually agreed that, considering my excellent references, and in light of my flexibility about compensation, they would let me take the vacation."

"With pay?" asked Lucy, fanning herself with some press releases.

"Of course. I'm a salaried employee. I don't get paid by the hour."

"Well, thanks for clearing this up," said Lucy, reaching for a tissue to mop her sweaty face.

"I'd call it a win-win situation for everyone," said Darleen.

"Thanks again." Lucy ended the call, thinking that only time would tell. She knew that the town's citizenry included plenty of folks who did get paid by the hour and would certainly resent Darleen's extremely generous compensation package. Win-win situation? No way. More like a pot about to boil over.

Chapter Four

Phyllis suddenly stood up, wobbled on her feet, and collapsed back in her chair.

"I don't feel so good," she said.

"It's the heat," said Lucy, moving as quickly as she could through air that felt as thick and sticky as cheese fondue into the tiny bathroom, where she grabbed a wad of paper towels and held them under the cold-water faucet. Carrying the soggy mass, she went straight to Phyllis and slapped it onto the back of her neck. "Hold it," she instructed, slogging in slow motion over to the water cooler and getting a cup of water. "Sip on this," she said, holding the flimsy paper cup to Phyllis's lips.

Gradually, Phyllis seemed to perk up. Her eyes began to focus, and her breathing became more regular. "I'm taking you home," said Lucy, making an executive decision.

"Ted wants us to keep the office open," protested Phyllis, weakly.

"I don't care what Ted wants; this is intolerable. I'll put a sign on the door with my phone number; if anybody needs something, they can call."

Lucy helped Phyllis to her feet and supported her as

they left the office. Once in her SUV, Lucy cranked up the AC, and they sat, waiting for it to kick in. It wasn't long before they felt the cool air wafting over them, and they both began to feel more normal. Lucy shifted into drive and made the short trip to Phyllis's house, where she parked in the driveway. "How's the house? Can you keep cool?"

Phyllis nodded. "Wilf got an air-conditioner for the bedroom. I fought Wilf about it, but now I'm glad he insisted."

Lucy gave Phyllis a hand to help her get out of the SUV and escorted her on the short walk in the broiling heat of the driveway to the house. Wilf greeted them at the door, a somewhat startling sight as he was shirtless, revealing a hairy chest and a massive belly that hung over his shorts. "What's this?" he asked, concerned.

"I think Phyllis has heat stroke. You've got to get her cooled down and hydrated."

"Righto," he said, taking his wife by the arm and drawing her inside. "Are you okay, Lucy?"

"Yup. The car's got AC, and we always get a breeze up on Red Top Road." She wasn't actually convinced about the breeze, but she figured the drive would give her a chance to cool down.

"Well, thanks for taking care of Phyllis," he said, with a smile as he closed the door.

The SUV sat in the drive, heat waves radiating from the hood and roof, but it was blessedly cool inside. Lucy drove slowly through the largely deserted town and up hilly Red Top Road to her antique farmhouse. She parked in the shade, grateful for the big maple that cooled the driveway and porch, and went inside to see how Libby was doing. She found the dog sprawled on the cool tile floor, panting heavily. "I know, girl, it's hot," she said, dampening a dish towel and laying it over the elderly dog. She then treated herself to a big glass of water and grabbed an ice pack from the freezer, which she alternately held on her forehead and the back of her neck. She'd been sitting there at the kitchen table for a few minutes when she heard Bill's truck crunch on the gravel drive.

"Too hot to work?" she asked, when he came in.

"You said it," he agreed.

"Do you want lunch?" she asked, without enthusiasm.

"Too hot to eat," he said, grabbing a cold bottle of beer from the fridge. Sitting down at the table, he held the bottle to his cheek, then took a long drink.

"I have to take the dog to the vet," said Lucy, checking the clock.

He studied the aged black Lab, who was lying motionless on the floor. "It's probably the heat."

"Probably," agreed Lucy. "It's harder on old people—and old dogs, too."

But later that afternoon when it was time to go and she grabbed the leash, Libby didn't respond. "C'mon, girl," she urged, clipping the leash onto the dog's collar, and Libby scrabbled weakly on the floor, trying to get up. Lucy grabbed her by her hips and hoisted her up, and the dog stood, legs splayed out beneath her. "Easy does it," urged Lucy, leading the dog slowly to the door and out onto the porch. They made it to the SUV, but Lucy knew there was no way that Libby was going to leap into the wayback, so she carefully slid her arms beneath her belly and lifted her up. It was much easier than she expected, realizing with a shock that Libby had lost quite a bit of weight.

Once at the vet's, she explained the situation to the receptionist, and Libby was transported inside on a small gurney. While she waited with Libby in the air-conditioned examining room, Lucy felt her anxiety rising. The dog was in bad shape, and she was worried. Also drowning in guilt, wondering why she hadn't noticed sooner. But she'd blamed the heat wave for the dog's lack of energy; in fact, she remembered, she had enjoyed a nice long walk with Libby the day before the heat arrived.

"So what have we got here?" inquired the vet, Sam Shapiro, when he entered the room. He was a middle-aged man, often seen out for a run in the early morning, with a trim brush cut and an easy smile. "Libby's not feeling well?"

"She's very weak; we needed to wheel her in."

Dr. Shapiro was stroking the dog's head, looking into her eyes, checking her ears. He listened to her heart and palpated her abdomen. He took her temperature, getting no protest at all from the motionless dog. Finishing his exam, he made eye contact with Lucy.

"She's old, Lucy," he began, "and she's had a good, long life."

Lucy felt as if her heart had stopped. "What do you mean? Isn't this heat stroke?"

"I'm afraid not. Her vitals are very low; her body is shutting down."

Lucy couldn't believe what she was hearing. "She's dying?"

Dr. Shapiro nodded. "I'm sorry, Lucy."

Lucy blinked back the tears that were filling her eyes.

"If you want, I can euthanize her now. Sometimes that's easier . . ."

"Oh, no!" Lucy wasn't ready to say goodbye to Libby. "Isn't there anything you can do?"

"No, Lucy. Prolonging her life would only be cruel and

cause her to suffer." He nodded sympathetically. "She isn't in pain; she's just very, very tired. If you want, you can take her home to die naturally."

Lucy leaped at the idea. "That would be best. She'd be in a familiar place, with people who love her." Lucy paused. "How long?"

"It's hard to say. Maybe a day or two; that's my best guess."

"This is not what I expected to hear," said Lucy, struggling to process this difficult new situation. Libby had been part of her life for so long that she couldn't imagine losing her.

"I understand." Suddenly brisk, the vet called in the receptionist, and together they wheeled the dog back to Lucy's car and laid her inside. The rear door came down, and Lucy got behind the wheel, taking Libby home for the last time. She was blinking back tears before she got out of the vet's parking lot.

When she got home, she discovered Bill had set up a fan in the kitchen and was seasoning some haddock, which he planned to throw on the grill. "Where's the dog?" he asked, anxiously.

"She's in the car. The vet said she's old and there's nothing he can do. He offered to put her down, but I, I don't know. I couldn't do that. I brought her home to die."

He took a minute to digest this information. "There's nothing we can do?"

She shook her head. "Just make her comfortable. I'll get some pillows for her doggy bed, then you can carry her in. She's too weak . . ."

"I'm on it," he said, heading for the door.

Libby was soon settled on her extra comfy bed, snoozing, while Lucy and Bill got supper ready. While they ate, they found themselves reminiscing about Libby. "Remember when Toby and Molly gave her to us?" said Bill, naming their son and his then-girlfriend, now wife. "They thought she was a he!"

"And we thought she was going to be a chocolate Lab," added Lucy, glancing over at the doggy bed, where Libby's furry black chest rose and fell ever so slightly with each breath. "She was always full of surprises."

"Like the time she ate all the Christmas cookies," said Bill, spearing a piece of tomato with his fork.

"What were we thinking, leaving that platter on the coffee table?"

"I think Santa came to visit and we all ran to see him, leaving Libby alone with the cookies."

"That's right! It was Sid Finch, in a Santa suit. The kids were thrilled."

"So was Libby, apparently," chuckled Bill.

"I thought she'd die of chocolate poisoning! She ate all those chocolate-covered buckeyes, complete with the foil cupcake papers." Lucy pushed a bit of haddock around on her plate. "I thought at the very least she'd be sick, but she didn't even burp."

"She was so good with the kids. Remember the time the coyote came into the yard? Zoe was playing alone out there," he said, naming their youngest child, "and Libby went right after the coyote, didn't hesitate for a second. That coyote turned tail and ran."

"Yeah. After that, Zoe always wanted to let the dog sleep with her, much to Sara's disgust." Zoe shared a room with her older sister, Sara, in what was at best an uneasy alliance. "They'll both be upset, I think."

"Elizabeth won't care," said Bill, naming their oldest daughter, who lived in Paris. "She was never a dog person."

"She barely tolerated Libby," recalled Lucy, thinking how the dog had grown in importance to her and Bill after all the kids had flown, leaving them with an empty nest. Elizabeth was in France; Toby and Molly lived in Alaska with their son, Patrick; Sara was in Boston; and Zoe, the baby of the family, had settled in Portland. "The house is going to feel so empty." She pushed her plate, mostly un-eaten, away. "No wagging tail to greet us when we come home. No walking companion." She looked at Bill. "Just you and me."

"I'll wag my tail for you," promised Bill, with a half smile.

"It won't be the same," said Lucy, standing up and clearing the table. Bill went off to the family room to watch the Red Sox lose another game, and Lucy finished loading the dishwasher. Libby seemed comfortable enough, but Lucy dampened a clean sponge and dribbled some water on her muzzle, which the dog lapped up with her pink tongue. When she stopped lapping and closed her eyes, Lucy scratched her behind her ears. She'd always loved stroking the silky-smooth fur on Libby's floppy ears. Then, with a big sigh, Lucy straightened up. She didn't want to leave Libby alone, so she decided to set up her lap-top and start writing the story about Millicent and her Civil War quilt.

The story proved harder to write than she expected, probably because she couldn't quite concentrate on the quilt when she was so worried about Libby. Every once in a while, the dog would twitch, or snort, and Lucy would start in her chair, convinced that this was the end. She'd stop typing and check the dog, always finding she'd re-sumed her slow, labored breathing.

Bill came through, on his way to bed, announcing that

the Red Sox's best batter had likely torn his ACL trying to stop a ground ball, so there was no chance of them making the postseason. "Coming to bed?" he asked, hopefully.

"No. I want to wrap up this story, and"—she glanced at Libby—"I don't want to leave her."

"Okay." He went up the back stairs, and Lucy stayed at the golden-oak table, staring at the letters on the screen and occasionally adding a word. The windows were all open, and the fan was humming; the temperature had dropped, but it was still very warm and humid, and her head grew heavy. She could hear the clock ticking, the fan whirring. Her chin dropped to her chest, and she nodded off; when her head hit the laptop, she jerked awake. She turned to check on the dog and saw that she was motionless.

Rushing to the dog's side, she fell on her knees and reached for her chest. It was still. Libby was gone. "Goodbye, old girl," she said, then used a chair to pull herself up, feeling the stiffness in her knees. She went into the downstairs bath and found a towel, which she laid over the dog's body.

Pausing at the table, she saved the little bit she'd managed to write of the story, then shut down the laptop. She glanced around the kitchen, making sure the stove was off, the door was locked, the dishwasher was quietly humming. She turned off the fan, switched off the light, and went upstairs to bed.

Chapter Five

The temperature fell in the night as a thick blanket of fog arrived that lingered into the morning, blocking out the sun. The gray day mirrored Lucy's mood as she drove to work, leaving Bill to deal with Libby's lifeless body. As sad as she was about losing her faithful companion, she had to admit she felt the tiniest bit of relief. She was grateful the dog's passing had been peaceful; she'd made the right decision to bring her home to die in a familiar place, comforted by her humans. And now Lucy no longer had to worry about getting home in time to let Libby out, expensive annual checkups, renewing her license every year, dealing with ticks and fleas. But she still felt the loss; she had an empty place in her heart and in her home.

Phyllis noticed something was wrong the minute Lucy stepped into the office, announced by the jangle of the little bell on the door. "Oh, my gosh. You look like you lost your best friend," she said, pouring herself a cup of coffee and going to stand in front of an open window that was letting in a faint cooling breeze.

"I kind of did," admitted Lucy, noticing with amusement that Phyllis had dressed in defiance of the gray weather. She was wearing a gaudy paisley tank top and bright pink pedal pushers, and matching pink pom-poms dangled from her ears. "Libby died last night."

"Oh, I'm so sorry. She was a good dog. I know you'll miss her."

"She was only a dog," offered Lucy, with an apologetic shrug. "It's not like losing a person."

"She was part of your family," asserted Phyllis, watching as Lucy crossed the office and set her bag down on her desk. "Do you want some coffee?"

"No, thanks." Lucy sat down and powered up her computer, staring at the screen as the aged machine groaned and clicked and eventually produced three moving dots.

"Have you told the kids?" asked Phyllis, carrying her mug back to her desk behind the reception counter.

"Not yet." The computer now informed her it was in the process of loading her emails. She knew from experience that it was going to take a while. Dot-dot-dot.

"I suppose they'll want to have some sort of funeral."

This idea had not occurred to Lucy, who knew Bill was planning to borrow a small Kubota from a friend who was a landscaper to dig a grave in the backyard. It was her fervent hope that the entire process would be complete by the time she returned home. "Do you really think so? We've always buried our deceased pets in a corner of the backyard."

"Without any sort of observance?"

"Well, I do remember that Zoe insisted on a funeral when her pet turtle died. It was a small family affair. Toby was the minister, and Sara painted a stone marker. Elizabeth sang a sad French song about the pain of love."

"See? If they did all that for a turtle, they'll certainly want a ceremony for poor Libby."

"It was kind of a joke, just to make Zoe happy."

"But it worked, right? At the very least, they'll want to comfort you and Bill. But I bet they'll be pretty upset about Libby themselves."

Lucy was skeptical; it seemed to her that the kids were a pretty unsentimental bunch. Just getting them to make birthday cards for each other had been a struggle, and using precious allowance dollars to buy gifts for one another was a nonstarter. At best, when they were young, she got a hastily prepared breakfast in bed on Mother's Day and nowadays, sometimes, a last-minute delivery of flowers. But, she decided, it wouldn't hurt to send them each a text about the dog. Not that she expected any sympathetic replies.

She was busy texting, hitting those tiny little letters on her phone and missing the one she wanted as often as not, which required backspacing and trying again, when Ted barged into the office, breathing fire.

"Phyllis! I don't mind you having coffee, but you could at least pretend to work while you drink it," he fumed, hands on hips and eyes afire. "And Lucy, since when is Wordle part of your job? It's a deadline, not a guideline, you know!"

Lucy debated informing him that she wasn't playing Wordle, she was texting her kids about their beloved pet's sad demise, but she suspected Ted would not see much difference between personal texting and gaming. "For your information, I spent most of last night working on the Civil War quilt story while I watched my dog die."

"Is the story finished? I didn't see it. Did you send it to me?" he demanded, completely ignoring Libby's death.

"It's not finished," admitted Lucy. "I was distracted. Like I mentioned, my dog died last night."

"Well, I need it ASAP. All I've got for the front page is

the grand opening." He snorted. "A smelly, old dog's death is hardly breaking news."

Lucy set her elbow on her desk and rested her cheek on her hand, studying Ted. He was often demanding and abrupt, even rude, but this was a bit much even for him. What was going on? She decided to ask. "Is everything OK, Ted? You seem upset."

"I'm upset because I've got a bunch of lazy employees," he declared. "I know you closed the office yesterday, in spite of my clear instruction to remain open."

"Yeah, we're lazy," agreed Phyllis, "and we did close the office because of the heat, despite your clear instruction"—she paused to make quotation marks in the air, then continued—"to keep it open. But, face it, we hardly ever pay attention to what you say, and you don't usually get this hot and bothered about it."

"That's true," said Lucy, nodding in agreement.

Much to her surprise, Ted collapsed in the chair she kept for visitors, grabbed a handful of tissues from the box on her desk, and, shoulders heaving, wiped his teary eyes.

"Oh, my. What's the matter?" she asked, making eye contact with an equally shocked Phyllis. Feeling something more was needed in the way of response, she reached out and cautiously squeezed his arm.

"It's Tim," he finally said. He paused to give his nose a good blow, then tossed the soggy tissues into the wastebasket. "He's relapsing. He refused to go to work this morning. Wouldn't even get out of bed. Turned his head to the wall. Won't speak, refuses to eat. Just lies there, motionless. It's like he was when he came home, after the, you know, incident."

"I know how he feels," offered Phyllis, trying to make light of the situation. "Sometimes it's all I can do to get out of bed and come to work."

"But you do," said Ted. "We all do. We get up and shoulder our burdens and carry on."

"But we're able to function, more or less," suggested Lucy. "Sometimes we get laid low with a virus and can't carry on; we need to rest and recover. Maybe Tim needs some R and R."

"It's just so hard. Pam and I thought he was making real progress, what with the job and all."

Lucy bit her lip, wondering if she ought to mention the way Darleen had scolded Tim. It was no wonder he didn't want to face that every day. Instead, she asked if Pam was coping.

"She's pretty devastated," he said. "Also frustrated. She kind of saw it coming and has been trying for days to get him an appointment with a therapist."

"Maybe this is what it takes to get an appointment," offered Phyllis, in a burst of optimism.

"Face it, he'll have to get up eventually," said Lucy, in a bright tone. "He'll have to pee."

"Ah, Lucy, you always do manage to utter words of wisdom. With that," he said, clapping his hands on his thighs and standing up, "I'm off to Gilead. They're an even lazier, more miserable bunch than you two are."

"Aw, thanks, Ted," said Lucy, batting her eyes. "You know I'm a sucker for flattery."

"Don't let it go to your head," he muttered, heading for the door. "Get that story to me by noon."

After he'd gone, leaving the bell on the door jangling behind him, Phyllis spoke up. "You've gotta feel bad for him and Pam. This thing with Tim, it's a tough one."

"Yeah," agreed Lucy. "And it's so hard to get treatment. Maybe we should do a spotlight story about the lack of resources for folks struggling with mental illness."

"Not a bad idea," said Phyllis, as the phone rang. She

picked up, then sent the call to Lucy, who immediately recognized the voice. She'd heard it many times through the years, and it always brought back the same mix of emotions: grief, anger, hopelessness. Just what she needed today, on top of her worries about Tim and the loss of her pet.

"Hi, Susan, what's up?" she asked, adopting the gentle tone she always used when speaking to Corinne Appleton's surviving sister. It had been more than a decade since Corinne, only sixteen years old, had disappeared from her summer job as a lifeguard, apparently vanishing into thin air. Sometime later, hunters found a few bones and a scrap of cloth that were identified as Corinne's; the hunt for the killer intensified, and a suspect was named and confessed to the crime.

"It was this time of year, to the day, in fact. Corinne disappeared on this day, thirteen years ago."

"That's right. Thanks for reminding me. We'll definitely run a short piece, a look back."

"That would be great; it would help a lot. You see, there's been a new development. Martin Wicker, the guy who did it—well, you know he got life in prison."

"That's right," agreed Lucy, wondering where this was heading.

"Well, he's applying for a retrial. He's retracted his confession, says the police mistreated him, forcing him to make the confession. He says it isn't true; he never did it."

"There's no chance . . ." protested Lucy.

"Times have changed, Lucy. People don't have the same faith in the justice system that they used to. A lot of convicted felons have turned out to be innocent; sentences are overturned all the time. I can't let that happen, not to Corinne's killer. All we have left of Corinne is that scrap of cloth, that little bit of the flowery shirt she was wearing that day. It was chilly, you know."

"I remember," said Lucy.

"Yeah. It was sunny, but breezy. She wore the shirt over her swimsuit. Mom said she should wear a sweatshirt, but Corinne didn't want to, she said she didn't have time; she was running late and the shirt was enough." Susan paused. "I've often wondered, if she'd come back in the house for the sweatshirt, if she'd been late, maybe he wouldn't have been there. Maybe he would have grabbed some other girl."

"What's past is past," said Lucy. "We can't change what happened."

"But I sure don't want Martin Wicker out of jail, on the loose, going after other girls. That's why I'm asking you to help rally opinion against the possibility of a retrial. It can't just be our family; we need more people to speak up against him."

"We have photos and clips. I can put something to-gether," said Lucy. "People were horrified at the time, and we can jog their memories."

"That would be great. Just what we need. Thank you so much." She paused to take a quavery breath. "We can't—my mom especially—we can't go through a trial again."

"No problem," said Lucy. "We were all heartbroken."

"My mom, myself, we'll never get over it. I miss Corinne every single day. I pray he didn't abuse her, that she didn't suffer."

"I hope not, too." Lucy paused. "I'm sorry you have to go through this."

"I have no choice," said Susan.

"Okay," said Lucy. "I'll do what I can."

Deciding this was an unpleasant assignment that she

might as well get over with, Lucy went into the morgue and pulled out the huge bound volume that contained all the *Pennysaver* newspapers from the year Corinne was murdered and set it on the big table they used for meetings and interviews. Nowadays the paper had been renamed the *Courier*, following Ted's acquisition of the *Gilead Gabber,* and they covered the whole county, not just Tinker's Cove. Lucy rather missed the relaxed *Pennysaver* days, when she had one deadline, noon Wednesday, instead of constant pressure to provide stories for the *Courier's* ravenous online edition. Newspapers all over the country were suffering, and Lucy knew they would have to keep up with the times to survive, but as she flipped through the pages of the *Pennysaver*, she felt a bit nostalgic. Also a bit shocked at how old-fashioned the little weekly seemed, after little more than a decade. These days, things changed so fast that thirteen years seemed like an eternity.

It was toward the end of July, in the issue of July 20, that Lucy found the headline she was looking for, as well as Corinne's yearbook picture. She stared at the pretty girl, with her big smile, round face, and shining hair, and sighed. Beneath the fold, she saw a picture of Corinne's mother and her desperate plea for her daughter's return quoted in the caption: "Please, please, don't hurt my daughter. I love her. I need her."

It was enough to break your heart, thought Lucy, trying to remember when Corinne's remains were discovered. Two years later, she thought, and it was fall, because they were found in woods off an abandoned logging road by a couple of hunters. Late fall. She pulled out another heavy volume, laid it on the table beside the first, and opened it. The pages parted on the story she wanted; they'd referred to it often throughout the years. There was a photo of the two hunters and an account of their discovery, which at first they'd thought were animal bones.

"It was the cloth," said Butch Guzman. "When we saw that cloth, we knew it had to be a person."

And there, next to the photo of the hunters, was a photo of the scrap of cloth. It was black and white, but Lucy remembered taking the photo in the police station. The fabric was cotton broadcloth, the sort of fabric used for shirts, and it was printed with flowers, pink flowers with green stems and little leaves on what was once a white background. It was no longer white; it was kind of gray and brown and spotty, but a button had survived intact. It was bright pink plastic, shaped like a flower. Looking at the image before her, gray and black and white, she saw the sweet pink and green pattern on the torn scrap of cloth, and she felt a hard bubble of grief growing in her chest and tears threatening to spill from her eyes.

She flipped quickly through the subsequent issues, blinking hard, and soon found the booking photo of Martin Wicker. That day, the day he was arrested and all the days that followed when he was tried, he was always carefully groomed, freshly shaved, with his black hair slicked back, showing the comb tracks, and carefully dressed in plaid shirts and pressed jeans. But what she always remembered was his smug expression, as if he were proud of what he'd done. Staring at that photo, Lucy knew that if, by chance, Martin Wicker were there in the room with her, she would struggle to restrain herself from smacking him hard and trying to rip that awful self-satisfied expression from his face.

It didn't take long for Lucy to wrap up the recap, even getting a quote from DA Phil Aucoin, who had prosecuted Wicker. That job behind her, she finished up the Civil War quilt story and sent it to Ted minutes before noon. Duty done, she decided to head for home.

She was in a somber mood. She'd gotten a "Sorry" text from Toby, which was all she'd expected, and only a slightly longer message from Elizabeth: "So sad, she was a good dog." Sara and Zoe had been more sympathetic, however, actually calling and expressing shock and grief over Libby's passing. They had both brushed aside Lucy's claim that she and Bill were coping, and insisting that they must be in need of comfort and consolation, both had immediately announced plans to come home for the weekend.

The rest of the week seemed to pass slowly as Lucy impatiently awaited the arrival of her two daughters. It would be almost like the old days, she thought, when the house was full to bursting, cluttered with book bags and sports equipment and rocking to loud pop music.

Zoe was already at the house when Lucy got home Friday evening, and Sara had texted she was on the way in a car borrowed from a friend. She actually arrived at the same time as Bill, and after hugs and a few tears, the girls announced that they had invited a few family friends for Libby's memorial service, which they had arranged with Reverend Marge to take place the next day, graveside, in the backyard.

"Isn't this a bit much?" asked Lucy, who had deep doubts about the propriety of holding a funeral for a dog.

"No, Mom!" exclaimed a shocked Zoe. "Libby was a member of the family."

"Your furry child," added Sara.

Lucy looked at Bill, who gave a resigned shrug.

Realizing no help was coming from that quarter, she made a last-ditch effort. "Well, I think we should call it off. Libby was a dog, not a child, not even a furry child. She was a pet, not exactly a member of the family."

"I loved her," said Zoe. "She saved my life."

"She used to lick my toes," confessed Sara. "It was weird, but it felt really good."

"We haven't had folks over in a long time," said Bill. "Think of it as an excuse for a party."

"Okay," agreed Lucy. "Whatever."

So, after a busy Saturday morning baking lemon bars and brownies, and picking up sandwiches and drinks at the IGA, the Stones and their friends gathered at Libby's grave in the shady back corner of the yard. Gazing at the freshly turned earth, Lucy thought how Libby was not alone but was accompanied in the tiny cemetery by several cats, two parakeets, a number of guppies, and, of course, Zoe's turtle, Zippy. Zippy's grave was the only one with a marker, a lavender stone that would have gone unremarked if you hadn't been there for Zippy's funeral and realized its significance.

Reverend Marge made it official, dressed in her ministerial robe and offering appropriate remarks about the special, blessed relationship between humans and dogs. Ted and Pam were both sorrowful, but Lucy doubted it had anything to do with Libby and more to do with Tim. Rachel and Bob Goodman were quietly thoughtful; Lucy figured Rachel was thinking about the stages of grief, and Bob was trying to remember an article he'd read in a law journal about the burgeoning field of animal rights. Sue Finch was struggling to contain herself, pressing her lips together so as not to laugh, and her husband Sid was sneaking admiring peeks at the Kubota tractor that Bill had used to dig the grave and hadn't yet returned. The brief service ended when Zoe and Sara led the group in singing the hymn "All Things Bright and Beautiful." Duty done, there was a collective sigh of relief as they all made their way to the deck for a light luncheon.

Beer and wine were distributed, everyone dug into the chips and sandwiches, and Lucy was relieved to hear most everyone congratulating Reverend Marge on a moving and appropriate service. All except Sue, that is, who took Lucy aside and expressed her surprise that Lucy had gone along with the notion of a dog funeral. "It was what the girls wanted," she said, sipping on her chardonnay. "And Bill wanted a party."

"Well," admitted Sue, who was a connoisseur of chardonnay, "any excuse to drink with lunch. Or for lunch, for that matter." Lucy knew she wasn't joking; she suspected Sue survived on a diet of white wine and black coffee.

After everyone had discussed the weather—the heat was forecast to return as soon as the clouds dissipated—conversation turned to the upcoming special town meeting, and all were agreed the community center was a beneficial, although costly, addition to the town. "Cost overruns are to be expected," said Sid, who, like Bill, was in the building trades.

"We spent the money; the bill's got to be paid," said Bob. "If folks turn down the override, it will be disastrous for the town's finances. It's got to pass."

"I agree," said Ted, "and I'm working on an editorial supporting the override. The problem is, a lot of folks have got the override confused with that fat salary of Darleen's."

"And that vacation!" exclaimed Sue. "She's barely started the job when she goes off on a paid vacation! It is not going over well."

"The Personnel Committee is getting a lot of blowback,"

said Reverend Marge. "I assume they will learn their lesson and not make the same mistake again."

As the food began to run out and folks remembered Saturday chores that needed to be tended to, they began leaving. Lucy was carrying an empty platter into the kitchen when she noticed Pam collaring the two girls and stopped to listen.

"Tim's home, you know, but he's been a bit down lately," she was saying. "It would be great if you girls would get together with him while you're here. I think it would really cheer him up."

"Uh, well, I'd love to, but I'm not here for long," Sara was saying.

"That's right," added Zoe, "we've both got to get back for our jobs."

"I understand," said Pam, in a resigned tone. "It's just that you all were such good friends, back in high school. Those were happy times, weren't they? It would be good for Tim to reconnect with his old friends."

"Well," began Zoe, revealing a chink in her usual emotional armor, "we can probably fit something in, before we leave tomorrow."

"I'll give him a call and see if we can fix something up," promised Sara.

Pam gave them a relieved smile. "That would be great. Thank you so much. You're good girls."

Then she was gone, and Sara and Zoe were obviously regretting their acquiescence to Pam's request. "C'mon, girls," urged Lucy. "These plates and glasses aren't going to wash themselves."

Many hands made light work, and the leftovers were soon wrapped and put away, the dishes were loaded in the dishwasher, the cans and bottles carried outside and added to the bin of recyclables. Lucy was alone in the kitchen, wiping down the counters, when she found herself automatically picking up Libby's water bowl, intending to fill it with fresh water. She was reaching for the tap when she realized the bowl was no longer needed, and tears filled her eyes. Standing there at the sink, she let them come. Libby, after all, had been her best friend.

Chapter Six

Bill liked to cook up a hearty breakfast on Sunday mornings, and the delicious scent of bacon drew the girls to the breakfast table. Along with bacon, he'd made blueberry pancakes and scrambled eggs and had added the remains of a bottle of prosecco left over from Libby's funeral to the orange juice, making weak mimosas.

"Some spread, Dad," said Sara, eagerly loading up her plate.

"That's a lot of calories," warned Zoe, sipping her mimosa. "I think I'll skip the pancakes."

"I know what your refrigerator looks like," said Lucy. "Yogurt, salad, and more yogurt. You ought to fill up for the lean times ahead."

"Okay, Mom," agreed Zoe, laughing, and adding a couple of pancakes to her plate. "I never can resist real maple syrup."

"No substitutes are allowed in this establishment," declared Bill, delivering a platter mounded with eggs and bacon to the table and joining them. "So what are your plans for the day? You're going to stick around for a while, aren't you?"

"Yeah, we promised Mrs. Stillings that we'd get together with Tim," grumbled Sara.

"She was saying how we were all such good friends," began Zoe, in a puzzled tone. "I don't remember it that way at all. Tim was always a weirdo."

"Yeah," added Sara, "remember how he wore black every single day and sat in the back of the bus, grunting along to some awful head-banger music."

"He'd argue with the teachers all the time. He told Mr. Fitz that there was no sense learning math since he had a calculator; he refused to dissect a frog . . ." remembered Zoe.

"And he wrote his senior paper on people he claimed were political prisoners jailed by the government . . ."

"Which Ms. Reynolds did not find amusing," added Zoe.

Sara took a bite of bacon. "What's there to do with him? I need to get going after lunch, and the only thing happening in Tinker's Cove on Sunday morning is church."

"Like Tim would go to church!" scoffed Zoe.

"How about a walk at Quissett Point," suggested Lucy. "It's going to be hot today, but there's always a sea breeze out there."

"Good idea," said Sara. "But it's got to be this morning."

"I bet he won't come," said Zoe, reaching for another pancake. "He'll want to sleep in."

"For sure," agreed Sara.

But much to the girls' surprise, Tim agreed to the walk. He promised to be dressed and outside the house, ready to be picked up for the short ride to the trail in fifteen minutes. The girls were a bit late, but they were soon off, leaving Lucy and Bill at the table. Lucy was reaching for the Sunday paper when Bill stood up, announcing he was meeting Bob Goodman at the golf course and leaving her to clean up the kitchen.

Bill was a notoriously messy cook, so it took Lucy quite

a while to scrub the greasy pans, mop the drips of batter off the counters, and clean the stove top. She'd finally gotten back to the paper and the crossword when her phone rang. It was Sara, sounding out of sorts.

"Mom, we don't know what to do. Everything was okay until we got to the lighthouse, but then, all of sudden, Tim ran off and disappeared."

"Did you guys have a disagreement or something? Was he upset?"

"Nope. Everything was fine, and then one minute he was there, the next he was gone. What should we do?"

"I bet it's just some sort of prank; he's probably waiting for you back in the parking lot."

"I hope so." Sara sounded doubtful. "I feel responsible for him, but I really can't waste a lot of time waiting around for him."

"Well, remember, he's going through a difficult time. He needs understanding . . ."

"And I need to prepare for a departmental meeting."

"I'm sure he'll be in the parking lot," said Lucy, crossing her fingers.

Zoe called when they reached the parking lot, reporting that there was still no sign of Tim and Sara was really anxious to get going. Lucy suggested they wait fifteen minutes and then leave, with or without him. Ending the call, Lucy stood by the window, drumming her fingers and staring out at the trees, where not a leaf stirred. The thermometer outside was inching up to ninety degrees. Dangerously warm for a long run or even a walk.

Right on time, fifteen minutes later, she got another call reporting that Tim had not shown up and they were coming home. Lucy decided she'd better let Pam know what had happened.

"Oh, well," sighed Pam. "Best-laid plans, eh? It was good of the girls to try."

"But what about Tim?" pressed Lucy. "He's out in the heat. Does he have water? A hat? Sunscreen?"

"I doubt it," confessed Pam. "There's no point worrying. Chances are he'll be fine. He's probably already on his way home by foot. He thinks nothing of walking miles and miles; he does it a lot."

"Ted was very worried last week," said Lucy.

"Well, he didn't make it to work on Wednesday—wouldn't get out of bed, in fact—but he was better on Thursday. Up and out of the house before I woke up, in fact."

Poor Pam, thought Lucy, as she heard the gravel in the driveway crunch, announcing Zoe and Sara's return. She didn't for a moment believe Pam wasn't worrying, she knew she was putting up a brave front. Tim was not the only one struggling; he was bringing his parents down with him.

Back at work on Monday, Lucy spent most of the afternoon covering a lengthy Finance Committee meeting. The committee was working to prepare a presentation in support of the override that was the main purpose of the upcoming special town meeting, and the members knew only too well that opposition to the increased spending was growing.

"Folks voted for the community center, but now they don't want to pay for it," complained Beatrice Popper.

"Well, the center did go over budget," reminded Bill Smithers.

"Buyer's remorse," said Phil McDermott. "Seeing the plans was one thing, but now that it's built, folks are wondering if they really needed air-conditioning or such a big gym."

"Or if they even needed a community center at all," added Melanie Woods.

Apart from the members, the meeting was sparsely attended. Besides Lucy, the only citizens in the audience were Dot Kirwan, her daughter Deirdre, and self-appointed citizen watchdog Natalie Withers. The Kirwans had a family interest in Tinker's Cove's finances, as many members of the clan were employed by the town. Natalie, however, was a new arrival; she'd moved to Tinker's Cove when she retired from her job as a claims adjuster for an insurance company. She was somewhat jaundiced by this experience and had come to believe that humans—all humans except herself—were dishonest by nature. This conviction had driven her to shoulder what she believed was the singular responsibility of making sure that tax dollars in Tinker's Cove were spent appropriately and there was no finagling.

Lucy knew that Natalie was upset about Darleen's unusual vacation arrangement, and she tried to avoid her by ducking out of the meeting the moment Phil raised his gavel to adjourn, but Natalie blocked her at the door. "Did you follow up on that Darleen woman?" she demanded.

"I did," said Lucy, attempting to edge around Natalie's substantial figure. "It's all aboveboard. She had booked the vacation before she got the job and made it a condition for accepting the position. She had already paid for it and made all the travel arrangements."

"Likely story," scoffed Natalie. "Considering her inflated salary, it seems she could have taken the loss and rescheduled the trip."

"I think the Personnel Committee wanted to get off on

the right foot and have a positive relationship," said Lucy, who was growing impatient. "If you don't mind, I have to get back to the office, and you're blocking the door."

"I'll walk with you," declared Natalie, stepping aside. "It's not just the Personnel Committee, mind you," she continued, as they made their way down the hall and out to the parking lot. "The whole town is mismanaged. This override is just one example. If there had been keener oversight, it wouldn't be needed."

"Natalie," began Lucy, stopping outside the door and facing her unwanted companion, "I hate to tell you this, but Tinker's Cove got along for three hundred years without you, and it's managed just fine."

"Well, that's definitely not the case nowadays," declared Natalie. "If you were doing your job properly, you'd be investigating that town hall, which, thanks to rampant nepotism, is filled with incompetents and crooks. They're all related, and they all cover for each other. The only way anybody gets a town job is if they know somebody and their family's been here for three hundred years."

"That's not true," argued Lucy, who knew only too well that Natalie had a point, although a small one. "Well, not entirely true," she continued, amending her position. "I work closely with town employees to cover local news, and I've found them to be hardworking, responsible, honest folks. It's true that a lot of them are related and come from families that settled here centuries ago, but that doesn't make them corrupt. If anything, they feel strongly about their hometown and want it to keep it robust and healthy."

Natalie cocked her head and gave Lucy a skeptical look. "I see you've been drinking the Kool-Aid," she said. "Maybe you need to examine the contents of the stuff you've been swallowing." With that, Natalie marched off toward her modest sedan, leaving Lucy completely speechless.

She made her way to her car, where she sat for a moment, waiting for the AC to kick in. While she sat, she watched the committee members begin leaving, accompanied by Dot and Deirdre. They were all chatting, commenting on the heat in the parking lot, presenting a picture of easy conviviality. Lucy had always thought that the way people got to know each other was one of the benefits of small-town life, but now she wasn't so sure. Maybe Natalie was on to something; maybe that closeness made them reluctant to challenge each other. It was easier to get along when people went along.

She shifted into drive, intending to head back to the office, wondering how on earth she could begin a deep dive into the town's finances. She found explaining the annual town budget to readers challenging enough. Besides, she wasn't sure she wanted to risk offending town employees with whom she'd spent years cultivating cooperative relationships. But that, she realized, was exactly the sort of thing Natalie was accusing her of.

She was passing the office of Bill's accountant, Jack deRossi, and impulsively decided to pay him a quick visit. She did have a question about her quarterly tax payments, and maybe she could get some idea about how to identify fraud. Jack had a one-man operation, and his office was always filled with stacks of paper; he never had time to properly file the various statements and accounts that flooded in, but somehow he always managed to find exactly what he needed, when he needed it. He was at his desk when Lucy walked into his office and greeted her with a smile.

"How's it going, Lucy?"

"Business is good, which is why I need some advice about the upcoming September 15 quarterly payment," she began.

His answer, which he delivered with a smile, was not at all what she wanted to hear.

"That much?" she asked, incredulous.

"Sorry," he said, with a sympathetic smile.

"Oh, well," she sighed, resigned to emptying her checking account. "There's something else I want to ask you. Some locals have been suggesting that all is not as it should be in town hall, that there's not enough oversight and employees could be cooking the books."

Jack gave her a surprised look. "Really?"

"I'm with you. I don't believe it. But if I did have to do some digging around, what should I look for?"

Jack leaned back in his chair and scratched his chin. He was middle-aged, and years of sitting at a desk had taken their toll; he had quite a belly. "It's hard; that's why these things go on for years and years before they're discovered. It usually takes a major audit . . ."

"Well, I'm no auditor," admitted Lucy. "I can't even balance my checkbook."

He smiled. "I could do that for you . . ."

"For a fee, I suppose," countered Lucy. "I'm actually quite comfortable with my method. As long as the bank says I have more money than I think I have, it's all good."

Jack smiled and clucked his tongue. "That's no way to run your finances."

Lucy shrugged. "But say I ran short and had access to some petty cash . . ."

"That's often how it starts, I think. Somebody needs ten

dollars to contribute to a retirement party or something, and they pull it out of the petty-cash drawer, fully intending to pay it back. But they forget, and it becomes a habit, and before you know it, they're padding expense accounts and making up phony receipts. Trouble is, these small amounts add up over time."

"And nobody's going to let me examine their petty cash," said Lucy.

"Not without a warrant," said Jack, chuckling. He leaned forward, propping his elbows on his desk. "Then there's 'pay to play' schemes. They're dangerous because word tends to get out, and if it's big enough, like that mayor in Massachusetts who collected hundreds of thousands of dollars to issue licenses to sell recreational pot, well, then the feds get involved."

"That would be easier for me to investigate," suggested Lucy, thinking out loud. "If the building inspector, for example, was shaking down contractors to issue occupancy permits, sooner or later somebody would start complaining."

Jack was doubtful. "Do you think that's really happening?"

"Not at all," admitted Lucy. "Just a hypothetical example."

"Keeping folks honest is one strong argument for paying competitive salaries," observed Jack. "And it was something we were mindful of when I was on the Personnel Committee. Let's face it, it can be very tempting for people who handle lots of money but may be strapped financially to help themselves. It's easy to rationalize that they deserve it; they're underpaid, after all, and it won't be missed."

"Especially if they don't like their boss," said Lucy.

"Always a factor," said Jack.

"Thanks for your expertise," said Lucy, swinging her bag onto her shoulder.

"Remember, if you get in trouble with that checking account . . ."

"I'll give you a call," promised Lucy, giving him a smile and a little wave.

Chapter Seven

Lucy was thoughtful as she left the accountant's office, and she paused on the sidewalk, gazing down Main Street, past the town hall, police station, and fire department. Through the years, her job had taken her into them all, and she'd gotten to know each and every one of the town employees. She'd watched Chief Buzz Bresnahan and his crew battle fires, risking their own lives to save others; she'd covered the transition from a volunteer force to a professional one. She'd seen Jim Kirwan's police department handle everything from a bike-safety clinic to a hostage situation that required calling in the state police SWAT team. And as for the folks in town hall, she knew they were on the front line when property assessments went up, or the snow plows didn't clear the roads as quickly as expected, or a beloved tree was cut down. The town's workers were easy targets and all too often heard the familiar taxpayer's refrain, "I'm the one paying your salary, y'know!"

It seemed that every year, at the annual town meeting in May, somebody had an issue with an employee's salary. It was usually the more highly paid workers who took the heat, like the school superintendent or the police chief, but even the summer hires on the road crew were often called out for "leaning on their shovels" and failing to properly "put their backs into their work."

Lucy found it understandable that people who were juggling two or three low-paying jobs and had skimpy or no benefits at all resented town employees with their thirty-five-hour week and paid vacations, as well as health and retirement plans. The pensions were a real source of irritation, as most folks in Tinker's Cove lived paycheck to paycheck and were unable to fund IRAs; they knew they would have to rely solely on Social Security in their not-so-golden years. Adding to the rumblings of discontent was the fact that most town employees managed to stay on the job for years and years, accruing seniority and sizable pension funds. And all the numbers for pension and health-insurance costs were there in black and white when the Finance Committee presented the annual budget at town meeting.

There was also a growing sense of resentment toward the Kirwan clan, who seemed to get special treatment when there was a rare job opening. No matter that they were usually the most-qualified applicants; to many folks, it seemed that the only qualification that mattered was having Kirwan for a last name. Dot, who was a cashier at the IGA, was widowed at a young age and had raised her large family alone. She often felt forced to remind folks that her cash drawer at the store always came out to the penny at the end of the day, and she had raised her kids to be every bit as honest and reliable as she was. As a young widow, she had taken a long, hard look at the available options and had concluded that town jobs offered her kids the best security in a capitalistic boom-and-bust economy and encouraged them to major in subjects like criminal justice, education, building management, and public health that would qualify them for town jobs. There were now three Kirwans, two sons and a granddaughter, in the police department and a couple of grandkids in the fire department; a daughter-in-law headed the Council on Aging, and numerous nieces and nephews had jobs in the schools.

Lucy knew that being smarter and more successful didn't necessarily make you popular, especially with people who were struggling with poverty, drug addiction, domestic violence, and other social blights. Tinker's Cove was a lot more prosperous now than it had been when she and Bill first moved to their antique farmhouse on Red Top Road, but the gap between the haves and have-nots had continued to grow.

Lucy was thinking about social divisions and the rising costs that were making Tinker's Cove unaffordable for young people as she got back into her car for the short drive to the office. She could understand why some less-advantaged folks were jealous and resentful of town employees, but Natalie Withers seemed to have retired at the top of the heap. Her motivation was different, perhaps simply a desire to make sure things were done properly, or maybe she got some sense of power by pointing out others' deficiencies. She couldn't be certain exactly what motivated Natalie, but she did know that, sooner or later, she'd have to deal with her accusations.

Driving down Main Street, she realized she was passing the former Boxer's Pharmacy, where folks used to get prescriptions filled and could enjoy a root-beer float from the soda fountain while they waited. Boxer's, alas, had been closed for years, and now Bill had been hired to renovate the space into a trendy shop that would offer soaps, lotions, and healthy smoothies. She knew that the local contractors were incorrigible gossips, sharing bits of news as they loaded up at the lumberyard or unloaded at the dump, so she impulsively pulled into an empty parking space in front and went in to say hi.

"Looks great," she said, stepping into the space, which now boasted fresh paint on the tin ceiling, polished wood paneling, a repaired tile floor, and a restored soda fountain, sans stools. Bill was on his knees, nailing in baseboard.

"What happened to the stools?" she asked, remembering the row of tall chrome models that swiveled.

"They're getting refinished and reupholstered," he said, getting to his feet. "Some of the soda fountain fittings are getting replated, too. It's gonna be nice."

"But no frappes or lime rickeys?"

"No," said Bill, shaking his head. "As I understand it, wheat-grass-and-kale smoothies to go with your sea-salt scrub."

"Sounds delicious," said Lucy, somewhat sarcastically. "And probably expensive."

"Yup, they're investing quite a bit in this redo."

"Oh, good." Lucy was thinking that their checking account could use a boost. "That reminds me," she began, "you know a lot of folks are talking about the override, and I've even heard accusations that some town employees are corrupt. Have you heard anything?"

"Maybe," said Bill, idly swinging his hammer. "I've heard rumors that the new building inspector, Rob Jackson, can be real tough. Some guys think he's looking for a little"—he brushed his thumb against his fingers—"you know, to guarantee passing inspection."

"Has he done that to you?" asked Lucy.

"No. But I play by the rules." He smiled. "He was pretty involved in the community center, you know. He put up quite a fuss about the asphalt parking lot, wanted gravel, and got shot down by the highway superintendent. I also heard he insisted on different shingles. He didn't like the ones the architect chose; he said he wanted more eco-friendly ones that were quite a bit more expensive. He might've had genuine concerns about the original ones, or maybe he was looking for a kickback from whoever was selling the ecological ones."

"Kickback?"

"Yeah. The seller inflates the price, then gives a cut to the buyer. The inflated price goes on the invoice."

"So the town pays more, and the inspector gets a cut?"

"Yeah."

"And people are saying this happened?"

Bill flipped the hammer in the air and caught it. "Some people."

"Do you think it's true?"

"Haven't made up my mind," he said, with a slow smile.

"Well, if you hear anything more about it, let me know, okay?"

"As long as I don't have to reveal my sources," he said, teasingly.

Lucy gave an exasperated sigh. "See ya later."

Ted was in the office when she got back, so she recounted the rumors she'd been hearing, asking if he thought she should attempt an investigation. Ted didn't seem all that interested, but Phyllis leaped at the idea.

"It's about time!" she declared, her zebra-striped cheaters slipping off her nose and dangling from their gold chain to rest on her ample bosom. "Taxes keep going up at the same time they're cutting back on services. Last winter, the plow only came down my street once after that big storm; it was an icy nightmare. And the sidewalk in front of my house! It's crumbling away, and I have to walk in the street when I go for my morning constitutional. And Elfrida," she continued, naming her niece who was a single mom, "Elfrida tells me that come fall there won't be reading and math specialists at the elementary school; they've all been laid off."

"So what do you think, Ted? Bill tells me a lot of contractors aren't happy with the new building inspector, and, of course, there's the whole Darleen thing at the community center."

"I don't know," mumbled Ted, who was staring out the window. "Nobody's ever happy about paying taxes."

"But it's more than that," argued Lucy. "I've been hearing specific allegations about town employees. We've got to get on top of this before the special town meeting so that folks know what's really happening. Whether they're getting ripped off or not."

"Hmm," said Ted, scratching his chin.

Lucy pressed her boss for an answer. "Well, what do you want to do, Ted?"

"Do what you think best," he finally said, standing up and walking over to the water cooler. He stood there, staring at the big blue bottle as if he'd never seen it before.

"Uh, Ted," began Phyllis. "Is something bothering you?"

He pulled a paper cup out of the holder. "Yeah. It's Tim."

"What about Tim?" asked Lucy, wondering how long it would be before he actually filled the cup with water.

"He hasn't come home," he said, staring at the empty cup. "He went out with your girls yesterday but never came home."

"They went to Quissett Point," said Lucy, feeling she had to defend her kids. "The girls were upset; they said that when they got to the lighthouse he ran off, leaving them. They waited a while but finally had to leave. I checked with Pam; she said he takes long walks, thinks nothing of walking miles."

"That's true." Ted pushed the blue lever, letting water fill his cup. Lucy watched, holding her breath, fearing he would let it run over, but he took his hand off the lever in the nick of time. "He's never done this, though. Staying out all night."

"Do you think he spent the whole day and night walking?"

Ted stared at his cup of water. "I have no idea. It doesn't seem possible, does it?" He lifted the cup to his lips, then lowered it without drinking. "We have absolutely no idea what he does or where he goes."

An unpleasant thought occurred to Lucy. "Do you think it's drugs?"

Ted looked once again at the cup of water, then decided he didn't want it after all. He went over to the pothos plant that rambled over the reception counter and dumped the water into the pot. "He never tells us what he's been doing, and I'm not sure he knows. I think it's some sort of walking amnesia." Just then his cell phone rang, and he yanked it out of his pocket and slammed it against his ear. "What's up?" he demanded.

Lucy and Phyllis waited with bated breath, hoping it was Pam, calling with good news. When he nodded and gave a little smile, they figured it was. "He's home?" asked Phyllis.

"Yeah." He put the phone back in his pocket. "Crisis averted." He tossed the empty paper cup in the trash and headed for the door, marching out without bothering to explain where he was going.

"Must run in the family," observed Lucy.

The rest of the week was quiet as Lucy covered the usual town committee meetings and interviewed a local amateur meteorologist for a feature about the record-breaking heat. Without getting an approval from Ted, she didn't pursue the corruption angle, but she had been studying the town budget closely and did ask various committee members about items that seemed out of line compared to last year's budget. Howard Wilcox, a former selectman now serving on the planning board, had a few questions of his own. "What are you up to, Lucy?" he asked.

"There are a lot of rumblings about town finances," she said. "I'm trying to get the facts out before things get nasty."

"I think the special town meeting is going to be very contentious," said Wilcox. "I do think the Personnel Committee made an unwise decision to pay that Darleen woman such a big salary. That's a fact, and there's no way of sugar-coating it. This vacation is a real slap in the face to hardworking folks."

"So it seems," said Lucy, struck by his reaction. Wilcox had devoted many years to Tinker's Cove, serving on practically every town committee. The fact that he was worried about the growing discontent among taxpayers only confirmed her suspicion that trouble was brewing.

Town finances were uppermost in her mind a few days later when she joined her friends for their usual Thursday-morning breakfast at Jake's Donut Shack; she'd noticed a large increase in several town department budgets over last year's amounts, and it was nagging at her. Was it simply inflation, or was Natalie Withers on to something? But when she joined Sue, Pam, and Rachel at their usual table, they were talking about Corinne Appleton's tragic death.

"That was some story, Lucy," said Sue, swallowing hard. "It never fails to get to me. That pretty young girl . . ."

"It's her family I think about," said Rachel. "How awful it must have been, almost two years of not knowing what happened. You'd never be able to forget; it would take over your life. The wondering, and the fear." Her big brown eyes brimmed with sympathy. "And they still don't know what happened, only that Corinne died. Wicker pleaded guilty but didn't give any details. They don't know how long he kept her, what he did to her, nothing."

"It's the picture of that scrap of cloth that always gets to me," confessed Pam.

"That little pink flower button—that does me in," added Lucy.

"Poor you, having to deal with it all over again," said Pam. "It must be hard."

"It is, but it's worth it to keep that monster in jail," said Lucy, as Norine approached to take their orders. That business completed, Pam announced her new project.

"I'm making a quilt—a crazy quilt, no pun intended—about Tim's life," she declared, pulling out her smartphone and presenting them with a photo of the partially completed quilt top.

"That's gorgeous!" exclaimed Sue. "You clever thing! I didn't know you could sew."

"I'm not really a sewer, but I did learn to operate a sewing machine in home ec, a zillion years ago. I pulled mine out of a closet and discovered it's like riding a bike: once you learn, you never forget."

"What about the embroidery?" asked Lucy, remembering crazy quilts she saw at the quilt show. "Can you do that?"

"Yeah. I can do a simple blanket stitch." Pam's face fell. "What I'm having trouble with is the way each scrap of fabric reminds me of Tim's childhood. He was a happy kid, wasn't he? He was a Cub Scout, he played Little League; I've got the proof. The Cub Scout shirt, the baseball uniform, his favorite pajamas. Every bit takes me back, and I can't figure out where I went wrong."

They were silent as Norine arrived with their orders and then returned with a fresh pot to top off their mugs of coffee. When she had gone, Rachel picked a bit off the top of her Sunshine Muffin and chewed thoughtfully. "You didn't do anything wrong, Pam," she finally said. "You didn't cause Tim's illness."

"Easy for you to say," countered Pam. "I've got to live with constant worry. Will he go to his job or will he stay in bed all day? Will he go out and stay out, doing who knows what for days at a time? And the worst part is thinking that somehow I'm responsible."

"They still don't know much about mental illness," declared Sue. "They don't know why two people can go through the same traumatic experience and have completely different reactions. One person recovers quickly, while another struggles with PTSD."

For once, Rachel admitted that psychiatry did not have all the answers. "Psychiatrists can't even agree on definitions for various conditions, like schizophrenia, manic depression. Even simple depression can be difficult to treat."

"If you ask me," volunteered Lucy, "it's all about chemical imbalance."

"Or genetics," chimed in Sue. "Some naughty little chromosome."

"You're both right. There's any number of things that can cause mental instability," said Rachel, reaching across the table to clasp Pam's hand. "The important thing to remember is that there's no one to blame. It's not your fault; it's not Tim's fault. We don't blame people for catching colds or a stomach virus, and it should be the same with mental illness."

"Well, if you ask me," grumbled Pam, "somebody should figure this thing out."

Chapter Eight

That night, after she'd finished cleaning up the dinner dishes, Lucy decided to clear out the dog's things. Libby's bed and her food and water bowls were all sad reminders that she was gone, but the object that Lucy found hardest to face was the old leather leash hanging on its hook by the door. All she had to do was reach for that leash and Libby would be on her feet by her side, tail wagging, ready to go. Libby loved a walk, but even better, from her point of view, was a ride in the car. A ride in Bill's truck, however, was doggy bliss. She would sit proudly by his side, tongue lolling in the breeze and enjoying the passing scenery. She really came into her own, however, when he parked the truck at the lumberyard and left her in charge. Then, aware that she was now the boss of the truck, she kept a wary eye on all comers as she waited patiently for his return.

Lucy intended to donate the dog's things to the Community Church thrift shop, but when she gathered up the dog's bedding, she decided it was too smelly, and too matted with fur, to appeal to anyone and decided to throw it away. She was bundling it into the trash when a red, white, and blue bandanna fell loose, and she snatched it up. It was Libby's Fourth of July accessory, worn when she marched with her family and all the other dogs in the annual parade. That, Lucy thought, was possibly her finest moment, when she joined her people and the other dogs in a huge pack and they all marched together down Main Street. Being a dog, she conveniently forgot about the booming fireworks that inevitably followed the parade and sent her scuttling frantically under the bed for refuge.

Oh, well, thought Lucy, setting the carton on the kitchen table so she wouldn't forget it in the morning, Libby had a good life. As good a life as any dog could expect, and that thought comforted her. But she still missed Libby's presence, the clicking of her nails on the wood floor, the way she would lean her shoulder against Lucy's leg when she wanted something, and, most of all, stroking that whiskery chin and those silky ears. Somewhat ashamed of herself for giving way to her emotions, she decided to indulge in a good, long soak in the bathtub. She could have a good cry in there all by herself.

Next morning, she tucked the carton in the back of her SUV, dropped it at the thrift shop as planned, and went on to the community center to see how things were going now that it was up and running. Darleen was an enthusiastic guide, taking her through the building where yoga was taking place in the gym, volunteers were offering Medicare counseling at the Council on Aging office, and preparations for the senior lunch were well underway in the kitchen. "Today it's beef stew. Doesn't it smell delicious?" she exclaimed. Lucy had been snapping photos of everything and was attempting to convince one of the cooks to pose with spoon in hand when she heard a crash. She turned around and saw the source of the noise; Tim had apparently knocked over a stack of chairs. He was attempting to replace them, an awkward job at best, when Darleen went for him like a guided missile.

"What do you think you're doing?" she demanded, angrily, wagging a finger at him.

"Uh, the chairs fell, and I'm putting them back," he said, as if it was completely obvious, which it was. He was wearing the blue work shirt and matching pants required for the town's custodial crew, but Lucy was relieved to see he hadn't suffered any ill effects from his night away from home. He was freshly shaved, in fact, and had made some attempt to tame his shaggy head of hair.

"Well, don't you think our senior citizens would like to sit down when they eat their lunch? Hunh?" demanded Darleen, tapping her foot.

"Uh, I guess so," admitted Tim.

"So maybe instead of stacking the chairs, you should be putting them by the tables?"

Tim's face reddened, but he maintained a cool attitude. "Okay."

Darleen placed both hands on her hips. "I don't like your attitude, Tim. You don't seem to care about your work. You're simply not interested in doing a good job."

Tim's head dropped, and he stared at the floor.

"Don't you have anything to say for yourself?" she demanded.

Tim didn't look up. "Um, you can fire me, if you want. Or I could quit."

"I don't want to fire you!" she growled, through clenched teeth. "I want you to try harder!"

Tim nodded. "Okay. I'll try harder."

"Good. Because, believe you me, buddy, you're on borrowed time here."

"But I just said I'm happy to quit . . ." began Tim, confused.

Darleen's eyes were blazing. "Don't get wise with me, mister!"

"Uh, sorry," he mumbled.

"You better be!" snarled Darleen, marching back to join Lucy, who had retreated to the doorway. Lucy wasn't sure what to expect, but Darleen smiled pleasantly and took her elbow, leading her into the hallway. Once there, she gave a nervous little laugh. "Good help is so hard to find," she said, as if she were the lady of the manor, apologizing for a lackadaisical maid.

"I happen to know Tim's family quite well," said Lucy. "I'm not sure you're aware that he's recovering from a mental crisis and needs positive support. This job is an important first step toward recovery for him. He's highly educated, you know, and was a curator at the Farnsworth, where there was a more collegial atmosphere."

Darleen was quite tall, Lucy realized, and towered above her in her very high-heeled shoes. She looked down on Lucy from her high eminence and condescended to explain herself to Lucy. "This center is funded by the taxpayers, Lucy, and I am determined to make sure the taxpayers receive good value for their hard-earned dollars. This is a community center, not a rehab facility, and I expect everyone who works here to earn their salaries. I will not tolerate slipshod work."

Lucy found herself struck by Darleen's hypocrisy and wondered if she really did not understand how she was perceived by many citizens. "Speaking of good value, there's a lot of talk in town about your paid vacation, and your salary. A lot of people aren't very happy that you're going off on a vacation after only a couple of weeks on the job, especially considering your generous salary."

Darleen rolled her eyes. "People can be so quick to judge," she said. "The Personnel Committee members were most understanding when I explained I'd already booked and paid for this trip. I'm long overdue for a vacation, and I explained that I would be better able to give my all after a much-needed hiatus. We all need time to renew and refresh. I'm sure you would agree."

Actually, Lucy didn't feel she was in a position to agree. She hadn't had a vacation in years and could never count on having time off on weekends and holidays. News broke at all hours, and she had to cover it, whether that meant waiting up at town hall until all the votes were finally counted in the wee hours of the morning or if a fire broke out inconsiderately on a holiday.

"Well, there's no rest for the wicked," said Lucy, shrugging off the negative aspects of the job she loved. "Where will you be spending your vacation?"

"It's a dream come true, starting tomorrow, when I'll be off and away," began Darleen, with a big sigh. "I've always wanted to stay at this resort in California, the Hotel del Coronado in San Diego. It's one of those grand old hotels, probably the grandest. It's right on the beach; I'm finally going to see the Pacific Ocean, maybe even swim in it. They actually shot the movie *Some Like It Hot* there! I'm going to spend two entire weeks doing absolutely nothing except relaxing." She paused. "Well, I am planning on treating myself to some spa treatments."

Lucy couldn't help it; she was envious. "Boy, that sounds great," she admitted. "I can't think of anything nicer than letting somebody else make the bed."

"I'll send you a postcard," promised Darleen, by way of farewell as she saw Lucy to the door.

Once she was back in her car, Lucy took a moment to check her phone and found another voice mail from citizen watchdog Natalie Withers. The woman must have extrasensory perception, she thought, listening to her list of complaints, which began with Darleen's salary and ended with a request for a return call as she had other important information.

In for a penny, in for a pound, thought Lucy, hitting the call button. Natalie answered on the first ring. "Thanks for returning my call, Lucy," she said, immediately moving on to Darleen's salary. "I find it hard to understand what the Personnel Committee members were thinking. Do you realize that woman is making more than the fire chief, the police chief, or the superintendent of schools? Have you asked any of the board members about this?"

Lucy felt a bit guilty since she hadn't actually spoken to any board members. "Even better, I spoke to Darleen directly," she said, attempting a counteroffensive. "Darleen said they were impressed with her excellent references and qualifications, and the salary they offered was less than what she'd been earning at her previous job."

"What was that job?"

"Running a big charity somewhere in Connecticut. I think it was the United Way, but I'd have to check."

"Hmm," responded Natalie.

"Darleen also said they were worried about insulting her with the lower figure, but they knew it was the most the town could afford. She also said they told her they didn't want to lose her; she was by far the best-qualified candidate, and that's why they sweetened the deal with the vacation arrangement."

"Well, it's very unfortunate, if you ask me, and sets a bad precedent," insisted Natalie. Lucy could have sworn she heard the wheels turning in Natalie's head, prompting her to pose another question. "I wonder how thoroughly they checked those references? Job applicants often pad their résumés, you know."

"I can't vouch for all the committee members, but I know that nothing much gets past Lydia Volpe."

"Still, it's worth looking into," suggested Natalie. "Darleen's not the only town employee living high on the hog. I saw that new building inspector, Rob Jackson, driving a fancy electric SUV that I happen to know sells for well over sixty thousand dollars. Now where did a building inspector get that kind of money?"

"I don't know," said Lucy, growing impatient. "Not everyone lives from paycheck to paycheck. Maybe he has a trust fund or got an inheritance. Won the lottery. It's really none of my business." She paused for breath. "Maybe we should congratulate him for investing in a car that's good for the environment as well as a practical choice for his job. The town reimburses employees for gas they use on the job, you know. Just think how much he's saving the town."

"I suppose," admitted Natalie, in a grudging tone of voice. "But that elementary school principal—I don't know her name, but I'm sure it was her because I've seen her directing traffic at pickup—she's toting around a Louis Vuitton handbag. Those bags cost over a thousand dollars, you know."

"I didn't know," laughed Lucy, who was presently toting a bag she found on sale for nineteen ninety-nine. "But, again, maybe it was a gift from her rich mother. Maybe she saved up because she always wanted one. I really don't think that working for the town means an employee has to take a vow of poverty and explain every purchase."

"I agree, Lucy, and I don't expect them to. But I do see these luxury purchases as possible indicators of corruption. I don't expect you to start examining employees' charge account bills . . ."

"That would be illegal, even if I could somehow gain access," said Lucy, shocked at the very idea.

"Of course," admitted Natalie, "but I do think it's possible that not all is quite right with the town's finances. That's where you should start, with the treasurer's office."

Lucy jammed her key into the ignition and started the car. "I'm a reporter, not an auditor," she said. "I can barely make sense of my own checkbook; simply reporting on the town budget every year stretches my skills to the limit. What you're asking for would require a forensic audit, and those are very expensive and take a long time." Lucy paused. "Frankly, I think you need to think twice before accusing people of dishonesty. They tend to take it personally, and they don't like it." With that, she ended the call and shifted into drive. The car lurched forward, and she quickly braked. Whoa, she told herself. Calm down. Try to get to work in one piece. Breathe.

Driving the quarter mile to the office, she struggled to control her emotions. She didn't like the way Darleen treated Tim; it had been painful to watch her scolding him. Was it abuse? Darn close, she thought, wondering if she ought to tell Pam and Ted about it. For all she knew, they thought the job was going to help Tim, while it seemed more likely to harm his fragile recovery. And why did Darleen behave in such a negative way? She was supposed to be a highly qualified professional. Was it a simple personality conflict? Or was Darleen really a bully at heart? It seemed to

Lucy that the woman had some issues of her own, but in her defense, it was early days in a new job, and she was bound to make some mistakes. Everyone made mistakes, Lucy told herself, and she was well aware that she had made a goodly number herself. Tolerance should be her byword.

And why was Natalie so convinced that Tinker's Cove was a pit of corruption? Did she simply have a suspicious nature, or was she really on to something? And perhaps she shouldn't have ended the call so abruptly. It was her job to listen, and maybe Natalie was handing her the scoop of the century. Well, in the larger scheme of things, corruption in a small Maine town was hardly an earth-shaking revelation and was unlikely to be of interest to anyone who didn't happen to live in Tinker's Cove. But, Lucy decided, as she parked in her usual spot in front of the *Courier* office, it would certainly interest the town's citizens. She turned off the engine and picked up her phone, dialing Natalie.

"Hi," she began, speaking to voice mail, "this is Lucy, and I'm really sorry I was so abrupt. I want you to know I've been thinking over what you said, and I'm going to see what I can find out. So, thanks for the information, and I'll be in touch."

Chapter Nine

Lucy and Bill spent a quiet weekend that included a re-freshing afternoon sail on Bob Goodman's boat. Ted didn't come into the Tinker's Cove office on Monday or for the rest of the week and limited his communications with Phyllis and Lucy to brief text messages. That wasn't all that unusual, especially during a quiet news period. Lucy knew he preferred the Gilead office, which was more modern and where there was a handful of male employees he liked to pal around with. She didn't give it much thought, but when Pam skipped the usual Thursday breakfast, she began to suspect something was wrong.

"She said she's coming down with a summer cold and didn't want to spread it," explained Sue, sounding doubtful.

"Don't you believe her?" asked Lucy, joining Sue and Rachel at their usual table in Jake's.

"You can always tell if someone's got a cold; you can hear it in their voice, and she sounded just fine."

"Well, we all make polite excuses sometimes when we don't want to do something," said Rachel. "I usually say my sciatica is acting up."

"I didn't know you have sciatica," said Lucy, as Norine approached with the coffeepot.

"I don't," admitted Rachel, laughing, as Norine filled her mug.

"Where's the yogurt granola parfait?" demanded Norine, noticing the empty chair and referring to Pam by her regular order. "Are we waiting, or do you want to order?"

"Pam's not coming," said Sue.

"Regulars for everybody?" she asked, cocking an eyebrow.

Sue and Rachel nodded agreement, but Lucy hesitated. Somehow her usual order of hash and two eggs over easy didn't appeal on a muggy, hot morning. "I'll have a blueberry muffin instead," she said.

"Do you feel okay?" asked Norine, surprised. "Some sort of flu is going around."

"I'm okay. Just want a change."

"What about Pam? Has she got this flu?" Norine kept tabs on all her regulars.

"Maybe," admitted Sue. "She said she was coming down with something."

"Well, I hope she feels better soon," said Norine, tucking her pencil behind her ear and going off to place their orders.

"I still don't think Pam has the flu, or a cold," said Sue, after Norine had gone. "I think she's got Tim trouble."

The three friends exchanged looks. "So do I," said Rachel.

"So what do we do?" asked Lucy, as Norine returned with their orders.

"I packed up a yogurt parfait to-go for your friend," she said, plopping a paper bag containing Pam's regular order down on the table. "Maybe one of you could take it to her?"

"Sure thing," said Lucy, pleased to have an excuse for dropping by. "I'll do it on my way to the IGA."

When she arrived at Ted and Pam's ranch-style home, Pam greeted her in the doorway with a big hug and immediately burst into tears. "I'm a wreck," she admitted, brushing at her cheeks. "Tim's been gone since Saturday. I don't know what to do."

"Oh, my," said Lucy, stepping inside and shutting the door. "All week?" Horrible thoughts flooded her mind: Tim dead, Tim hurt somewhere and suffering, Tim lost and confused. She started to hug Pam, then remembered the little bag in her hand and held it up. "Norine insisted on sending you a yogurt parfait."

"Oh, that was nice of her," said Pam, operating on automatic. She took the bag and set it on the hall table. Then she stood, looking puzzled, as if trying to decide what to do next. "Oh," she finally said, "I was working on the quilt. Want to see?"

"Sure," said Lucy, following Pam's lead. She wanted to help and support her friend anyway she could, and right now, the quilt seemed to offer much needed distraction. "But first let me put this in the fridge."

"Oh, right," said Pam, wandering down the hallway. "The quilt's in the spare room."

Lucy stowed the yogurt in the fridge, her mind still struggling with frightening, dire thoughts. Pam must certainly be terrified for her son, but didn't want to discuss it. So she joined Pam in the third bedroom, which contained a guest bed and a table that had previously served as a nightstand but was now open, revealing her sewing machine. The neatly made bed was strewn with colorful bits of fabric, and the partially completed quilt top was on the extended leaf of the sewing machine cabinet. Pam lifted the machine's pressure foot and slid the fabric out, holding it up for Lucy to see. "What do you think? It's a crazy quilt—appropriate, right?"

"It's beautiful," said Lucy, who was not about to pick up on the "crazy" reference. Pam had produced a modern version of the Victorian favorite, made back then with oddly shaped scraps of velvet and silk, stitched together with decorative embroidery. Her quilt was made with bits of Tim's outgrown clothing, and Lucy recognized pieces from his Little League uniform, his blue Cub Scout shirt, some blue flannel that she thought was once a baby blanket, and a patch of red-and-green plaid she remembered as a favorite shirt. "You've got his whole life here."

"That's the idea," said Pam, snatching up some fabric from the bed. "See these? I found out you can print photos on fabric, see! This is his favorite stuffed toy!" She waved a square printed with a stuffed fox. "He called him Pilgrim. And here's a club he joined in high school, the Earth Day Club." That square showed a group of kids, including Lucy's daughter, Zoe. "I've even got his college graduation, see?" Lucy saw a handsome young man, dressed in cap and gown, with a big smile.

"Those are really going to make the quilt special," said Lucy.

"I know!" crowed Pam. "And I'm going to pick out details from the photos with embroidery. Like the tassel on his graduation cap and the tree on his T-shirt—here, see?" She jabbed at the image of her son, and then, pressing the fabric to her chest, collapsed on the edge of the bed. "Here I am, making this thing for Tim, and I don't know if he'll ever see it. I don't know where he is or what he's doing. I don't even know if he's alive or dead."

Lucy sat beside her and held her close. "Tell me all about it. When did you last see him?"

"He never came home last Friday night. He'd slept late that morning, which was bad because he was late for work, but I did get him to take his meds, and he was home for supper. Then when I was clearing up the dishes, I think he got a text or something, 'cause off he went. I watched him run down the street, then he turned the corner . . ."

"And no word at all from him since then?"

"No. I checked with the community center, and Sheri at the Council on Aging said she hasn't seen him all this week."

"Did she mention anything out of the ordinary? Was he upset? Was there some sort of conflict?"

"Not according to Sheri."

Interesting, thought Lucy. "What about the police?"

"Well, they're aware of the situation, that he's got some issues. But unless he commits a crime or becomes a danger to himself or others, there's not much they can do. Officer Sally said they'll keep an eye out for him, but even if they spot him, all they can do is advise him to call home."

"He's done this before, right? Like that day when he left my girls out at Quissett Point. Has he said anything about what he does? Where he goes?"

Pam looked up and stared blankly out the window, where white curtains with ball fringe framed the view of the opposite house. "He doesn't say. I'm not sure he re-members."

"He just comes home as if nothing's happened."

"Yeah. Ted thinks he's got walking amnesia, whatever that is." She patted the quilt top. "If it is something."

"Have you asked him what he was doing?"

"We're not supposed to pepper him with questions; that's what the doctors said."

"Oh." Lucy sat beside her friend, harboring deep doubts

about the advice she'd been given. "Do you think that's right?" she finally asked.

Pam shrugged and shook her head. "That's why I decided on the quilt. Go at it indirectly. Sideways. I hoped it would help him to open up."

"I think that's a good idea," said Lucy, patting Pam's knee.

"Hasn't worked so far."

"I wonder," began Lucy, thinking back to the weekend. "I wonder if he talked at all to the girls . . ."

Pam jumped on the notion. "Could you call them and ask?"

"Sure," said Lucy. She pulled out her cell and tapped Sara's name, but she didn't answer, and, not surprisingly, her voice mail was full. Calling Zoe, she had better luck.

"I'm here with Pam," Lucy began. "Tim's disappeared . . ."

"Disappeared! For how long?"

"Since last Saturday."

"Ohmigod!"

"Yeah. We're all very worried, and since you and Sara spent some time with him that Sunday, we wondered if he said anything that might give a clue to where he might be?"

"Maybe," said Zoe, speaking slowly as she formulated her thoughts. "At first, he was real quiet, just marched along. Then he grabbed a fallen stick covered with lichen and started in, kind of manic, really, saying it was a sign of climate change. I said something about wishing I knew what to do that would help, that I felt so helpless since it's such a big problem. He got kind of puffed up, sort of like he was high on something, and he said there were people. That's what he said, 'I know people who are doing something,' but when I asked what they were doing and if I could join, well, that's when he ran off."

Pam grabbed the phone. "Do you think he's with them? Maybe a bunch of survivalists? Or activists, like Greenpeace?"

"Maybe," admitted Zoe. She fell silent, and they heard a distant voice. Then Zoe came back. "Look, I gotta go. Good luck with Tim."

Pam returned the phone to Lucy, giving her a quick hug. "I think we're on to something here. He's always been involved with the environment, starting with kindergarten. He won the recycling award. I couldn't throw anything away; we had a compost pile, he and was really into zero waste. I used to have to smuggle the trash out of the house."

"Do you really think he's hooked up with a bunch of radical undercover climate activists?" asked Lucy, who thought she certainly would have heard if such a group was active in the region. "So far, the only climate-change activity I'm aware of is the garden club, urging us to plant native species and avoid using chemical fertilizers."

"I've got something to show you," said Pam, jumping to her feet. "Follow me." She dashed out of the room and down the hall to Tim's room, where she threw open the door to reveal an untidy mess. But strewn over the unmade bed and scattered among the clothes and shoes on the floor were books and magazines, many dealing with global warming and climate change. Flipping open one of the books, she displayed the notes Tim had made in the margins, along with charts and mathematical calculations. "He's really been obsessed with this," she said. "I wouldn't be surprised if he's out in the woods somewhere, living on weeds and trying to make zero impact on the ecosystem."

Maybe, thought Lucy, harboring doubts. From what she'd observed, Tim didn't seem to have the energy or initiative required to construct a zero-impact lifestyle. If anything, his focus seemed entirely inward; he couldn't even muster up enough resistance to stand up to Darleen. She thought of the way he'd reacted that Friday at the center, head bowed, as she'd showered him with insults. It was a purely defensive posture, and she feared that he was curled up, fetal-style, in some hole somewhere, licking his wounds.

"I'm sure he'll turn up soon," said Lucy, trying to be reassuring but fearing the worst. He'd attempted suicide once and failed; she feared a second attempt might be successful. But that was a thought she didn't dare utter.

"Well," she said, standing up, "I've got an empty fridge, and Bill's going to want dinner."

"You better go, then," said Pam. "Thanks for coming by."

Lucy wrapped her arms around her friend and gave her a long hug. "It's going to be okay."

Pam nodded, then walked with her to the door. "Thanks again."

"Let me know if you hear anything," said Lucy, reluctant to leave.

"I will," said Pam, looking grave and not bothering to put on her usual brave face. "I will."

Lucy's heart sank as she made her way down the walk to her car, but she told herself she'd done as much as she could to comfort Pam. Truth was, she decided, as she started the car, she could be of more use out and about, keeping her ear to the ground. Tim couldn't disappear into thin air; he had to be somewhere, and that meant somebody would have seen him. So she kept an eye out as she drove through town to the grocery store, just in case she caught a glimpse of Tim. If he was living rough, in the woods, perhaps she'd catch sight of him stealing veggies from somebody's garden or helping himself to berries from a back-yard patch. He might even snag some clothes that an energy-conscious housewife had hung out to dry. But even though she drove slowly, casting her eyes from side to side and peering into backyards, there was no sign of Tim.

There had to be another way, she decided, but didn't know what it was. Organize the whole town in a search? If anything, a crowd of people yelling his name might drive Tim deeper into hiding. She thought again of Corinne Appleton's family and how they had lived every day with dread for more than two years before learning that their worst fear had come true. She hoped that wasn't the case for Pam and Ted; she hoped this situation would come to a conclusion, a happy conclusion, sooner rather than later. But now, approaching the IGA, she attempted to shift mental gears and turn her focus to the task at hand.

There was plenty of parking at the IGA, where the weekly three-day sale didn't begin until Friday. Shopping on Thursday, which was usually her day off, meant she missed the loss-leader sales, but Lucy was willing to trade economy for convenience. She preferred being able to zip through the largely empty store and getting right through the checkout without waiting in line.

She had a big list today, so she grabbed a cart and started loading it in the produce department, went on to the deli counter and the fish counter, and zipped down the coffee and cereal aisle, skipped the canned vegetables, checked out the meat counter and came to a full stop in the bottled water. There, an elderly, bearded man with long white hair had blocked the aisle with his cart as he struggled to lift a shrink-wrapped case of spring water.

"Whoa, there," said Lucy, leaping to catch the package as it slipped from his hands.

"Good catch," he said. "This plastic is hard to hold 'cause of my rheumatiz. Can't grip like I used to."

"I'm surprised you're buying bottled water," said Lucy, who recognized the old fellow as Wild Willy, who was making a rare visit to town. His last appearance, as far as she knew, was at the community center grand opening when he railed against the building's air-conditioning. "Aren't you opposed to plastic bottles?"

"I am, that I most definitely am," said Willy, scratching his beard, "but we're having a drought, and the crick's real low."

"Well, this ought to hold you for a while, 'til we get some rain," said Lucy, who had successfully wrestled the heavy bottles into his cart. She stood back and grabbed her cart handle, expecting him to roll his cart out of the way, but he didn't move. He remained in front of the tower of bottled water that was taking up half the aisle. She was a bit leery of getting too close to Wild Willy, who she didn't imagine had easy access to a hot shower and probably bathed in that crick, which was low. But, taking a closer look, she realized he was quite neat and clean. His hair and beard were carefully groomed, and his clothes, though worn, had been washed recently. His farmer's overalls were neatly patched, and all the buttons were present and correct on his plaid shirt. "Well, pardon me," she said, attempting to squeeze past him.

"Mebbe you could do me another small favor?" he asked.

"Mebbe," replied Lucy, with a chuckle.

"Could you wrestle some more of that water for me?"

Lucy looked at him in surprise. "Really?"

"Yeah. I could use four more of them cases."

"You must have a powerful thirst," observed Lucy, bending to the task. When she'd piled the additional four cases into the cart, she leaned against it to catch her breath. "What's it all for, Willy? It can't all be for you. Have you got a regiment out there in the woods?"

He knitted his flamboyantly wavy brows together. "I'm seein' the signs all around; there's gonna be trouble. Crick's low, leaves on the trees are curlin' up and fallin' early, I'm not seein' as many birds as I used to."

"It's climate change," said Lucy. "It's happening. We've never had a string of heat waves like we're having this year."

"Planet's in trouble," agreed Willy. "We've gotta get prepared."

"So you're stocking up for the future drought?"

"Future? It's here."

"You might well be right, Willy," said Lucy, as a small lightbulb clicked on in her head. Hadn't Zoe remembered Tim talking about people who were "doing things" about climate change? Maybe Willy did have a regiment of climate activists out there in the woods. "By the way, do you know Tim Stillings? Ted's son? Tall and skinny with long hair?"

"Mebbe," said Willy, narrowing his eyes suspiciously.

"Well, if you do see him, could you tell him to give his mom a call? She's real worried about him."

Willy took his time to think this over. "He's a good kid," he finally said. "Loves the woods. I used to see him in the woods."

Lucy's heart leaped. "Have you seen him lately?" asked Lucy. "In the woods?"

But Wild Willy was on the move, pushing his heavy cart

down the aisle. She was thinking that he hadn't even thanked her when he stopped abruptly and turned to face her. "I forgot to say thanks. Thanks for giving me a hand."

"No problem," said Lucy, wondering if Willy had consciously made a decision to avoid answering her question, or if he had simply decided to get a move on. That was something a lot of folks seemed to be doing these days.

Chapter Ten

Friday morning found Lucy back in the *Courier* office, glumly scrolling through her social-media feeds in search of an interesting story. She was hoping for a nice human-interest item she could work into a feature, something that would catch readers' interest. A woman giving birth to a third set of twins, a dog that dialed 911 and saved his owner from a stroke, a five-year-old who could sing the alphabet song backward. But, unfortunately, all that was on offer today were the usual meeting notices, along with an announcement from the water department banning outside watering.

"They've banned watering," she told Phyllis.

"About time, if you ask me." Phyllis didn't look up from the sudoku she was working on.

"Do you think it's a story?"

"Up to you," said Phyllis, with a marked lack of interest.

"I guess I'll post a notice in the online edition, give people a heads-up."

"Everybody knows," said Phyllis, erasing a seven and replacing it with a five.

"Looks like we're going to have to let the guys in Gilead carry the ball this week."

From her expression, it didn't seem that Phyllis had a lot of faith in the Gilead crew. She furrowed her brow and chewed her lip, then exclaimed "Aha!" and added the final number, completing the puzzle. "This one was rated 'challenging,' " she bragged.

"I don't know how you do it," said Lucy. "I don't like numbers."

"You're more a word person," observed Phyllis, as the police scanner sputtered into life with a burst of static. She leaned forward to better hear the garbled noises coming from the small device on her desk. "Hmm, hard to make out, but I think a dog walker found something."

"Tim's been missing, you know," said Lucy, already on her feet and hoping against hope that *something* was not Tim's body. "Did you catch where?"

"The Audubon, I think."

"I'm on it," said Lucy. "Maybe you should give Ted a call."

Phyllis bit her lip. "I don't want to panic him; it could be a deer or something."

Lucy nodded agreement. "Right. A deer. Let's hope it's a deer."

When Lucy pulled into the parking area at the Audubon Sanctuary, she knew immediately that she was in the right place; both of the town's police cruisers, as well as the ambulance, were already there. She started off down the trail but didn't have to go far before spotting a couple of officers, two EMTs, a man in a bucket hat, and a very pretty Irish setter, gathered in a knot and staring at the ground. The setter barked, announcing her arrival.

"Oh, hi, Lucy," said Officer Barney Culpepper, greeting

her. "Heck of a thing," he added, hoisting his belt to a more comfortable location beneath his substantial belly. He was red-faced and sweating.

Beside him was Officer Todd Kirwan, also suffering from the heat with dark circles beneath his armpits. "This is Fred Norton," he said, indicating the man in the hat. "Lucy is from the local paper," he added, introducing her. "Mr. Norton was walking his dog, Siena."

"Yup," said Fred, who was looking rather pale and shaky. "I couldn't believe it. The dog brought it, plopped it right down in front of me."

He pointed to the ground where Lucy saw what looked like a human foot, in perfect condition, lying among the brown leaves and pine needles. It looked like an actual foot, but her mind resisted the thought. It was probably a prosthetic, or maybe part of a shoe-store display. It could even be from a mannequin. "Is it real?" she asked.

"Oh, yeah," said EMT Ethan Kirwan, chiming in. "It looks pretty fresh."

"And sliced quite neatly," added the other EMT, Jeremy Bumpus. "Not what you expect in your typical dismemberment."

Lucy studied the foot, hoping it wasn't Tim's. He was tall, and she remembered seeing his shoes scattered about in his room. Large shoes. This foot was definitely not Tim's, which was a relief. Nevertheless, she found herself growing a bit queasy and swallowed hard. She remembered wishing for an interesting story, but now she thought perhaps she should have been more careful about what she wished for. But, she realized, given that this is what she had to work with, there were definitely interesting possibilities. She turned to Fred and opened her reporter's notebook. "Can you tell me what happened?"

"Well," he began, "I usually walk Siena out at the point, but I thought that since it was so hot and steamy, maybe the woods would be cooler. Shady, you know?"

Lucy nodded.

"But we'd hardly stated out when she started to go crazy, barking and pulling at the leash. It caught me by surprise, and I let go. I wasn't holding tight; I was thinking about letting her off leash anyway, even though I know you're not supposed to. So she bounded off, trailing the leash, and I'm calling and calling; I wanted to get her back under control. But she's off somewhere in the brush, barking and barking, and finally she comes back, and I see she's got something in her mouth, and she dropped it." He pointed. "Right there. She was real proud of herself . . ."

Lucy could see that Siena was still quite pleased about her find and all the attention she was getting. She was sitting on her haunches, tongue lolling, smiling a doggy smile. She remembered how Libby used to adopt a similar pose, presenting her with a stick to throw, and she felt a wave of sadness roll over her.

"I didn't want to touch it or anything, and as soon as I got her back on the leash, I called 911." He looked at the foot and the dog. "They told me to stay here."

Lucy closed her notebook and pulled out her phone. "Okay if I take a photo?" she asked the cops.

Barney and Todd exchanged glances. "What do you think?" asked Barney.

"Maybe somebody'd recognize it," said Todd, sounding doubtful.

"There's nothing really distinctive about it," observed Jeremy.

"Yeah. It's a pretty ordinary foot," added Ethan.

"Still, it might jog somebody's memory."

"I don't think it's a man's foot," said Fred. By now, Siena was growing bored with the situation and was on her feet, tugging at the leash.

"I agree," said Todd. "Maybe a woman . . ."

"Toes aren't polished," observed Barney. His wife, Marge, was big into pedicures.

"A kid? A teen maybe?"

Lucy felt a sudden resurge of fear and checked out the foot again, just to be sure, and compared it again to those enormous boat shoes and sneakers scattered on Tim's bedroom floor. She let out a sigh of relief. This foot could not possibly belong to Tim.

"I think we got all the information we need," Todd was saying to Fred. "You can go, if you want."

Fred definitely wanted to go and promptly headed back to the parking area; Siena wasn't sure and gave a backward glance over her shoulder before continuing, tail held high, down the trail.

"So, what do you want us to do?" asked Ethan. "Bag it?"

"Nah," said Todd. "We're waiting for the medical examiner."

"Right." The two seemed to come to the same conclusion. "No sense us sticking around."

"Yeah," agreed Todd. "We'll make sure it doesn't go walking off."

They all groaned. The EMTs picked up their cases of equipment and left. Lucy figured she ought to stay, in case the ME had something to say. Oddly, she thought, somewhat shocked at the discovery, her primary reaction, now that the shock had passed, was curiosity. That foot must have belonged to a person, and presumably that person was dead, but lacking information about that person, the foot in the woods seemed ridiculous and rather macabre.

"Any ideas?" she asked the two remaining officers.

"Not at the moment, but this is clearly not the work of a wild animal," said Todd.

"Yeah. Whoever did this had a sharp saw and knew where to cut," added Barney. He ran his fingers through his sweaty hair and sighed. "This is probably just the beginning."

"What do you mean?" asked Lucy.

"Mark my words," said Todd, grimly. "There'll be more bits and pieces turning up."

Suddenly, Lucy felt rather nauseous and decided she didn't really need to wait for the ME, who she knew rarely commented until after she'd completed her autopsy—or, in this case, forensic examination of the foot. All things considered, Lucy decided she'd wait for the press conference.

Sure enough, DA Phil Aucoin announced the press conference for five thirty, obviously hoping to make the local TV station's evening news. Lucy was usually cracking open a bottle of chardonnay at five thirty on Friday, but that bottle sitting in the fridge would have to wait. Truth be told, she didn't really mind. The discovery of the foot had upset her; it lurked in her mind like a spider crouched high in a corner by the ceiling, ready to pounce. That waiting spider was only the beginning of the story that would have a gruesome ending for some bumbling bug. And Lucy agreed that where there was a foot, there was a body, a body that had met a similarly gruesome ending.

Aucoin, she suspected, would definitely hype the discovery. This was big, and he would want to play it up. Sitting among the boxes of supplies in the police department basement that served as the local emergency management headquarters, Lucy remembered the days when Aucoin, a young assistant DA, had been pathetically shy and practically hid from reporters. But now, twenty years later, he'd come to love the spotlight. And this, he knew, was going to get him a lot of publicity. Voters would remember and would, once again, reward him with another four years in the job.

Aucoin had also learned the art of the late arrival, which had the advantage of impressing everyone with the heavy demands of his job as well as allowing suspense to build. So it was nearly six, when Lucy would have been pouring herself a second chardonnay and turning on the local TV news, when he finally entered the emergency command center, accompanied by the medical examiner and police chief Jim Kirwan.

"Well," he began, taking note of the assembled reporters, those who were present and those who were not, as well as the TV crew from NECN. "As you know, I'm DA Phil Aucoin, and here with me is the county medical examiner, Sharon Oliver, and Tinker's Cove police chief, Jim Kirwan. The main purpose of this meeting is to inform the public of a disturbing discovery and to give them the facts. I'm well aware that there is a lot of misinformation out there, and we want to clear that up. So, first and foremost, let me say that a citizen, a dog walker, discovered a detached human foot in the Audubon Sanctuary. The discovery was reported to 911 at eleven fifty-seven a.m. Two officers responded to the call, along with the rescue squad, and the medical examiner was subsequently called. Now I will turn this over to our medical examiner, Dr. Oliver."

Sharon Oliver was new on the job. Lucy guessed she was in her early thirties, and she had adopted an extremely brusque, no-nonsense attitude that made it clear to doubters that she was a fully qualified, consummate professional, even if she happened to be drop-dead gorgeous. It must be quite a burden, thought Lucy, having to cope with that head of natural blond hair, that glowing complexion, and a slender body that had curves in all the right places. Today, as usual, she was dressed in scrubs that managed to send a dual message: sexy as well as professional.

"Today I was called to the Audubon Sanctuary in Tinker's Cove by Cove PD officers Culpepper and Kirwan to examine a human foot. After examining and photographing the foot *in situ*, I transported it to the county lab for further examination. The foot was in good condition, a woman's size eight, and was partially frozen. There were subtle indications of tooth marks and saliva on the foot, which were consistent with the fact that it had been found and transported by a dog.

"The foot had been neatly separated from the leg with a sharp instrument, cut through the interstice between the tibia and the talus. It is fair to say that a certain degree of anatomical knowledge was employed, as the fibula also needed to be detached." She looked up from the paper she was reading and gave a curt nod. "I will now answer questions."

The room exploded as reporters' hands shot up and they shouted out their questions. "One at a time," said Oliver. "Ah, Lucy Stone."

"Is it possible that the foot was surgical waste? Perhaps from an amputation?"

"Uh, no. The foot was healthy; apart from a mild case of toenail fungus, there was no reason to amputate it. And, furthermore, there are protocols in place to properly deal with amputated limbs."

She next recognized the cub reporter from the Portland TV station, Jake Roberts. "Do you know if a search was made for other body parts?"

Sharon glanced at Aucoin, who stepped forward. "That's a very good question," he said, "and I will refer it to our police chief."

"Ahem," began Jim Kirwan, stepping forward to the mic. "The officers who responded to the 911 call made the determination that the foot was the only body part in that locale. They based that judgment on the dog's behavior, which was solely fixed on the foot."

Catching the pun, everyone groaned, and Kirwan continued. "However, at the suggestion of DA Aucoin, we instituted a search of the Audubon Sanctuary this afternoon. It was a difficult search, as the sanctuary is maintained as habitat for birds and is thickly planted with brush and trees. A body-sniffing dog from the county sheriff's department was deployed and was unable to find any more body parts."

"How long had the foot been detached?" asked Deb Hildreth, the stringer for the *Boston Globe.*

Kirwan stepped back, making way for Sharon Oliver to take the mic. "It's hard to tell, since the foot was frozen and quite well preserved."

"Does that mean that somebody around here has the rest of the body in their freezer?" shouted Andy Green, from NECN, causing a sudden silence in the room.

Sharon considered the question, then answered. "It's definitely a possibility," she finally said.

"So you're going to be finding more body parts?" demanded Green.

"I can't answer that question," said Sharon. "I can't predict the future."

"Well, I can," said the police chief, stepping forward and standing beside her. "If the owner of the foot was murdered, which I think is a fair assumption, we can expect the murderer to continue to work at getting rid of the body. The body is the primary evidence of the crime. You've all heard of *habeas corpus*, right? It's very hard to convict someone of murder if you don't have the body. So I think we can expect to find more bits and pieces showing up, and I want to ask the public to be aware and, if anybody does come across another dismembered part, to please, immediately, call 911."

"And," said Aucoin, determined to get the last word, "I can guarantee that my department will offer whatever support the police department needs to discover the perpetrator of this dastardly deed."

Chapter Eleven

Leaving the police station after the press conference, Lucy crossed the street and went back to the *Courier* office to write up the story and post it online as breaking news. Staying late on Friday night was definitely not great, but she wanted to get it out of the way so her weekend would be free. That was the plan, anyway, but she knew it could all change in a minute if another body part was discovered. And, having the office to herself, she'd be able to get the story done without any interruptions.

So it was quite a shock when she found the door unlocked and Ted sitting at his desk, the old-fashioned roll-top he'd inherited from his grandfather. "What are you doing here?" she asked. "Don't you know it's Friday?"

"Of course, I know it's Friday. I also know that Tim's been missing for a week and that my wife is frantic with worry."

"There's been no word from him, then?"

"Not a peep."

"And nobody's seen him?"

"If they have, they're not saying."

"It's hard to believe somebody can just drop out of sight," said Lucy.

"I guess it's not all that hard when the police don't take your troubled kid's disappearance seriously. They're more worried about this foot, one rotten little foot, than my entire son."

"I know," said Lucy, sympathetically. "It doesn't seem as if they've got their priorities straight, but you know as well as I do that they're very reluctant to classify healthy adults as missing persons. They are keeping an eye out, but without clear evidence of some sort of mischief, that's about all they can do."

"Mischief? Is that the best you can do? Pam's terrified he's going to try to kill himself again." Ted sighed. "Maybe he already has."

"No, Ted. If he had, he would've been found."

"How can you be so sure?"

"Because bodies can't move; they can't hide themselves."

"But now we've got somebody who's cutting up bodies . . ."

"A foot, Ted. A woman's foot. For all we know, it may not have anything to do with Tinker's Cove at all. Maybe it was just dropped off here. Nobody's missing from Tinker's Cove except Tim, and it's a whole different matter trying to kill a healthy young fellow like Tim."

"But Tim's not healthy; he's not capable of taking care of himself."

"I think he's stronger and more capable than you think," said Lucy, trying to believe it.

"I hope you're right," said Ted, slowly getting to his feet. He exhaled. "It's going to be a long weekend unless he shows up."

"Give my love to Pam," she said, opening her laptop.

"Will do," he said, making his way slowly to the door. "Don't forget to lock up."

"You can count on me," she said, already clicking away on the keyboard.

Lucy struggled with guilt all weekend, questioning her reluctance to tell Pam and Ted about Darleen's harsh treatment of Tim. As a reporter, she'd learned there was always more than one side to a story, and she wasn't sure that her reaction to what she'd seen was entirely justified. Maybe Tim was sloppy and lackadaisical. She'd raised a whole houseful of kids who constantly shirked their assigned chores, so she knew firsthand how frustrating it could be when the garbage wasn't taken out or the table wasn't set. She'd seen for herself the mess in Tim's bedroom. It was entirely possible that Tim had driven Darleen to distraction, and she'd been unable to control her growing frustration with an unsatisfactory employee.

Lucy sensed that her unwillingness to report what she'd witnessed between Darleen and Tim went deeper, however, and was rooted in the uncomfortable feeling that she'd seen something she wasn't supposed to see. She felt a bit like a voyeur who'd seen more than she should have. There was something about the relationship between Darleen and Tim that bordered on sadism, with Darleen being the dominant and Tim the submissive. It had been uncomfortable watching as Darleen scolded Tim, who had mutely accepted her criticism. Why hadn't he spoken up for himself? Why did he let her abuse him? That was the question that bothered her, that lingered and made her feel strangely protective of him.

But was remaining silent the right thing to do? Would it be better to get the whole messy situation out in the open? Or was her reaction overblown? Were things really as she thought? There was only one way to find out, and now that Darleen was away on her controversial vacation, it would be a good time to go over to the community center and ask a few questions. So first thing on Monday morning, that's what she did.

The place was already busy when she arrived; the kitchen crew were cooking up lunch for seniors, a group of knitters had gathered in one of the meeting rooms, and a Zumba class was in progress in the gym. Lucy was on her way to chat up the lunch ladies when she encountered Sheri Thurston, the Council on Aging director, outside the dining room. Sheri's abundant brown hair was tumbling out of the clip that held it, and her flowery blouse was slipping out of her waistband. "Hi, Lucy!" she exclaimed, brimming with energy and greeting her with a big smile. "What can I do for you today?"

"Just wondering how everybody's settling in," said Lucy.

"Come on into my office," Sheri said, leading the way down the hall. "This is such a luxury, being able to invite folks into my office. Do you remember that closet I had in the basement of the town hall?"

"I do indeed," said Lucy, laughing. "Not room enough to swing a cat, as my mom used to say."

Sheri opened her office door, with a big "Ta-da!"

"Wow," said Lucy, taking in the spacious, windowed room where there was plenty of room for a desk, a file cabinet, and several captain's chairs for visitors.

"I can grow plants on the windowsill," enthused Sheri. "I've already brought in my Swedish ivy and spider plant. I want it to be homey and comfortable, welcoming. I'm thinking of bringing in a braided rug and putting some pictures up on the wall."

"Nice," said Lucy, sitting down. "Comfy chair," she

added, approvingly. "So everybody's happy, it's all ship-shape?"

Sheri seated herself in her fancy desk chair, swinging about playfully. "Sorry, I just can't resist."

"I get it," said Lucy, thinking of the somewhat grubby, tired *Courier* office. "It seems as if things are running smoothly while Darleen's away."

"Ah, so that's why you're here!" Sheri laughed. "Checking up on us while Darleen's gone. She's a force of nature, you know. She has high expectations, and she makes sure everybody's on their toes, if you know what I mean."

"Could you be more specific?"

Sheri took a moment to gather her thoughts. "Well," she finally began, "at our very first staff meeting—and that's important, the fact that she's instituted weekly staff meetings so we all get a heads-up on coming events and have a chance to air any concerns; they've been really good—anyway, at the first staff meeting, she pointed out that town employees are fair game for disgruntled taxpayers, and that our best defense is a good offense. Do a good job; don't give them reasons to complain."

Lucy nodded, impressed. Darleen was doing a better job than she expected. "How did the employees react? Did this go over well?"

"Yeah. I think we all felt that Darleen had our back, that she'd stick up for us."

"But she can be demanding, no? I heard her laying into Tim Stillings one day . . ."

"Oh, that. Tim's a sweetie, but he's not been reliable. He drops in when he feels like working or doesn't bother to show up if he's got something better to do. I don't think he came in at all last week, you know, and he hasn't shown up yet today."

"Maybe he couldn't handle Darleen's criticism?" suggested Lucy.

Sheri shrugged. "You know what they say: If you can't take the heat, stay out of the kitchen. Tim did a good job when he applied himself, but he wasn't consistent. His heart wasn't in the job."

"So you think he's done here?"

"It's not my decision, but the most basic job requirement is showing up . . ."

Lucy really couldn't argue the point. "Well, is it okay if I snap a few pictures, just to remind folks that the center is up and running?"

"Good idea, Lucy. We've still got to get that override passed at the special town meeting."

Leaving the center, Lucy decided her suspicions about Tim's troubles on the job were confirmed. From what Sheri had said, it seemed clear that the job had not worked out and was most likely a factor in his disappearance. This was something his parents needed to know, and she decided to drop by the Stillings' house on the chance that Pam might be home.

When Pam opened the door, Lucy thought she was a mere shadow of her former self; she'd lost weight and had dark circles under her eyes. "Hey, you," Lucy said, wrapping Pam in a big hug. "Let's go out for coffee. I've heard they've got amazing chocolate croissants at that new place, Coffee Connection."

"Sorry, Lucy. I don't feel up to it."

"All you've got to do is get in my car; I'll take care of the rest," urged Lucy.

"I don't want to leave the house. What if Tim came home and I wasn't here?"

"You could leave a note."

Pam shook her head. "I know it's crazy, but I just can't. I've got to stay here."

"Okay," said Lucy. "But you've got to eat something. You're fading away. What have you got?" Lucy marched into the kitchen and opened the refrigerator door, hoping to find something inside. Much to her surprise, it was packed to the gills. "Wow. Somebody's been shopping."

"Ted."

He must be worried about his wife, thought Lucy. "You know what I'd like?" she said, suddenly inspired and grabbing some packages. "How about homemade egg sandwiches? With ham and cheese and drippy egg on English muffins?"

Pam was sitting on a stool at the kitchen island. "Whatever you want, Lucy."

Lucy got to work, clanging a black cast iron frying pan onto the stove, slicing English muffins and sliding them into the toaster, cracking some eggs into the pan. In minutes, she'd made fair facsimiles of McDonald's Egg McMuffins. Climbing up on an adjoining stool, she took a big bite. "Mmm," she announced noisily, hoping to encourage Pam to eat her eggy muffin.

Pam picked hers up, nibbled at a bit of ham that was hanging out the side of the muffin, and smiled. "It's good, Lucy."

Noticing that Pam had put her egg sandwich back on the plate, she chided her. "You've got to eat more than that."

"I will," said Pam. "Later. I'm not very hungry now."

"You've got to eat these things when they're hot," advised Lucy.

Pam shrugged. "I've almost finished the quilt." She picked

up her sandwich, took a tiny bite, and put it back. "Do you want to see it?"

"Sure," said Lucy, who had already consumed her egg sandwich. "I'd love to." She followed Pam down the hall to the spare room, where the quilt top was spread out on the guest bed. She was shocked at how much these scraps of fabric seemed to embody Tim; somehow Pam had captured his whole life in these lovingly stitched bits of cloth. "This is amazing," said Lucy, leaning close to study the quotations Pam had embroidered on some of the pieces.

"I put in bits from things he wrote," said Pam. "Like this from a Mother's Day card he made for me. 'You are my hero.' I'm sending it right back to him." Pam's legs gave way, and she landed on the bed, next to the quilt top. "I wonder if he'll ever see it." She sniffed and brushed away tears. "Oh, Lucy. There are so many signs we missed. We should have realized he was in trouble, that he was suffering."

Lucy folded the quilt top carefully and sat next to Pam, taking her hand. "Hindsight is always twenty-twenty," she said. "You can't blame yourself. Tim did a good job of hiding his distress. He was successful in school, got a great job at the Farnsworth; he seemed to be doing fine."

"But he wasn't. I'm his mother, I should have known."

"Pam, did he ever say anything about his job at the community center? Did he like it?"

"Sort of. He didn't seem to mind it. I always had the sense that he was kind of ashamed that being a janitor was the only job he could get."

"I don't think it was going well. One day when I was there, I overheard Darleen scolding him."

"Like a bad boss kind of thing?"

"That's what I thought, but it could've been that he really wasn't doing a good job." Lucy squeezed Pam's hand. "He's AWOL there, too."

"I'm not surprised," admitted Pam. "He'd never done that kind of work before. I'm sure he found it demeaning, even though Ted and I tried to encourage him. We told him it was a big step toward recovery. But if that woman was undermining him, well, it was the opposite. It just reinforced his sense of inadequacy."

"Maybe that's what prompted him to take off. He didn't want to admit the job wasn't working out."

"Could be," agreed Pam. "But he knew Darleen was going on vacation and wouldn't be there to bother him. I know he liked some of the people at the center, especially the old folks who came for the senior lunch and the free meal they always gave him." She shook her head. "I don't think it was the job. Something else was going on, something . . ." she paused, reaching for the right words and finally came up with "secret." "Something very secret and important to him."

That gave Lucy pause. How many times had she read about a young man who'd got hold of a gun and acted out his most disturbing and destructive fantasies. "Pam, you don't think . . ."

"Oh, no," replied Pam, reading her mind. "No way. Tim deplores violence. He would never; he hates guns."

"Right," said Lucy, somewhat relieved. But if Tim had secrets, how could Pam be so sure they weren't terrible, violent secrets? It suddenly seemed to Lucy that there was no time to waste and it was imperative to find Tim. But how? That was the question she was mulling over as she left Pam and headed to the office. How could she find Tim?

Chapter Twelve

Lucy was pulling into a parking spot in front of the office when a patrol car, lights flashing, tore down the street, immediately followed by the town's ambulance, also with lights flashing plus siren blaring. Probably a crash on Route 1, thought Lucy, immediately abandoning the parking spot and taking off in pursuit. Ted loved crashes, especially if the vehicles happened to burst into flames, in which case the photo went on page one, accompanied by a detailed account of the accident. He would expect Lucy to get as much information as possible: how the collision occurred, who was involved, their injuries, and, even better from his point of view, the fatalities. But as Lucy followed, driving as fast as she dared in order to keep up, she realized they were not headed for Route 1. Instead, the cruiser and ambulance careened around the corner onto Quissett Point Road.

The narrow, twisty road wound its way around various rock formations and only led to one place, scenic Quissett Point, where there were a lighthouse and trails that attracted occasional sightseers, hikers, and bird-watchers. A crash on this quiet, winding side road seemed unlikely, and she wondered if the first responders had been called to a heart attack or some other health emergency. That's what seemed to be happening when she arrived in the parking area and spotted Officer Barney Culpepper and a couple of EMTs gathered around two people seated at one of the picnic tables.

This was lucky, as Barney was an old friend and unlikely to send her packing, as some of the other police officers would. Nevertheless, she decided she'd get the most information if she quietly joined the group, keeping her eyes and ears open while keeping her mouth shut. She got out of her parked car and closed the door gently, then casually approached the group in the picnic area. Drawing closer, she saw that Jeremy Bumpus was again on duty, but with a different partner, Jeannie Kirwan. The two were attending to a young woman who looked decidedly green. Her companion, a man with a pair of binoculars dangling on his chest, was talking to Barney.

The victim didn't seem to be injured in any way; Jeannie was taking her pulse, and Jeremy was ready with a bottle of water. Determined to find out what was going on, Lucy turned her attention to Barney, who was commiserating with the other hiker. "Must've been a terrible shock," he said.

"What was a shock?" she asked, forgetting she had planned to simply observe and snap photos.

"Oh, hi, Lucy," said Barney, greeting her with a smile. He towered over her; he was well over six feet, with a substantial belly that stretched his blue uniform to the limit. He and Lucy had met years earlier when Lucy was a Cub Scout den leader and Barney's son, Eddie, was in her den. "Looks like you've got a scoop."

"Yeah? What's up?"

"Well, these folks were out here bird-watching . . ."

"We saw a bunch of sooty shearwaters, and lots of gulls and cormorants, of course," said the man.

Somehow, that didn't seem like "scoop" material to Lucy. "Can you tell me your name?" prompted Lucy. "I'm from the local paper."

"Sure. I'm Carl Wyman, and this is my wife, Edie. We'd decided to call it quits and were stopping here at the picnic table for a little snack and a drink of water; it's so important to stay hydrated, you know . . ."

Also not breaking news. "Did your wife suffer dehydration?" asked Lucy, noticing that the EMTs were moving her to another picnic table that was shaded by a scrub pine and encouraging her to drink the bottled water.

"No, not dehydration. It was the shock of what she saw when she took our wrappers over to the trash bin."

"Not at all what you want to see," said Barney, with a sharp nod that jiggled his jowls.

Lucy had an idea what Edie had seen, but needed confirmation. "Not another . . . ?"

"No. Not a foot," said Barney. "This time it's an arm."

Lucy felt a bit woozy, and things were going dark when Barney grabbed her and had her sit on the picnic-table bench. "Head between your knees," he instructed, and she obeyed. When she raised her head and had regained a bit of color in her cheeks, he continued. "I was gonna show you, but mebbe better not."

Lucy definitely did not want to see the arm, but she was pretty sure Ted would want a photo. "Would you mind taking a picture for me?" she asked, holding out her phone.

"No problem," said Barney, trotting over to the trash bin and taking a snapshot of the interior. "Better check it," he advised, returning the phone. "I'm not a great photographer."

Somewhat warily, Lucy glanced at the screen on her phone, noting the presence of a very real arm among the discarded fast-food wrappers, disposable diapers, and dog-poo bags. "Definitely an arm, but there's no hand," she said.

"Hands can be used for identification," said Barney.

"Right," said Lucy, thinking that this killer knew what he or she was doing. She waved the camera. "Thanks for the photo."

Carl had gone to join his wife, who was doing much better, shaking her head ruefully and smiling at him. "Okay if I interview the Wymans?" she asked Barney, noticing that the EMTs were returning to the ambulance.

"Sure. Get them while you can. The ME is on her way, along with the DA and the state cops."

Carl and Edie were sitting together at the shaded picnic table, so Lucy joined them, reporter's notebook in hand. "Hi, Edie. I'm Lucy Stone from the *Courier* newspaper. I've already met your husband. Would you mind telling me what happened?"

Edie was holding tight to Carl's hand, and they made an attractive if somewhat shocked couple. He was tall and blond, while she was petite and dark-haired. They were both togged out for bird-watching in long pants and sleeves that offered protection against sun and ticks, hiking boots, bucket hats, and, of course, binoculars. She had a Peterson bird guide tucked in one of the many pockets of her practical vest. "Well, I guess Carl told you about the, um, arm?"

"Yes. But let's go back a bit. Where are you from? Are you here on vacation?"

Edie looked at Carl, who spoke right up. "Well, we're from Braintree; that's a suburb of Boston. Edie's folks have a cabin on Biscay Lake, and we're visiting them. We're both rather keen bird-watchers, and this is a great spot, so we came out early because that's when the birds are most active."

"We added quite a few new birds to our life lists," said Edie. "It was a great morning, until . . ."

"Yeah. Things were quieting down, and we decided to call it quits. We'd brought water and granola bars, and we sat over there, at that picnic table, talking about the shearwaters and how they skim along above the waves."

"Nature is just so amazing," added Edie.

"Well, we finished eating, and Edie went to dispose of the wrappers . . ."

"Take only pictures, leave only footprints, that's what we always try to do. But a little wind came up, and I wanted to make sure everything went into the barrel, so I leaned over to look, and there was this arm! I mean, a human arm! Right in the barrel! I've never been so shocked in my life. It's not at all what you expect to see."

"A dog walker found a foot last week," said Lucy.

"I had no idea!" exclaimed Edie.

"Does that mean there's some sort of psycho running around, dismembering people?" asked Carl.

"Are we in danger?" demanded Edie, clutching her husband's arm.

"I don't think so," said Lucy. "For one thing, nobody seems to be missing. It's likely that the actual murder took place some distance from here."

"Maybe this killer is picking on tourists, on visitors like us. Then nobody local would be missing," suggested Edie, wide-eyed.

"I guess that's a possibility," admitted Lucy, as a number of vehicles began arriving in the parking lot, including the medical examiner's white van. Barney went to meet the officials and update them on the discovery; Lucy decided it was time to make herself scarce before she was ordered to get out of the way or, worse, was forbidden to report the story before the DA's official announcement.

That announcement came at a press conference held in the county administration building in Gilead the next morning. Aucoin began by briefing reporters on the latest discovery, but was quickly upstaged when reporters began shouting questions at the ME, Sharon Oliver. Today Sharon had abandoned the scrubs in favor of a professional business suit, and her hair, newly cut in a particularly fetching style that kept slipping in front of her left eye, required frequent sexy head tosses.

"Did the arm match the foot?" "Was it frozen, like the foot?" "Any distinguishing characteristics?" were among the questions. Sharon held up a hand for silence and began delivering a prepared statement.

"Yesterday, I was called to the Quissett Point Reservation, where a body part had been discovered by a couple of bird-watchers in a trash barrel located in the picnic area. This body part was an entire arm, minus the hand. It seems likely that it came from the same body as the foot found last week, but we will have to wait for DNA analysis to confirm this hypothesis. The arm, like the foot, was frozen. When discovered, it was partially thawed. Like the foot, it was dissected by a skilled person, perhaps a hunter, doctor, or butcher, someone familiar with anatomy. This person took advantage of the natural separations between bones to effect the dissection and may have used a power tool or even an electric carving knife.

"There were no distinguishing characteristics, such as a birthmark or tattoo, and only a light sprinkling of freckles. I was able to determine that the arm belonged to a woman of above average height, somewhat overweight, between thirty and fifty years of age." She paused and folded the sheet of paper she had been reading from. "Copies of my complete report are available; you can grab them as you leave. So now, if you have any questions . . ."

The gathered crowd of reporters had plenty of questions, especially the TV journalists who wanted to get airtime, but the questions didn't reveal any new information. Oliver, however, patiently answered each one, most often repeating the results of her examination as presented in the report.

Lucy guessed she was taking a page from Aucoin's book, using the press conference to build name recognition and credibility. She might even have her sights set on an elective office. Lucy couldn't blame her; she actually admired her. This was a woman who was determined to succeed in what had been a male preserve. More power to her, she thought, as she snapped a final photo before heading back to the office in Tinker's Cove.

"What's the story, morning glory?" asked Phyllis, looking up from her computer screen when Lucy arrived, setting the little bell on the door jangling. Phyllis was in fine form, actually resembling a blooming flower, having colored her hair bright pink, which contrasted with her neon green tunic and leggings.

"Same old, same old," said Lucy, with a sigh, settling in at her desk. "The arm probably belongs to the same poor soul as the foot, pending DNA analysis. It was partially frozen and separated from the body by somebody who had knowledge of anatomy. Sharon Oliver said they could have used some sort of power tool, even an electric carving knife."

"I've never approved of those things," said Phyllis, with a disapproving sniff. "A bit too mechanical for the dinner table."

"I know. I remember my grandfather wielding a steel to sharpen his knife before carving up the Sunday roast. It was sort of a ceremony."

"Those were the days, when people came home from church and had Sunday dinners," said Phyllis, with a fond smile. "I wonder, do you think the killer might be a hunter? Hunters sometimes butcher their kills themselves and store the meat in a freezer. I don't imagine it's much different cutting up a deer or a person, when you get into the bones and stuff."

"I suppose one joint is a lot like another," said Lucy, thinking Phyllis might be on to something. Hunting was a popular pastime in Tinker's Cove, where people shot ducks, turkeys, and deer. When hunting season was over, they practiced their marksmanship at the Rod and Gun Club. "The Rod and Gun!" she exclaimed.

"Yes, Lucy. The Rod and Gun Club; it's out on Bumps River Road."

"I know where it is, thank you very much. I was just thinking that maybe somebody out there might have a lead on the killer."

"Worth a try," admitted Phyllis, with a shrug. "But you better be tactful. I don't think any of those guys . . ."

"And girls," added Lucy.

"Right." Phyllis rolled her eyes. "I'm just saying, there's a lot of emotion about guns these days, and it wouldn't go over very well if you start making accusations, that's all. Better watch what you say."

"I'm pretty sure I can conduct an interview without ruffling any feathers," said Lucy, somewhat huffily. She grabbed her bag and headed for the door. "If you don't hear from me in an hour, send the cavalry."

Once she was seated in her car and had started the engine, Lucy belatedly thought that, since it was a weekday, there very well might not be anybody present at the club to interview. While waiting for the AC to kick in, she made a quick call to the club's president, Mike Doucette.

"Come on down," he urged, in a hearty tone. "I'm at the club; we're getting ready for our annual game dinner."

When she arrived at the club, which was in an old one-room schoolhouse that had been rehabbed and now featured a locker room for gun storage, a meeting and dining area, a small bar, and a commercial-grade kitchen, she found Mike sitting at one of the dining tables. He was retired, compensating for his bald head with a lush beard, and was wearing a camo T-shirt. Hearing her footsteps, he looked up from the paper he was writing on. "Hi, Lucy. Good timing. I'm writing out a press release about the upcoming game dinner. It's open to the public, you know; anybody can come and try some new foods. We've got rabbit, bear, venison, wild turkey, duck, and goose, and for the brave, there's raccoon ragout and skunk punch."

"Skunk punch?" asked Lucy, not at all sure anybody would want to taste skunk.

"Gotcha!" he crowed. "It's not actually skunk at all; it's a killer brew that's heavy on the bourbon."

"That sounds good," admitted Lucy. "I'll be sure to put it in the listing. But you know, it isn't the game dinner that brought me out here. I've got some questions for you about these body parts that are turning up."

"Just a foot, right?"

"Uh, no. Today some picnickers found an arm in the trash bin out at Quissett Point."

Mike pressed his lips together and tugged on his beard. "And what do you think that has to do with me? Or the club?"

"Well," began Lucy, choosing her words carefully, "the medical examiner says these bits and pieces were removed quite skillfully, by someone who has a bit of anatomical knowledge. She mentioned the killer might possibly be a butcher, or a medical professional, or maybe a hunter."

"It's this anti-gun stuff; anything bad happens, they blame the gun owners."

"I don't think anybody's making any accusations; she was just providing examples. People who might know how to easily separate a joint. Like when you cut up a chicken, you wiggle the knife until it goes through between the thigh and the drumstick bone."

"I don't have any experience myself, but I suspect cutting up a person is a lot trickier than a carving a chicken."

"That's why she mentioned butchers and hunters as people who know their way around a large animal," said Lucy. "She says the victim is a middle-aged woman."

Mike grinned. "Well, as far as I know, none of the members have killed their wives, or even their mothers-in-law. All present and accounted for, and most of 'em are busy cooking up their specialties for the dinner." He paused. "In fact, Lois Bryan is here right now, in the kitchen. Maybe you'd like to talk to her? She's the gal who's in charge of the dinner."

"I would, thanks," said Lucy. Mike pressed his hands against the table and pushed himself up, revealing his camo hunting pants, belted low under his belly. He gave the belt a tug, then led the way through the bar and into the kitchen, where he introduced Lucy to Lois. She was an older woman, with neat white hair, dressed in shorts and a T-shirt with a buck pictured inside a bull's-eye, and was stirring up some sort of fragrant stew in a giant pot.

"Lucy here is gonna write up a piece on the game dinner," he said, with a wink.

Before Lucy could explain that she was thinking of an events listing, not a feature story, Lois gave her a big smile. "That would be wonderful! In fact, why don't you come? You could take photos and sample some of the most delicious food you've ever eaten."

"That does sound interesting, and whatever you're cooking does smell delicious," admitted Lucy, "but I'd have to run it by my editor."

"I know Ted," said Mike, pompously announcing his intention to work the good ol' boys network, which Lucy knew was still annoyingly effective. "I'll have a word with him."

"Okay. You've got a deal," said Lucy, managing not to roll her eyes. "But what really brought me here is the body parts that keep showing up."

"I heard about the foot; now, that's very puzzling, isn't it?" offered Lois, removing her spoon and placing a cover on the pot. "What would that have to do with us?"

"Well, yesterday they found an arm," said Lucy, going on to explain the ME's report and her hypothesis about the killer possibly being a hunter.

"My goodness," said Lois.

"Like I told her, we're not missing any ladies, are we?" demanded Mike.

"Not that I know of," said Lois. "I was able to contact all the cooks on my list; of course, there are some wives who don't contribute. They say they're too busy, working moms, you know." She paused, struck with a horrifying thought. "You don't think it could be one of them, do you?"

"If someone like that were missing, I think we'd have heard by now. If Mom doesn't come home, it gets reported." Lucy paused, figuring she'd run out of questions. "Well, if anything changes, if you think of anything suspicious, please let me know."

"Will do," said Mike, pulling his phone out of his pants pocket. He looked at it, announced he had to take the call, and left the kitchen.

Lucy lingered, noticing that Lois seemed to have something to say. She did.

"Mike wouldn't want me to say anything, but, you know, I have noticed somebody lurking in the edge of the woods, by the shooting range. It's probably kids; that's what he thinks. I said we should do something; it's dangerous, right? But he said kids will be kids, and they're smart enough to not get themselves shot. But it worries me. I don't want to see anybody get hurt, especially a kid. But maybe it's not a kid. Maybe it's somebody who wants to steal the guns or ammo? Some members keep their guns here—in lockers, of course—but it's not exactly Fort Knox. It would be easy enough to break in, and then we could have more than one body turning up."

"What exactly have you noticed?" asked Lucy.

"A shape, that's all. And when I went out to check, there were some broken branches. Somebody was definitely out there."

"An animal, maybe?"

"No. Definitely a person."

"Probably just a bird-watcher," said Lucy, trying to reassure Lois.

The pot cover began to jiggle and steam, and Lois ran to

the stove to lower the heat. "I hope it's not ruined," she moaned, stirring the contents.

"I better leave you to it," said Lucy. "Thanks for your time."

When she walked out through the bar and the meeting area to the door, there was no sign of Mike. She hoped he was staying around; she didn't like to think of Lois, all alone in the club and vulnerable. Not when a killer was on the loose.

Chapter Thirteen

Lucy was walking to her car when she heard the scream of a red-tailed hawk and looked skyward to see the bird circling high above her, wings outstretched and motionless as it soared on the rising air currents. She stood for a moment, wondering what it would be like to be a bird, lifted and carried by nothing more than air. As she watched, another red tail joined the first, and the two circled around each other; gazing up from below, it was easy to imagine their delight as they displayed their mastery of the sky. Or not, she decided, wondering if birds experience emotions like delight. Maybe when they swooped down and successfully snatched a sparrow, rather than when they were simply circling, eyes out for their next meal.

Somewhat deflated as she considered the kill-or-be killed reality of bird life, she heard another screech from the hawk, which broke the silence as she reached for the car door. Out here, far from town, she realized she heard nothing but the hum of cicadas and the occasional bird call. Nobody was shooting; the range was empty. A little exploratory tour seemed safe enough, especially since she wondered if the kid Lois saw might actually be Tim, so she turned around and walked over to the shooting range.

It was a cleared, grassy area about the size of a baseball field, with target stands at the far end. Little signs along the edges, which were bounded with woods, noted the increasing distances from the shooting stands. Checking once again to make sure they were empty and nobody was preparing to start firing rounds, she began walking along the edge of the range. She wasn't at all sure what she was looking for as she peered into the dense forest, but figured anyone who had been lurking in the area must have left some signs and maybe even dropped something that would identify them, so she kept her eyes peeled.

She didn't find much except for an occasional plastic shotgun shell, plus lots of fallen pine needles, pine cones, leaves, and quite a few tattered plastic bags that were snagged in the trees. An invention of the devil, that's what her elderly friend Miss Tilley called the single-use bags that were easily caught by the wind and blown not only into trees but into ponds and even the ocean, where they became hazards to marine life. She was thinking about sea turtles, which were said to mistake the bags for jellyfish and swallowed them with disastrous effects, when she heard an odd noise.

She stopped in her tracks, listening, and made out distinct rustling sounds. Somebody, or something, was in the woods quite close to her. Not a bear, she hoped, peering anxiously into the dimly lit forest and seeing nothing at all except trees and ferns and bushes. But she continued to hear the rustling, which was definitely growing louder. Whatever was making the noise was coming toward her. She instinctively backed up a few paces, wondering whether she should make her escape while she could, when a beam of sunlight suddenly illuminated a head of gray hair. The head had a lush beard and was atop a plaid shirt. Wild Willy!

"Hi!" she called, both relieved and curious. "What are you doing here?"

Willy came toward her, squinting. "Oh, it's you. The newspaper lady. What are you doing here?"

"Looking for someone."

Willy stepped out of the woods, onto the range, making sure the shooting stands were empty. "This isn't a safe place," he said. "You shouldn't be here."

"It's safe enough, now. Nobody's here but us." She paused. "So, how've you been?"

"Me?"

"Yeah, you. What's happening?"

Willy shrugged. "Nothing much. Just foraging." He swung his backpack off his shoulder and opened it, showing Lucy a mess of weeds. "Great stuff. Purslane, wild onions, Jerusalem artichokes."

"Good eating?" inquired Lucy.

"Oh, yeah," he said, with a sly grin.

"Actually," began Lucy, "I'm looking for Tim Stillings; he's still missing. He's in his twenties, a tall guy, brown hair. Have you seen him?"

"Mebbe," admitted Willy.

"I think you'd remember if you saw him," said Lucy. "He's good-looking, acts a bit shy."

Willy reached under his bib overalls and scratched his tummy. "You'd be surprised how many folks are poking around in the woods. Can't remember all of 'em. Mostly I just tell 'em to skedaddle. They don't belong in my woods."

"So these are your woods?" asked Lucy, who knew full well that the area was part of the town's watershed. "How is that?"

Willy puffed himself up. "By right of eminent domain."

"I'm not sure that's correct," said Lucy. "Maybe you're

thinking of adverse possession. You need to establish residency to claim that."

"I'm a resident."

"Really?"

"Yeah. I got a house. Built it myself."

"Can I see it?" asked Lucy, thinking that Wild Willy and his house might make a good feature story. Besides, she had a hunch he knew more about Tim than he was willing to admit.

Willy took a while to consider the matter, and Lucy suspected he wasn't eager to welcome a visitor to his humble abode. She was surprised when he suddenly said, "Okay," and began marching off along what Lucy had taken to be a deer track. She followed, struggling a bit to keep up as branches and even small saplings pushed aside by Willy snapped back and whacked her arms and chest. When one particularly vicious one hit her across the bridge of her nose, she decided she was following too close and slowed a bit. She was hot and sweaty; her hair was sticking to her face, and her nose hurt. "How much farther?" she asked.

"Just a mite. It's up yonder."

This better be worth it, she thought, as she struggled up a rise. But when she got to the top, the trees suddenly opened out into a clearing with a neat little shanty in the middle. The solar panels on the roof first caught her attention, but as she crossed the cleared area, she took in the tidy vegetable garden, planted as the Native Americans did with the three sisters: corn, beans, and squash. A couple of tall sunflowers were planted on each side of the door, and Lucy smiled, taking in the cleverly assembled, clearly recycled building components. The door was quite fancy, boasting a stained-glass window, but the window beside it, which opened outward, was meant to be a cellar window. A window on the other side of the door might have once graced a Tudor-style house as it contained numerous diamond-shaped panes. Mismatched and patched together it might be, but the tiny house had a definite charm.

"I guess you'll want to see inside," he said, grumbling. Lucy wasn't fooled; it was clear that Willy was proud of his home and wanted to show it off.

"This is amazing," said Lucy. "You have made a fabulous home for yourself. I'd love to see inside."

"C'mon, then," he said, opening the door and standing aside, bowing with a flourish.

Lucy stepped inside, looking about curiously at the surprisingly comfortable one-room interior. Pride of place was taken by the woodstove, made from an oil barrel. Arranged around it were a battered couch, a matching easy chair, and a table and chair under the window. A kitchen area contained a refrigerator, an electric stove, and a sink. "The solar panels power the fridge and stove, but how do you get water?" Lucy thought of the dozens of bottles she'd helped Willy hoist into his supermarket trolley.

"There's a crick nearby, and I rigged up a system of gutters that feed rainwater into barrels," he said. "Truth is, it's gettin' a bit low; we need some rain."

"Right," said Lucy, recalling meeting him in the IGA. "That's why you bought all that water."

Willy's eyes flickered for a moment, before he said, "Uh, yeah. That's right." He shifted a bit awkwardly on his feet, then asked Lucy if she'd like to see the greenhouse.

"Greenhouse! I wish I had a greenhouse!"

"Nuthin' to it, really. I got a bunch of old windows people were throwing out," he said, leading her behind the fridge and opening a pocket door that slid neatly into the wall. Beyond was a small, but serviceable space, entirely enclosed with the recycled windows. On the bench, Lucy saw, he had started seedlings for his fall planting of kale, parsnips, leeks, and turnips.

"Do you heat it in winter?" she asked.

"If I leave the door open enough, heat comes in from the woodstove, plus the sunlight, so I can grow cold-weather crops like lettuce and radishes."

"You've really got it all figured out," said Lucy, smiling broadly. "Do you mind if I take a few photos and write a story?"

"Well, I dunno," he answered, shaking his head. "I don't want anybody knowing where I live and coming 'round and bothering me."

"Do many folks come around?" asked Lucy, thinking again of Tim.

Willy scratched his beard and shook his head. "Not many. I just yell at 'em, tell 'em to scram. Don't chat with 'em."

"No problem," said Lucy, who knew she'd strayed from the subject at hand and didn't want to lose the story. "I don't have to say where your cabin is. I can just say 'somewhere deep in the hinterland and off the grid.' How about that?"

"Has a nice ring to it," said Willy, nodding. "You sure got a way with words."

"I do my best," said Lucy, fingers crossed, hoping he would consent. "It would be good for folks to learn how you manage without fossil fuels."

"Well, okay," he finally said, grinning and revealing a surprisingly white, obviously well-cared for set of teeth.

"And, uh, could you point me in the right direction? Back to the Rod and Gun?"

"Sure. I'll take you."

He was good to his word and escorted Lucy back to the shooting range, which was still empty of marksmen. She thanked him and set off, giving him a little wave, to her car. As she drove back to town, she began writing the story in her head, trying out various leads. She smiled, remembering his claim of eminent domain and made a mental note to check it out when she got back to the office.

But when she called Rachel's lawyer husband, Bob Goodman, he laughed at the idea. "No, no, eminent domain refers to the government's ability to take property it needs for public purposes—like a road, for example. And, of course, the government has to compensate the owner. Maybe you're thinking of adverse possession," he said, confirming her suspicion, "but in that case you have to pay taxes on the property as well as occupy it, and you certainly can't grab a piece of town property and call it yours."

"That's what I thought," said Lucy, deciding that she wouldn't mention Wild Willy's sketchy knowledge of the law in her story.

A little seed of doubt was planted, however, and she wondered how much of what he'd told her was true. As a result, she chose her words very carefully and relied heavily on quotes, letting Wild Willy speak for himself.

Chapter Fourteen

When the *Courier* came out on Thursday, Lucy was proud of her Wild Willy story, which was on the front page, accompanied by a full-color photo of the hermit himself, standing proudly in front of his door, between the towering sunflowers. Readers, however, did not react favorably to the story. It began slowly, with a few emails; then the letters began to arrive, and then a *Boston Globe* columnist picked up on the story calling Wild Willy a "social parasite." Tweets were written, posts went viral on Facebook, and Willy was parodied in skits on TikTok.

Ted loved the attention, repeating the old saw that there was no such thing as bad publicity. Lucy couldn't agree and found the negative reaction terribly upsetting. Completely chagrined, she decided to pay a visit to Willy and apologize. She timed her visit carefully, since the only way she knew to reach the homestead was by the deer track that ran by the shooting range. As she trudged along on a hot and humid morning, Lucy wondered why on earth the silly animals dared to come so close to the shooting range, but figured there must be some tempting opportunities for grazing in the area that they couldn't resist. And, she admitted as she pushed branches out of her way, the woods were certainly dark and thick enough to conceal their comings and goings.

Somebody was shooting, however, by the time she reached Willy's shack; she could hear the pops in the distance. Willy greeted her with a smile, commenting that "the guns are out today" and urging her to step inside.

"Don't you worry about getting shot?" Lucy asked, as he closed the door behind her.

"Nope. The guns are pointed the other way," he said. "Only someone with really bad aim could send a round in my direction, and they're pretty careful at the Rod and Gun."

"Could be an accidental misfire," said Lucy.

Willy shrugged. "Life is full of risk."

"Right," agreed Lucy, taking a deep breath. "Look. I want to apologize for any trouble you're getting because of the story. It certainly wasn't my intention to expose you to a lot of nasty commentary."

Willy raised his bushy gray eyebrows. "Ah, so folks don't approve of my lifestyle?"

"Afraid not," admitted Lucy.

"Well, I haven't heard a word. The squirrels, the birds, the chipmunks, they all seemed to like it when I read it to them. And I did, too. You did a real good job."

Lucy could just picture it: Wild Willy seated on a rock, reading the news to his furred and feathered neighbors, like a modern-day Johnny Appleseed. "Well, I'm glad somebody liked it."

"Take a look," he said, pointing to his rusty refrigerator, where he'd stuck the story on the door with magnets. "I'm famous."

"Well, don't let it go to your head," teased Lucy. "Fame's only supposed to last fifteen minutes."

"Can I offer you something?" asked Willy. "I've got some dandelion tea, or maybe you'd like to try some pemmican? Made it myself from a deer got hit by a car."

Lucy was quick to offer excuses. "Maybe another time; I just ate," she said. "And I really need to get back to the office."

"Well, suit yourself," he said, taking a tin off a nearby shelf and opening it, pulling out a strip of something and taking a bite. "Pretty tasty," he said, chewing.

"*Bon appétit*," said Lucy, making her escape.

While Wild Willy was insulated from the negative reaction to the article by his adoring circle of woodland friends, Lucy continued to have to cope with the flak as she went about her job covering the local news. Thanks to her story, Wild Willy became a meme, a laughable character everybody knew about, or thought they knew about, that persisted long after the fifteen minutes of fame allotted to most people. Lucy couldn't even escape it when she covered the weekly Monday select-board meeting a few days later.

References to Willy popped up during the public comment period, during the discussion of proposed tree cutting at the baseball field, while voting to install solar panels on town buildings, and in the town's natural resources director's presentation about removing invasive water plants from Blueberry Pond. At first, Lucy found her cheeks burning but soon adjusted to the new reality: Wild Willy had reached iconic status and was here to stay.

She was wondering whether, on the off chance that some ambitious TV producer actually managed to find Wild Willy, he would accept an invitation to appear on late-night TV. He could chat with Jimmy Fallon or maybe

Seth Meyers, who would nod approvingly as he described his lifestyle and joke about it afterward. Oddly enough, she could almost imagine him sitting on one of those couches, in his clean but worn bib overalls, earnestly preaching his anti-consumerist gospel.

"Lucy! Lucy!" A strident female voice broke into her train of thought. "Planet Earth to Lucy!"

Lucy snapped to attention, realizing that Natalie Withers wanted a word with her. She knew that Natalie was a faithful attendee at select-board meetings and was only too aware that she didn't hesitate to criticize Lucy's coverage. Instead of daydreaming, Lucy belatedly realized she should have beaten a hasty retreat. Now she was stuck and would have to answer to Natalie. "What can I do for you?" she asked, bracing for the onslaught.

"Well, Lucy Stone, instead of writing about weirdos who live in the woods, maybe you should write about the strange goings-on in town hall."

Lucy smiled. "You know, Natalie, I've been covering this town for quite some time, and, as I keep telling you, I've always found our town officials and workers to be hardworking, honest souls trying to do the best job they can for our citizens."

"Humpf!" Natalie looked at her in disbelief. "Well, you must be blind, that's all I can say. These wonderful town officials of yours are clearly mismanaging taxpayer funds! Why else would they need an override to pay for the community center. Why indeed?"

"I think it's all been explained by the town treasurer. Costs went up during the project and exceeded the initial appropriation. Surely you know yourself that every time you go to the grocery store, the prices go up or the packages get smaller. Like ice cream. Used to be a half-gallon, but now there's quite a few scoops less. Or cereal? Have you noticed how the boxes are slimmer? And don't even talk to me about the price of gas. Everything's going up. It's called inflation."

"A responsible treasurer would have anticipated inflation and included it in the proposal. It's not fair for taxpayers to vote one amount and then get hit with surcharges." Natalie sniffed. "And don't get me started about the Personnel Committee," she said, clearly only too willing to vent on a favorite topic.

"Natalie, I've been over this with you. If you're dissatisfied, you should take it up with the committee members, not me."

"Don't think I haven't tried. That Lydia Volpe's got an excuse for everything, except her incompetence."

This was more than Lucy was willing to tolerate. She had a high regard for Lydia, now retired, but who had taught kindergarten to all four of her children. "You need to be careful making unsubstantiated claims about town officials," she warned.

"Unsubstantiated? Well, for starters, how long was that woman's vacation—a paid vacation, by the way—how long was it supposed to be?"

"Two weeks," said Lucy. "And it was part of a negotiated compensation package that was approved by the HR committee and the select board."

"That's my point, exactly. They were taken in. She's taken the money, the vacation money, the signing bonus, and she hasn't come back."

"Really?" Lucy was doing the math in her head and counting the days since Darleen left on vacation and discovering that Darleen's two weeks were over.

"Really!" crowed Natalie, triumphant. "She should have

been back on the job today. I've called the center numerous times this morning, and my call always goes to voice
mail."

Maybe, thought Lucy, Darleen was dodging Natalie,
just as she herself often did. Or maybe Darleen was
AWOL and she needed to follow up. "I'll look into it," she
promised. "I hope she hasn't had some sort of accident."

"Accident, my foot," said Natalie. "That woman is a
grifter, mark my words. She took the town for a bunch of
suckers."

Natalie's choice of words struck Lucy as odd, and she
began to wonder if the foot and arm could possibly belong
to Darleen. It was a disturbing thought, especially since
everybody thought Darleen had gone on vacation, and nobody had considered she might actually be missing, even
murdered. She was beginning to feel rather sick at the idea
of the dismembered parts actually belonging to someone
she knew and decided to make sure that Darleen was actually missing in action. Pulling out her phone and making
the call as she walked down Main Street toward the
Courier, she punched in the number for the Council on
Aging.

Sheri Thurston answered, and Lucy paused under a
shade tree to ask if Darleen had returned as scheduled.
"Well, now that you mention it, no," replied Sheri. "She
was expected today, at least I thought she was, but I probably got it wrong. I thought it was a two-week vacation;
that's what I wrote in my calendar, but maybe she only got
paid for two weeks. Maybe she was planning to take some
unpaid time, too. That's what I think it must be."

"That's probably it," said Lucy, unwilling to alarm
Sheri, even though she clearly remembered Darleen telling
her she planned to do absolutely nothing at the resort in

San Diego for two whole weeks. "I'm sure she'll turn up, tanned and relaxed and rarin' to go."

Sheri laughed. "That's Darleen for you."

Lucy ended the call and continued on her way along Main Street to the office, then decided to take a short detour to Millicent's house, just around the corner. Millicent would surely know her daughter's whereabouts.

It was hot in the sun, and Lucy's hair was sticking to her forehead when she rang the doorbell at the Busby house, where a neat plaque beside the door announced it was built in 1760. Millicent answered promptly, greeting her with a smile, and inviting her in. "You look done in, Lucy. How about some iced tea?"

"Sounds lovely," said Lucy, stepping inside the cool hall, where a portrait of Captain Isaiah Busby in a blue and buff Continental Army uniform held pride of place above an antique console table.

"Let's go in the kitchen," invited Millicent. "It's more comfortable there."

So Lucy followed Millicent as she floated along on tippy-toes, like one of the aunts in *Arsenic and Old Lace*, through the dining room, past the shelf with the "Nantucket" basket and the cabinet with the "Paul Revere" teapot. They continued on into the kitchen, where Lucy took a trip backward in time as she viewed the old-fashioned linoleum floor and the Formica counters. Millicent invited her to take a seat at a small table, which was accompanied by two painted wooden chairs. It all reminded Lucy of her own grandmother's kitchen, right down to the house sweater hanging on the back of one chair.

"I hope you don't mind herb tea," said Millicent, taking a glass pitcher out of the round-top Frigidaire. "It's my own mixture: mint, chamomile, and lavender, all from my own garden."

"That sounds delicious," said Lucy, watching as Millicent wrestled with the handle on a stainless-steel ice cube tray. "Can I help you with that?"

"No need," said Millicent, yanking the handle back and loosening the ice cubes. She plopped them into two glasses decorated with painted daisies, then carefully refilled the tray with water and replaced it in the freezer compartment. "Do you take sugar?" she asked, closing the fridge door.

"No, thanks."

"I suppose you believe this modern nonsense about sugar, that it's practically poison," said Millicent, carrying the glasses of tea over to the table and setting them down. Seating herself in the opposite chair, she reached for the sugar bowl and dumped a couple of spoonfuls into her tea, mixing it in with a long-handled iced-tea spoon, the likes of which Lucy had not seen in a dog's age. "Darleen is always on a diet, but they never seem to work."

"That's actually why I came," began Lucy, sipping the tea and finding it delicious.

Millicent smiled mischievously. "To check on Darleen's diet?"

Lucy chuckled. "No. To check on Darleen. People are beginning to be concerned because she hasn't returned as expected to her job at the community center."

"That's right," said Millicent, as if the thought had just occurred to her. She took a sip of sweet tea and shook her head. "That's Darleen for you. Impulsive, especially if she's enjoying herself. Why, I remember how, as a little girl, if she was playing with her Barbie doll or reading a Nancy Drew story, you couldn't pull her away. Not even for dinner. I'd have to actually take the doll or the book away to get her attention."

"So you think she's simply extended her vacation?"

"I do." Millicent leaned forward and lowered her voice. "Just between you and me, I suspect she's met a man."

"And you think she would drop everything for a man? Even risk losing her new job?" Lucy took another big swallow of the tea, which she was finding positively addictive.

"She's been lonely," confessed Millicent, in a sad tone. "And I can't blame her. Her husband, Dan, has been gone for close to twelve years, and I know she misses him. He was a wonderful fellow. He agreed to hyphenate their name; they both went by Busby-Pratt. He had great respect for the Busby family traditions."

Lucy was beginning to suspect she was being gaslighted, so she pressed the issue. "So you've actually heard from Darleen? Did she tell you about this man?"

Millicent paused and stirred her tea, making the ice cubes clink in the quiet kitchen. "Yes, she called just the other day and said she was planning to stay on a bit longer. She didn't actually mention a man, but"—Millicent raised her eyebrows and gave a meaningful nod—"I definitely got the feeling something was cooking in that department."

Lucy gave an understanding smile. "How so?"

"She just sounded cheery, pleased with herself."

"Wouldn't she have told you if a man was taking an interest in her?"

Millicent shook her head, making her permed white curls bounce. "Ah, no, not Darleen. She holds her cards close to her vest, if you know what I mean. And, well, if she had, let's say, *misbehaved with some fella*," continued Millicent, her voice becoming sharp, "well, she knows full well that I most certainly do not approve of that sort of thing, so she wouldn't want me to suspect anything of that nature."

Lucy drained her glass and prepared to ask one final question. "So you're confident Darleen has simply decided to extend her vacation and is enjoying herself in San Diego?"

Millicent shrugged. "Sad to say, but it's typical behavior for Darleen. She's always been like a butterfly, flitting here and there, carried on the wind of her own impulses." Millicent giggled. "I didn't make that up. It was Dan, dear Dan, before, um, the accident."

Feeling somewhat overwhelmed by the information overload, Lucy stood up. "Well, thanks for your time, and the tea."

"Anytime, dear. Anytime. I love a bit of company."

Millicent accompanied Lucy to the door, where Lucy suddenly found herself eager to leave. But why, she wondered, retracing her steps through town to the office. Millicent had been nothing but generous and forthcoming, welcoming her and giving her iced tea. Why did she feel she had to escape?

"So what tricks are those selectpersons up to?" asked Phyllis, by way of greeting when Lucy arrived at the office. "Meeting went way longer than usual."

"Same old, same old," said Lucy. "Nothing new. I went to talk to Darleen's mother. Do you realize she hasn't come back from that controversial vacation? Natalie Withers thinks she's absconded with her signing bonus. Was there a signing bonus?"

"Not that I know of," said Phyllis, "but you better find out."

"That's what I intend to do," said Lucy, plopping herself down in her desk chair; she pulled her lunch from her bag and immediately called Lydia Volpe. After the preliminaries, in which Lydia required a detailed account of all her former students' doings, naming Toby, Elizabeth, Sara, and Zoe one by one, Lucy was able to ask about Darleen's alleged signing bonus.

"Signing bonus?" scoffed Lydia. "What do you think this is? The NFL? There was no signing bonus." She paused a moment. "Whatever gave you that idea?"

"A concerned citizen . . ." said Lucy, hedging, as she unwrapped her PB&J sandwich.

"So Natalie's been after you."

"Well, yeah. But the fact of the matter is, Darleen hasn't come back from her controversial vacation."

Lydia didn't sound happy. "Is that so?"

"Yeah. I checked with her mother. She says Darleen is most likely extending her vacation because she's met a man." Lucy took a bite of her sandwich.

"I suppose it's possible," admitted Lydia, "but it seems out of character. We interviewed Darleen several times and checked her references thoroughly, and everything checked out."

"I guess there's one way to find out," said Lucy, pausing to swallow. "I guess I'll call that resort and see if she's still there."

"Let me know," requested Lydia, sounding troubled. "I can't believe we misjudged her so . . ."

Lucy was quick to reassure her. "I'm sure you didn't." But she couldn't shake the feeling that something was wrong.

Lucy polished off her sandwich while she googled resorts in San Diego to find the Hotel del Coronado, a huge, old-fashioned beachfront resort that looked in the photos as if it had once welcomed Gibson Girls and straw-hatted gentlemen; it now claimed to have been thoroughly modernized. She dialed the number and asked to speak to guest Darleen Busby-Pratt and got the not-unexpected information that no one by that name was staying at the hotel.

When Lucy asked if Darleen had been there and checked out, she was told, very politely, that the hotel maintained a strict policy of respecting each guest's privacy. Lucy knew only too well that identifying herself as a reporter following up on a missing person story would not advance her cause; instead, it would only prompt the del Coronado to lock down any and all information about Darleen.

The woman she was speaking to had a very sweet voice and sounded young, however, which encouraged Lucy to continue trying, even if it meant resorting to desperate measures. She let out a big sigh, added a sniff, and proceeded to lie through her teeth. "Oh, dear. Darleen's my sister, you see, and I haven't heard a word from her since she left home a few weeks ago. She's been planning this trip for such a long time and promised to send postcards, but we haven't gotten any. And while she's gone, I'm taking care of Mom, who really relies on Darleen; she frets so when Darleen isn't home. And this is the first vacation Darleen's had in years and years, but she was supposed to come home a few days ago, and I need to get back to my kids and my job, too. So if you could tell me anything, anything at all about Darleen, it would be such a relief, rather than this uncertainty . . ."

"Okay," said the voice, in a whisper. "I see there was a reservation for Darleen Busby-Pratt, but she never checked in . . ."

"Never checked in!" Lucy remained in character. "Are you sure? She's been looking forward to this trip for such a long time! It doesn't make any sense."

"I'm sorry, I have to go now."

"Of course. Thank you. Oh, I hope nothing has happened to Darleen . . ." continued Lucy, but the screen on her phone went dark, indicating the call had ended.

"What now?" asked Phyllis, who had been listening in.

"It's time to inform the authorities," said Lucy, feeling rather sick. "We've got body parts and a missing person . . ."

"Could be a coincidence," said Phyllis. "Maybe you misunderstood; maybe Darleen is staying at some del Coronado hotel in Florida, or maybe you got the name wrong. Or maybe she misled you for some reason."

"She had a reservation that she didn't keep," said Lucy.

"Foolish, because they'll ding her credit card. But I bet she had a sudden change of plans and is relaxing on a lounge chair and sipping on a frozen margarita somewhere."

"Or maybe she never left Tinker's Cove and is scattered in bits and pieces all over town," said Lucy, dialing the number she knew only too well for the TCPD.

Chapter Fifteen

Oddly enough, she got put right through to the chief, which wasn't at all usual. Chief Jim Kirwan tended to dodge her calls, at least that's how she saw it. Maybe he really spent most of his time out on a call or in a meeting or at a conference, but she doubted it. Nevertheless, today she heard his voice coming right out of her phone.

"Uh, hi," she began, somewhat nonplussed. "It's me, Lucy . . ."

"I know, Lucy. What's on your mind?"

"Well, it seems Darleen Busby-Pratt hasn't returned from her controversial paid vacation."

"That so?"

"Yeah. People are starting to talk. She was supposed to get back to work today, but she never came in, so I called the hotel she told me she was going to be staying at, the del Coronado in San Diego, and they said she had a reservation but she never checked in."

"We haven't had a missing person report from her family," said the chief. "Are you sure about the hotel? Maybe she changed her mind and went somewhere else."

"Could be, but the fact remains that she was supposed to be back on the job at the community center today."

"Okay. Thanks for the info, Lucy. We will definitely follow up."

"Keep me in the loop?"

"Absolutely," promised the chief, but Lucy wasn't convinced. She knew that once the police began an investigation, a cone of silence descended over the department. She'd have to do her own investigating.

She was wondering who she could question next when she heard a shriek from across the room. Snapping to attention, she saw Phyllis had turned white, her eyes were huge, her mouth open, and she was clutching her phone to her ear, hanging on to every word.

"Ohmigod," she finally said, grabbing her purse and heading for the door.

"Hey, hey," yelled Lucy. "What's the matter?"

"It's Arthur . . ."

Lucy knew Arthur was Phyllis's grandnephew, her niece Elfrida's youngest child. "Is he okay?"

"I don't know. Elfrida's completely panicked. It seems she found a foot under his bed."

Lucy had expected to hear that Arthur had broken a bone or gotten involved in some sort of childhood scrape. This, however, was news. "Hold on," she instructed Phyllis. "I'll go with you."

Lucy drove the short distance to Elfrida's house, a rather tired ranch she'd inherited from Phyllis's late sister. While she drove, Lucy questioned Phyllis. "What happened? Did she actually find a foot?"

"That's what she says. She's really shaken up. She was changing the sheets and pulled the bed out from the wall, and there it was, on the floor."

"It was under Arthur's bed?"

"That's what Elfie says."

"And how old is Arthur now?"

"He's in second grade."

Lucy remembered Arthur as a careless little scamp who had, a couple of years ago, left his bike on the porch, causing Phyllis's husband, Wilf, to fall and break his leg. It had happened during a family crisis when Phyllis and Wilf were caring for Elfrida's five children, and Wilf had required surgery and several pins to repair his leg.

"Still the same naughty boy?" inquired Lucy, turning carefully into Elfrida's drive to avoid the scooter that was lying right smack in the middle.

"He's a typical little boy," said Phyllis, "by which I mean he's a menace to society and will eventually either end up in jail or win election to the U.S. Senate."

Elfrida had been on the lookout and was standing in the open doorway, anxiously tapping her foot. "Thank goodness, you're here. I just don't know what to do," she said, as they crossed a patch of grass that needed mowing.

"The kids are all in school?" asked Phyllis. With a start, Lucy remembered school had indeed resumed after the summer vacation. She hadn't been assigned to cover the first-day observances last week; Ted had taken that annual assignment himself.

"Even Angie. She's in class at the community college."

"They'll be home at three?" asked Lucy, following Elfrida through the living room, where toys were scattered on the floor. They proceeded down a short hallway to the bedroom Arthur and Albert shared, where one of the twin beds, covered only with a fitted sheet depicting assorted colorful superheroes, was pulled out at an angle from the wall. Angie pointed to the space, where a foot was lying among the dust bunnies and Legos.

"Pardon the dust," said Angie, apologizing. "It's actually Addie's job; she's supposed to push the Swiffer around once a week, but she's been busy at the fudge shop. She's got a part-time job, you know."

"Good for her," said Lucy, peering at the foot and deciding it was a good match to the other foot, the one found by the dog.

"I think I'm going to be sick," said Phyllis, dashing for the bathroom, where she proceeded to noisily lose her lunch.

Lucy was relieved to find her sandwich had settled nicely and was somewhat dismayed to discover she was no longer shocked or upset by finding body parts in unusual places. Sad to say, she was getting used to it.

"What should I do?" asked Elfrida.

"I'd start by calling 911," advised Lucy, who proceeded to do that very thing. When the call ended, with the promise that an officer was on the way, Lucy asked Elfrida the obvious question: "Do you have any idea how the foot got here?"

Eldrida was a remarkably attractive woman with a killer figure, and she looked quite fetching today, wearing a tight pink tank top and white short shorts, with her wavy blond hair pulled back by a bandana headband. Most people in town believed it was her looks, along with a chronic inability to say no, that had resulted in her five officially fatherless children. They had obviously each had a father, but Elfrida had either been unable or unwilling to name names. "I guess he found it somewhere and brought it home," she said, shrugging indulgently and smiling prettily. "Last week he brought a toad home; he said he found it in the woods."

Phyllis returned, looking rather wan, just as they heard a squawk from outside announcing the arrival of a police cruiser. Lucy went to the door to greet the officer, smiling when she saw Barney Culpepper easing his sizable bulk out of the car. Once he was clear and standing upright, he smoothed his brush cut and set his cap on his head. "Hey, Lucy. What's up?"

Lucy wasn't about to announce the discovery of the foot to the world at large, so she limited herself to inviting him inside. Barney was a big man, and he seemed to fill the whole house once he stepped inside. He waited politely, removing his hat, while Lucy closed the door behind him. "Dispatcher said you've found a foot?" he began.

"Follow me," said Lucy, leading the way down the hall.

"Hello, ladies," he said, greeting Elfrida and Phyllis. "What have you got here?"

He followed Elfrida's pointed, pink-tipped finger and saw the foot.

"Anybody touched it?" he asked, scratching his chin.

They all shook their heads.

"Whose room?" he asked, taking in the scattered Star Wars and superhero figures, the school photos hung on the wall, and the pile of well-thumbed comic books.

"Arthur and Albert's," said Elfrida. "This is Arthur's bed."

"And how old is Arthur?"

"He's seven."

"I'm going to have to talk to Arthur," said Barney, pulling out his radio. "Where is he?" He nodded, learning he was at school. "I'll send a cruiser for him, and I've got to call the medical examiner. You ladies better wait in another room."

Elfrida led the way to the kitchen, where she suggested they sit at the table where the family took all their meals. Elfrida fixed glasses of water for Lucy and Phyllis, and Lucy studied the cheap plastic placemats, printed with a faded gingham-check pattern. Elfrida fussed about, anxious and unable to settle. She finally blurted out her fears. "I think it must be that Maine Maniac. Remember that poor girl, Corinne? All they found was a few bones."

"There was never a Maine Maniac," said Lucy, drawing her finger through the condensation that was forming on her water glass. "Corinne's killer is in prison, and he's going to stay there. He was just denied a retrial."

"But what about those other women? The ones who were missing? They never found them, and that's probably because they were cut in pieces. And I've got two teenage girls to worry about. I don't want somebody to find bits of Angie and Addie under their picnic table."

"I think that's most unlikely," said Lucy, but Phyllis strongly disagreed.

"If I were you, Elfie, I would keep those girls close. No more hanging out at the coffee shop or at friends' houses. If they're not at work or in class, they should be here at home, with the doors locked. Wilf's been at loose ends lately. He can drive the girls to work."

"I really think you're overreacting," said Lucy, but her comment fell on deaf ears.

"They never caught that Maine Maniac," said Phyllis. "I always thought he'd resurface."

"It just makes your blood run cold, to think of somebody out there, chopping people up," fretted Elfrida. "My friend from Merry Maids—you know Janie?"

Lucy knew Elfrida worked during the school year cleaning houses, but didn't know Janie.

"The girl with the twins?" asked Phyllis.

"That's her! Well, she was moonlighting at the Quik-Stop for the summer, but she quit. She said it was too scary being there all alone at night, what with a diabolical killer running around."

"She's not the only one," added Phyllis. "My neighbor, Gerry, she owns the mini-golf and Frostee Freeze out on Route One. She says she can't find anyone to take the evening shift; they're too scared."

Arthur's noisy arrival ended this discussion, which Lucy was finding enlightening. She hadn't realized the level of fear that was gripping the town and knew she needed to cover it. But Arthur, who had found the foot, was apparently unscathed by the experience.

"Hi, Mom!" he yelled, bursting into the kitchen. "Guess what? I got to ride in a police car!"

Lucy couldn't help smiling at Arthur, who was a cute kid with a back-to-school buzz cut, a couple of missing front teeth, and a badly skinned knee.

"Wow, honey, that's great," said Elfrida, smiling at Officer Sally Kirwan, who had followed him into the house. "Thank you for bringing him home."

"No problem."

"She even put on the siren, and the lights!"

They all gave Officer Sally a questioning look.

"Just for a moment," she admitted, with a smile. She left the kitchen and went to have a word with Barney in the bedroom, then both returned. "We need to question Arthur," she began, speaking to Elfrida. "Do you have any objection?"

"No. But can I be there?"

"Absolutely," said Sally.

"What about me?" asked Lucy, who wanted to get the story firsthand.

Sally and Barney exchanged a look, then Barney shrugged. "Seems to me you've been in on this from the beginning. I don't have any objection."

"It's okay by me," agreed Sally, "as long as you just observe. Don't say a word, okay?"

Lucy nodded, and they all went into the living room, where Elfrida sat with Arthur in a big old squashy armchair. Lucy and Phyllis perched on the saggy couch, and Barney leaned against the wall, leaving the questioning to Sally.

Sally perched on a footstool and placed her phone on her knee, recording the conversation. "Okay, Arthur. You're not in any trouble; we just want to know where you found the foot. Okay?"

"Sure," replied Arthur, pleased to be the focus of attention. "I found it near where I found that toad, in the woods."

"What woods?"

"The woods behind the house."

"Okay. Did you see any other body parts? An arm or a hand?"

"No." He frowned in disappointment. "Just the foot."

"How come you brought it home?"

Arthur gave the officer a look that expressed dismay at this complete lack of understanding. "Well, it isn't every day you find a foot."

"Right." Officer Sally nodded, and Barney managed to restrain himself from laughing. "It's special. Did you tell anybody, or show them?"

Arthur shook his head. "If I told Mom, she wouldn't let me keep it, and if I told Albie, he'd want me to share it; maybe he'd even take it. And at school, I did tell Lily, but she didn't believe me. So I thought maybe I could bring the foot tomorrow, in my backpack."

Elfrida let out a little moan, then pressed her lips tightly together as Sally asked another question. "When did you find the foot?"

"Uh, yesterday. It doesn't smell," offered Arthur, helpfully.

Eldrida seemed to be growing faint, and Barney stepped forward, inviting her to get a breath of fresh air, which she gratefully agreed to. The two stepped outside, and Sally continued the questioning.

"So you were planning to keep it?"

Arthur was incredulous at this example of adult incomprehension. "Yeah!"

"Was anyone with you when you found it?"

"No. I was looking for my toad. Mom made me put him back, but I wanted to make sure he was okay. I named him Spotty."

"Well, I don't have any other questions," said Officer Sally, looking up as Elfrida and Barney returned. "We just have to wait for the medical examiner, and she'll relieve you of the foot."

"You mean she's going to take it?" demanded Arthur.

"I'm afraid so," admitted Sally.

"Shit," said Arthur.

"Arthur!" exclaimed his mother.

Chapter Sixteen

Lucy was quite pleased with her scoop and couldn't wait to tell Ted all about adorable little Arthur's big discovery, so she called him as soon as she got in her car. She was alone since Phyllis had decided to stay with Elfrida, who needed a bit of moral support. She smiled to herself as she tapped Ted's name, figuring he would certainly want to play it up big, putting little Arthur's gap-toothed grin on page one. But when she called with the news, Ted didn't react as she'd expected. "Listen, Lucy, I think this story needs to be handled carefully."

What was Ted getting at? "Are you kidding? This is real human interest, and I've got photos. You know what you say: kids and dogs sell papers."

"He's just a little boy, Lucy. And face it, finding a human foot is all kinds of traumatic. I think readers are going to worry about little Arthur. He's probably going to need years of therapy."

"Are you kidding? Arthur was tickled pink. He got a ride in a police car, for one thing. The only problem for him was having to give up the foot. He wanted to keep it."

Ted was not swayed. "No, Lucy. I've decided that Pete's going to cover the story . . ."

"Pete Popper?" Lucy was outraged. Pete was a veteran reporter who covered county news out of the *Courier*'s Gilead office and was a joke among his colleagues because, even though he regularly attended press conferences, he'd never once asked a question.

"Yeah. This is gonna be a county story, what with the DA managing the investigation and the obvious involvement of the ME, and Pete's got good relationships with the county officials. I want you to focus on the upcoming special town meeting. I think that's more in your ballpark."

Lucy couldn't believe what she was hearing. "The special town meeting?"

"Yeah, Lucy. That's the big story in Tinker's Cove, and I'm counting on you to do your usual excellent job." Then the call ended, and Lucy was left holding her cell phone and wondering if her career as a reporter was over. So instead of heading back to the office, she decided to drop in on Pam. If she was in trouble with Ted, Pam would certainly know.

But Pam greeted her with a big smile. "Hi, Lucy! C'mon in. I've got something to show you."

Lucy and her friends had noticed that, as the days turned into weeks since Tim's disappearance, Pam had gradually grown to accept the situation. "The only thing I have control of is myself," she'd told them at their last Thursday-morning breakfast. "Tim's gonna do what Tim's gonna do. I can't wrap him up in cellophane and protect him. I have to protect myself; I have to live my life. Ted and I talked it over with a counselor, and what really stuck with me was when she asked what's different today from before Tim's breakdown. That was when I thought about how, when he was in college, we didn't hear from him for weeks unless he wanted some money or something. And when he was working at the museum, when he was in the greatest danger and heading for the breakdown, I thought he was doing great. If this thing has taught me anything, it's that I have to have faith in my son. I have to let Tim be Tim."

Rachel had beamed approval at this pronouncement, and even though Lucy and Sue both doubted that Pam could truly divorce herself from Tim, they kept those thoughts to themselves. But today Lucy thought all signs indicated that Pam was definitely coping better. She followed her friend through the house to Tim's bedroom, where Pam proudly displayed the completed quilt top.

"Ta-da!" she crowed, unfolding it with a flourish.

"It's beautiful," said Lucy, amazed at how Pam had managed to create a work of art from the disparate bits of cloth. "I love the way you've brought it all together."

"It's the embroidery," said Pam. "The gold thread kind of winds its way through Tim's life, and there's a lot of blue. Blue and gold work well together."

"You started with his baby things, up at the top," said Lucy, "and as he grows older, the colors get deeper, toward the bottom. It's really very cleverly done."

"I only hope he gets to see it," said Pam, wistfully smoothing the quilt. "I wish this pattern wasn't called crazy quilt; maybe it should be a kaleidoscope quilt."

"Kaleidoscope quilt is better," agreed Lucy. "That's what you should name it when you show it at the next quilt show."

"Do you really think I should enter it?" Pan was doubtful. "It's not really finished, you know. This is just the top. It needs filling and a back."

"Absolutely. You've got a winner." Lucy had a thought. "Why don't we have an old-fashioned quilting bee? Wouldn't that be fun?"

"Thanks, Lucy. That's a great idea." Pam folded the quilt top and laid it carefully on the bed, giving it a loving little pat. "How about some iced tea?"

"Sounds great. And maybe a cookie? I only had a PB&J for lunch. At my desk."

"Oh, Lucy, you're working too hard," suggested Pam, heading down the hall to the kitchen.

Before following her, Lucy took a look around Tim's room. It was neat as a pin, and Lucy figured Pam had taken advantage of his absence to tidy things up. Apart from the bed, the room contained a desk, a bookcase, and a dresser; a few framed prints of paintings by Thomas Eakins hung on the wall, including his famous *Wrestlers*. It struck Lucy that the room was waiting for Tim to return; there was even a stack of books on his desk. She stepped closer to see what he had been reading before he disappeared and realized, with surprise, that there were several anatomy books among the others, which dealt with climate change and global warming.

Tucking this bit of information away for later, Lucy followed Pam. Joining her in the kitchen, she recounted little Arthur's big adventure. "So I don't know what to make of it," she concluded, climbing on one of the stools at Pam's kitchen island. "I thought Ted would love the story, but he's giving it to Pete Popper, which is practically the same as killing it."

"This whole situation with Tim has hit him pretty hard," said Pam, filling two glasses with ice and taking a pitcher of tea out of the fridge. "Ever since we saw that therapist, he's been reevaluating some of his attitudes toward other people, and how they might cause pain, even trauma." Pam slid the glass of iced tea across the island to Lucy, then piled some cookies on a plate. "It's kind of scary, really."

She chuckled. "A kinder, gentler Ted." She set the plate on the island. "I wouldn't worry, if I were you. It sounds to me as if he's trying to relieve you of such a heavy workload." She chuckled. "It certainly won't last."

"That's a relief," said Lucy, lifting her glass. "Here's to Ted. Do you think he'd be open to giving me a raise?"

"Uh, no, Lucy," said Pam. "No way."

Due to a printing problem, the papers weren't delivered until Thursday afternoon, when Lucy had the pleasure of reading Pete Popper's story about the investigation, which began with DA Phil Aucoin's assertion that there was no danger to the public. NO DANGER TO PUBLIC was actually the headline. Rumors had been swirling around town for days that the body parts belonged to Darleen, so it was hardly news when Pete got around to mentioning the medical examiner's identification in the middle of the story, which had been continued on page 17.

"Burying the lede," muttered Lucy, reading that a comparison of Millicent's DNA with that of the body parts, including the recently discovered second foot, had made it possible to confirm the identity of the dismembered woman as Darleen Busby-Pratt.

Pete had not mentioned Arthur in his story but had been more interested in parroting DA Phil Aucoin's promises of a "full and thorough investigation" and repeated assurances that the murder was an isolated incident and that finding the killer was top priority. "All of our county and state resources are being brought to bear," Aucoin had insisted, "and I have complete confidence that the killer will be brought to justice. No one is above the law in this county."

And even though Lucy knew from a colleague that Aucoin had been questioned several times at the press conference about the Maine Maniac, Pete had not mentioned it in his story, either. Lucy didn't know if Aucoin's answers would have made a difference, but rumors about the Maine Maniac were continuing to circulate.

Lucy well remembered how Corinne's disappearance had originally been linked to that of several others, two women who had been sex workers in Portland and a mother of six children, all under eight years of age. A Jack-the-Ripper type killer had been suspected at the time, but only Corinne's body had been found. It wasn't until sometime later that Martin Wicker, whose truck had been seen at the pond where Corinne was working, was identified as Corinne's abductor and killer. The other three rumored victims had never turned up, and it was eventually assumed that they'd simply gone on to forge new lives for themselves elsewhere.

But now, those stories had surfaced, and everyone seemed to believe the Maine Maniac had returned. All of a sudden, folks were looking over their shoulders, locking their cars in the IGA parking lot, and even locking their doors. Standing in line at the IGA, Lucy overheard two women discussing the situation, fretting that, even though they were now careful to lock their doors, it wasn't possible to lock the windows. "It's been so warm this September that I don't want to close them. It's not so bad in the daytime, but at night, I get so scared thinking that maniac could cut the screen and climb right into my bedroom."

"I know," said her friend. "I keep a baseball bat by my bed, but I don't know if that would stop a madman with a knife."

"How do you think he got Darleen?"

"I saw a TV show where the killer hid under a woman's bed; he got in the house in when she was out and waited . . ."

"I saw that, too. Oh, it made my heart stop when he slid out . . ."

"Next," announced the cashier, interrupting their fascinating conversation, which had stalled the line.

Meanwhile, Lucy was doing her best to follow Ted's instructions and was taking a deep dive into municipal finances in preparation for the special town meeting. There was only a single item on the warrant, an article for a budget override that would allow the town to fund remaining costs related to the construction of the community center. Finding the technicalities confusing, she had arranged to interview the town treasurer in his town hall office on Friday morning. He was making a sincere attempt to explain the complexities of municipal finance to her, when the sudden blare of a fire siren interrupted them. They listened as the truck thundered past, followed by another, and then the ambulance. "Accident on Route One?" guessed the treasurer.

"Maybe a forest fire; it's been dry," suggested Lucy. She looked at the treasurer, who was unfolding a large spreadsheet, and made a quick decision. "Um, thanks, it's been really helpful talking to you, but I think I better check out the fire situation."

"But I was just about to explain debt ratios in relation to expected revenues . . ."

"I'm afraid it will have to wait. I'll get back to you," said Lucy, tossing her notebook into her bag and swinging it onto her shoulder. "I'll call," she promised, dashing for the door.

As she looked down Main Street, there was no sign of

the fire trucks, so Lucy had no idea where they'd gone. She crossed and went into the *Courier* office, where she noticed that Phyllis hadn't come in yet. Briefly wondering if she was home sick, Lucy switched on the scanner and learned the fire was in the woods out by the Rod and Gun Club. She was on her way out the door, when the scanner squawked again, calling for mutual aid from Gilead.

This was big, she realized, deciding she'd better get herself out there, fast, before Ted got wind of it and assigned it to Pete Popper. She suspected that if Pete covered it, he'd start the story with a history of the club and get around to the fire when the story was continued on page 27.

Lucy could already smell smoke when she left the office, and the scattered tourists taking in the sights on Main Street were sniffing the air and looking worried. She was worried, too, fearing that the fire might get out of control. The Rod and Gun was in the forested town watershed, which provided plenty of fuel for the wildfires that were a growing concern these days. But when she got to the club, she found it was unscathed. The fire was in the adjacent woods, where a huge tower of smoke was rising into the sky.

She pulled into the parking lot at the Rod and Gun and got out of the car, camera at the ready. She snapped photos of the smoke and the growing number of first-response vehicles in the road. Spotting fire chief Buzz Bresnahan, she approached him, noticing he was speaking into his walkie-talkie. Seeing her, he raised a finger, instructing her to wait. When he finished, he turned to her. "Good news. It's under control; it seems to be a structure of some sort. A shack."

"Oh, no. That must be Wild Willy's place."

"You mean he lives there?"

Lucy nodded. "I hope he's okay."

Buzz was already issuing new orders to check the shack for a victim. "Unlikely he'd survive if he was home," he told Lucy. "The shack was fully involved when we finally got in. It's pretty deep in the woods. Had to lay hose quite a distance."

"Any idea how it got started?" asked Lucy.

"Unfortunately, I do," admitted Buzz. "Hooligans. We found a gas can and most of a twelve-pack. Looked like they were dropped in a panic; fire probably went up faster than they expected."

"You mean it was done on purpose?"

"Who knows what goes through these idiots' minds? They don't think things through. It seems like a good idea, a lot of fun, but then things get a little crazy, and they end up in a whole mess of trouble."

"I hope Willy's okay," said Lucy. "I know he goes into town for groceries."

"Let's hope that today's shopping day."

"Any chance I can get some photos?" asked Lucy.

Buzz shook his head. "Sorry. Too dangerous, and we want to preserve the scene for the fire marshal. There's gonna have to be an investigation."

"I understand," said Lucy, snapping a photo of Bresnahan and then making her way back to the parking lot. Once there, she remembered the path through the woods that she'd used to visit Wild Willy and decided to see if she could get close enough to get the photo she wanted. She also thought she might find Willy in the woods, where he might have fled from the fire. She'd be careful, she told herself, intending to make a quick retreat if she encountered any problems.

The air was thick, and she smelled smoke, but there were no signs that the fire had spread as she made her way along the narrow deer track. The birds were silent, but she could hear shouts in the distance, as well as the hum of diesel engines. Finally reaching the clearing, she remained out of sight as she surveyed the scene. The shack, Wild Willy's home, was completely gone. Nothing was left except a smoldering pile of ash, which firefighters were sifting through with rakes, occasionally directing a stream of water to put out a hot spot. The only piece of firefighting equipment that had been able to make it through was the county's brush breaker, but a number of hoses snaked through the woods, connected to the pumper trucks.

Looking through her cell phone camera, she couldn't find much to capture in a photo but snapped a couple of shots depicting the firefighters. Then she turned and retraced her steps back to the parking lot. As she whacked her way through the undergrowth, her thoughts turned to Willy. She had an awful feeling that she bore some responsibility for the fire. If she hadn't written that story, Willy would have remained anonymous, safe in his forest home. She'd drawn attention to him, which made him a target for violence from those who couldn't tolerate anyone who was different.

Returning to the office, Lucy discovered the door was locked and Phyllis was absent. This was somewhat disconcerting since Phyllis was very reliable and always called in on the rare occasions she was sick or had some family crisis. Digging in her bag for her keys, Lucy figured she must have missed the call and hoped everything was okay. She shelved that thought for later, intent on writing her account of the fire. She'd just settled at her desk when she got a call from the fire chief. "We found William Sorenson, aka Wild Willy. He appeared as we were leaving, asked for a ride back to town. He's safe and sound. Rob Jackson offered to put him up until he can find housing."

"That's good news," said Lucy, who was flooded with relief. She still felt guilty about exposing Willy to violence, but at least he'd only lost his house. Willy himself was safe. The shame of it was, however, that he'd lost everything. His home may have looked like a worthless shack to the hooligans who burned it down, but Lucy knew it had been lovingly and thoughtfully assembled out of discarded bits and pieces that Willy had gathered. Windows, doors, shingles, every component had been tossed out and left for trash, but Willy had seen their value and recycled them. It was a bit like Pam's quilt, thought Lucy. Something made out of nothing.

Her thoughts turned to Pam, and she smiled to herself. Pam was weathering the storm. Only a few weeks ago, she had been completely shattered by Tim's breakdown and disappearance, but now she had not only put the quilt together, she'd put herself back together. Now, if only Tim would give her a call or, even better, come back home. Back to his family, back to the house he'd grown up in, back to the room that was waiting for him and the books he'd been studying.

The books! Lucy tried to tell herself there was probably a good reason that someone as connected to the art world as Tim was would consult an anatomy book. Maybe he'd taken a course in figure drawing; maybe he'd wondered about the perspective in one of those Eakins prints. Eakins had famously studied cadavers to better understand the human body . . .

Lucy didn't want to go there, but the fact was she knew only too well that Tim definitely had a motive for killing Darleen. She had been abusive to him; Lucy had seen it with her own eyes. She'd homed in on his vulnerability, his instability, and proceeded to verbally flay him. Tim's apparent passivity seemed to inflame her, inciting her to ramp up her attack. It would not be surprising, thought Lucy, if Tim had snapped. Her eyes fell on her desk calendar, where she'd noted Darleen's vacation. The vacation she'd never gone on. Was it a coincidence that Tim had disappeared immediately afterward?

Chapter Seventeen

No doubt about it. Absolutely a coincidence, thought Lucy, unable to imagine Tim killing a spider, much less a woman. She remembered how he'd cringed when Darleen rained abuse on him, not even attempting to defend himself verbally. Of course, she acknowledged, that might just mean that he'd stored all his anger away for later, like a volcano that simmered deep beneath the earth's surface, until it finally boiled over and erupted. But Tim wasn't a volcano, she told herself, he was a troubled young man who couldn't seem to focus or settle on the simplest tasks. And furthermore, she thought with a huge sense of relief, he didn't have a freezer.

Then a truly terrible thought occurred to her. What if Tim was in this killer's freezer? What if he was also a victim? She remembered how he hadn't defended himself from Darleen's verbal attack. Would he fight back if someone attacked him physically? Lucy took a deep breath and tried to clear her mind. Killers, it seemed to her, fell into two groups: people who snapped when angry and lashed out at someone they had a relationship with, and people who got a kick from killing and planned and plotted their murders. Darleen, it seemed, had been a victim of the latter sort of murderer, someone who had hidden her body and was taking time to dispose of it bit by bit. That sort of killer usually went for the same type of victim, in this case a middle-aged woman who was easily overpowered. Tim most definitely did not fit that description.

No, she thought sadly, it was more likely that if he was involved in Darleen's death, which she doubted, it was because he had fallen under the control of another. He certainly seemed to have a secret life, and she suspected he must be sharing it with someone. Or a group, she thought, thinking of the militias and activist cells that were attracting disenchanted young men who were unhappy with the status quo. She had the impression from Pam that these disappearances were not a new thing; it seemed Tim had been dropping in and out of family life for some time. But where did he go? It didn't appear that he was living rough, sleeping outdoors like a homeless person, but was probably couch surfing, finding shelter with others. But who? Had he fallen under the influence of some crazy sect?

Lucy thought of her own kids and their networks of friends. Sara, she knew, had found it quite difficult to get started on her grown-up life in Boston when she took her job at the Museum of Science. She'd missed her old friends in Tinker's Cove, where she'd attended both high school and college. "I used to know everybody," Sara had complained. "But now I don't know anyone." Her solution had been to come back home most weekends to see her old gang, a strategy that Lucy had pointed out was self-defeating since it prevented her from seeking out and making new friends. And Sara had gradually formed relationships with coworkers and other new graduates who couldn't afford Boston rents and had settled in her Quincy neighborhood.

She was soon too busy on weekends to trek back to Tinker's Cove. She still stayed in touch with the old friends on social media, however, and could pick up as if she'd never been gone when she did come home for Thanksgiving and Christmas. So who, wondered Lucy, did Tim stay in touch with? She decided to give her son, Toby, a call; he and his wife, Molly, were both in Tim's class in high school and might remember the people he hung out with.

Toby, however, lived in Alaska, and Lucy always had a hard time figuring out the time difference. A look at the Willard clock on the wall indicated it was well past noon, which a growl from her stomach confirmed was the correct time. That meant she wouldn't be waking up her son; she might even catch Toby before he left for his job as a state fisheries official.

"What's up?" he asked, answering the call with a bright tone of voice.

"Nothing much," began Lucy. "Ted's got me working on the town budget."

"And you need a break," he suggested, laughing.

"You said it. I'm going out of my mind, what with debt exclusions and overrides."

"I have to submit a budget every year. It's awful. It's the only part of the job that I don't like."

"So how's everyone?" asked Lucy, referring to Molly and her grandson, Patrick.

"Molly's been volunteering at the animal rescue shelter; she's always threatening to bring home some poor creature or other."

"Patrick would probably love a dog," suggested Lucy.

"Yeah, he would. But we're too busy. Nobody's home most of the day, and dogs don't like to be alone."

"Yeah," agreed Lucy, thinking sadly of her old pal, Libby,

now buried in the backyard. "How're Patrick's swimming lessons going? Has he mastered the butterfly?"

"Still working on it," laughed Toby.

Lucy decided she'd better cut to the chase before Toby decided he really needed to get to work. "Do you remember Tim Stillings? You were friends in school . . ."

"Sure. He's got a job at the Farnsworth, right?"

"Well, yeah, he had a job there, but he had a breakdown, and he's been home for a while now."

"That's too bad."

"I was just wondering if he still hangs out with that Earth Day group? He was pretty involved with them, wasn't he? Are any of them still around, here in the Cove?"

"Not sure. Molly would know. She's active on Facebook and Twitter and probably stays in touch with all of them. She was a member of that group, too."

"Right, I remember. Can I talk to her?"

"No. She's at a team-building thing for work, completely offline for the entire day. She's probably got the shakes without her phone. But I'll ask her about them when she gets home."

"That'd be great," said Lucy, as her phone began beeping, indicating another call. "I gotta go. I think Ted's trying to call me."

"Love ya, Mom."

Lucy smiled. "Right back at you."

As she suspected, the caller was Ted, and he wanted her to write Darleen's obituary as an online follow-up to Pete's story. Things were pretty bad, she decided, when you actually got excited about writing an obit, but it was definitely preferable to wrestling with the town budget.

"I've got photos of the fire," she told Ted, as a further evasive action. "Do you want me to write it up?"

"No. I've got Pete on it; he's got a call in to the chief."

"I've already talked to the chief," said Lucy. "In fact, I was at the fire. I've already started and can finish up in half an hour."

"Like I said, Pete's on it. But I can use your photos." Lucy could practically hear the wheels turning in Ted's head. "How's that special town meeting story going? I haven't seen it yet."

"I'm on it," said Lucy. "Almost done."

"Great. And don't forget the obit. I want to get 'em both online today."

"Not a problem," said Lucy, ending the call and looking up as Phyllis came in. "Taking a day off?" she asked, puzzled. Phyllis was wearing a fishing vest, wellies, and a bucket hat decorated with fishing flies.

Phyllis was standing at her desk, looking for something in a drawer. "I'm not working today. I just came in to grab my sunglasses. I left them here yesterday; at least I thought I did." She pulled out another drawer and crowed in triumph. "Got 'em!" Then she turned to go.

"Mental health day?" asked Lucy.

"Not exactly," said Phyllis. "Ted cut my hours. I'm down to three days a week."

"No!" Lucy's mind was racing. First, it was giving her stories to Pete Popper; now he'd cut Phyllis's hours. That could only mean one thing: Ted was going to close the Tinker's Cove office.

"I'm next," she said.

"I'd start looking for another job, if I were you," agreed Phyllis. "Just in case."

"But I like this job," said Lucy. "I don't want to do anything else."

"Then you better make yourself indispensable," said

Phyllis, sliding the sunglasses onto her nose and heading for the door. "I'm going fishing."

"Good luck," offered Lucy.

Phyllis chuckled. "I'll need it. I never fished before."

"Really? Where'd you get the cool gear?"

Phyllis laughed. "Borrowed from Wilf."

Lucy watched her leave, then sat gazing at the wall. Pete Popper was hardly a threat to her, or was he? Had he seen cuts coming and decided to go after her job? Well, if that was the case, Pete Popper had another think coming, she decided, reaching for her phone. Darleen was going to get the best obituary anybody had ever written! She wasn't going to give up without a fight; if she was going down, she was going down swinging.

Reaching for her phone, she took a deep breath and punched in Millicent's number. Over the years, she'd interviewed plenty of grieving survivors but always found it difficult. Sometimes, the death had been completely unexpected, the result of a car crash or a drowning, and the survivors were absolutely shattered. Other times, it had been the result of a long, debilitating disease, and grief was mixed with relief. But she'd never, ever, interviewed a mother whose child had been murdered and dismembered. This was going to be difficult.

She was relieved, then, when she heard a young person's voice coming through the phone and quickly identified herself. "Oh, hi, Lucy. I saw your article about Aunt Millie's quilt."

"I'm afraid this is a much sadder story," said Lucy. "I'm afraid I need some information for Darleen's obituary." Lucy paused, thinking that whomever she was talking to didn't seem too broken up. "I don't want to bother her mother. Maybe you can help me?"

"That would be best. Aunt Millie is much too upset to talk. I'm Cassie, Cassie Wainwright, and I'm Darleen's cousin."

"Thanks for your help, Cassie. Let me begin by saying how very sorry I am for your loss. It's truly a horrible situation."

"Well, the police are working on it, trying to find whoever did this awful thing. It's really hard to believe. I mean, I remember spending endless summers here when I was a kid. Darleen and I had great times together. We used to dress up the dog. Sadie was a very old Airedale, and we'd stuff her in old baby clothes and push her around in this old carriage. And there were great things in the attic, chests of old clothes and stuff that we used to dress up in and put on little plays. Oh, we got up to no good, too. We used to hide when Aunt Millie wanted us to pick beans or weed the garden, and she'd get so mad at us."

"That sounds like fun," said Lucy. "Did you and Darleen stay close as adults?"

Cassie sighed. "It wasn't quite the same, you know. We both got married; we were bridesmaids for each other. Darleen married her high school boyfriend, Dan Pratt, but it didn't last, and they got divorced."

"I thought Dan Pratt died in an accident," said Lucy, recalling something Millicent had said.

"No, it was a divorce. First in our family, in fact. They didn't have any kids, so it was pretty simple. Nick and I, on the other hand, have four kids, so we were pretty busy raising our brood while Darleen was off being a single lady."

Lucy got some dates and other details from Cassie, who was proving to be a fountain of information. She pulled up Darleen's résumé, which the Personnel Committee had included when they announced her appointment, and began asking Cassie about Darleen's impressive career. "So she was the CEO of the United Fund in Fairfield County," began Lucy, referring to Darleen's most recent position. "Do you know why she left that job to come back to Tinker's Cove?"

"Uh, I don't know about that," said Cassie, in an uncertain voice. "I know she came back to be with her mom. I mean, I wouldn't put this in the obituary, but Aunt Millie's not getting any younger, and she really can't be entirely on her own these days. She doesn't need a lot of care, but Darleen was keeping an eye on her, making sure she took her meds, and made some adjustments in the house, picking up scatter rugs and installing grab bars, that sort of thing. She knew what to do because she worked as a home health aide in Portland. That's the last job I knew about. This Fairfield thing is news to me. And CEO? Darleen only had a year of college."

"Are you sure?" asked Lucy, checking the résumé and noting that she'd claimed to graduate from the University of Connecticut with a degree in business.

"Yeah. I remember it well because I was kind of jealous that she was going to the community college because I was already pregnant with Cindy. But Dan didn't like it, said she was always studying and didn't have any time for him, so she dropped out after a year and got a job."

"Well," said Lucy, struggling to maintain a calm tone of voice, "I must have the wrong information. Do you happen to know if she worked for a health-care agency in Portland?"

"I think she must have, but I don't know the name. I did hear her complain about her boss, said she always gave her the toughest cases."

"Well, thanks for your help," said Lucy, eager to check out cousin Cassie's information. "Is there anything you'd like to add?"

"Just that we're really shocked and heartbroken and that if anybody has any information that might help identify Darleen's killer, please call the state police tip line. Maybe Darleen was just the first; let's make sure she's this demon's last victim."

"Well said, Cassie. Thanks again."

Lucy didn't waste a moment but got right on to Google, searching for Portland health-care agencies. On the third try, she struck gold.

"Darleen Busby-Pratt, oh, I remember her well," recalled the director. Her voice was cheery, as if she was smiling at the memory.

"Can you tell me about her?" asked Lucy.

"Well, no," she said, sounding regretful. "I'm sorry, but our policy is to only confirm whether or not a former employee worked for us. We don't share job evaluations or anything like that."

"I completely understand," said Lucy. "But I'm sorry to tell you I'm writing Darleen's obituary."

"She's dead! How?"

"I'm afraid she was murdered."

"Oh, no! Poor Darleen."

"Yes, indeed. It's quite tragic, you know, leaving her aged mother all alone."

"I know she went back home to care for her," admitted the director.

"Perhaps you could tell me something about her as a friend, not as her employer?" coaxed Lucy.

"I must say I'm absolutely shocked and appalled to learn of her untimely death. My goodness, what is the world coming to? She was a great friend, and I was very sorry when she left Portland. And I can tell you that her patients were also very upset to lose her. They often say how they wish I could send them someone just like Darleen."

"Well, thank you," said Lucy. "That's a wonderful tribute."

"Are you absolutely sure it's Darleen?" asked the director, hoping there was some mistake.

"No question, I'm sorry," said Lucy.

Lucy sat for a moment after the call ended, absorbing this new information. Darleen, it seemed, had created an entirely false résumé and somehow had managed to convince the Personnel Committee that it was true. She had made them believe she had been the CEO of a major charity when she had actually been a home health aide. It was breathtaking. How on earth did she manage to do it? Lucy's next call was to Lydia Volpe.

"Of course, we confirmed her employment at the United Fund of Fairfield, the Boys and Girls Club of Bridgeport, and the New Haven Sports Center," declared Lydia, sounding insulted. "I, myself, spoke at length to the three individuals she listed as character references, all of whom gave glowing reports. The only thing that kind of bothered me was that I began to wonder if they were too good to be true. But it all checked out; it seems she was Phi Beta Kappa at the University of Connecticut!" She let out a long breath of air. "If what you're saying is true, and I don't see how it could be, I guess she fooled us all." There was a long pause. "But how could she possibly do it? Get friends to playact or something? It would've been quite difficult. We have a very thorough hiring process."

"I have some ideas," said Lucy, "and I'm going to get to the bottom of it."

Lucy had recently seen a TV show about a brazen imposter who had successfully defrauded a number of high-profile individuals by convincing them to invest in a Ponzi scheme. These were smart people who had checked out her references, including speaking to her banker and lawyer. Unfortunately for them, they'd been speaking to the imposter herself, who was using voice-altering technology. Lucy wondered if Darleen had also seen that show, which had aired for several nights and was probably still streaming. She turned once again to Google, typing in the names of the three charities Darleen had claimed to work for, one by one. And one by one, the phone numbers Darleen provided for the Boys and Girls Club, the New Haven Community Center, and the United Fund of Fairfield were all quite different from the numbers listed on their websites. It seemed that Darleen had indeed tricked Lydia and the others on the Personnel Committee.

Chapter Eighteen

There was nothing for it but to give Ted a call. This was big news, and she knew Ted would want to play it up big. So it was with a growing sense of impatience that she waited for the call to carom from cell tower to cell tower. "You're not gonna believe this, Ted, but it seems that Darleen was not who she seemed to be. I spoke to her cousin, who says Darleen went to college for just one year and her last job was working as a home health aide in Portland."

"Whuh?" asked Ted.

"It was all a big hoax! Her résumé, as far as I can determine, was entirely made up."

"That's not possible."

"It seems it is. I spoke to the director of the home health agency she worked for; it's called Silver Linings. She was sad to lose Darleen, she says, because she was such a good worker and the old folks absolutely loved her."

"My gosh. That's crazy." Ted fell silent, apparently processing this new information. "It's all got to be double-checked," he finally said. "I'll have Pete call the agency . . ."

Hearing this, Lucy literally saw red. This was not going to happen. She had a scoop, it was her scoop, and she wasn't going to hand it over to Pete Popper. "If you do that, I'm done," she said, speaking in a strangely quiet, calm voice. "I will quit. This very minute."

Lucy sat, staring at the wall and holding her phone to her ear, waiting for Ted's reply. It was slow in coming, but he finally spoke. "Okay. It's your story."

"I'm going to go to Portland Monday, talk to the lady at Silver Linings, get whatever documentation I can. Meanwhile, Phyllis can contact Darleen's references."

"Uh, a bit of problem," began Ted.

"No problem, because you're going to restore Phyllis's hours. This is a Tinker's Cove story, and we're going to cover it out of this office."

As expected, Ted wasn't willing to go down without a fight. "Lucy, this isn't like you," he said, sounding like a disappointed father. "I don't suppose, maybe you have some sort of, um, hormone thing going on?"

That approach did not go over well with Lucy. "I'm a professional, Ted, who happens to be a woman. This is not about hormones; it's about all the years I worked hard to establish my credibility. This is a big story, and I need to know you're behind me, giving me the support I need to cover it. It's not time to cut corners."

Lucy heard Ted exhale a long breath. "Okay," he finally said. "You're right. Follow the story wherever it leads."

"And Phyllis?"

"What about her?"

"C'mon, Ted, part-time isn't going to cut it. I can't staff the office and cover the news at the same time."

Lucy thought she heard a faint rumble, like heaving magma deep in the earth, but it was probably only Ted clearing his throat. "Okay," he finally said, "She's back, full-time."

Lucy smiled. "Good."

Monday morning, Lucy was on her way to Portland, zipping down Route 1, which offered glimpses of salt marshes and picturesque coves in between the gas stations, clam shacks, and souvenir stores. Her mind was elsewhere, however, as she negotiated the permanent traffic jam at Ray's in Wiscasset, whizzed past the Bath Iron Works, and eventually made her way onto the freeway in Brunswick. Her thoughts darted here and there, jumping from one idea to another, attempting to assemble a narrative that made sense. What was true? What were the connections? Had Darleen's lies resulted in her gruesome death? Was Tim involved? And what about Wild Willy and the fire? Was that an entirely separate incident, or was some evil mastermind at work, terrorizing the community? And to what end?

Silver Linings was housed in a strip mall located in the outskirts of Portland, so parking was no problem. Stepping inside, Lucy was greeted by a friendly receptionist who quickly referred her to the director, Venetia DiZoglio. While she waited for Venetia to appear, Lucy took in the waiting room atmosphere, the fake plants and the posters picturing attractive nurses and home health aides caring for smiling senior citizens. It was worth noting, thought Lucy, that the pictured seniors all seemed to be exceptionally fit and glowing with good health, which made her wonder why they needed health-care assistants.

Venetia, when she appeared, was warm and friendly, almost comforting, as she greeted Lucy and invited her into her office. Lucy thought this was probably due to a misconception that she was a potential client needing help with her aged mom, which she was quick to deny. "I'm Lucy Stone, from the *Courier* newspaper in Tinker's Cove.

We spoke yesterday," she said, taking the seat that Venetia had offered.

"Oh, I remember. You asked about Darleen."

"Right. She was the victim of a particularly horrible murder, and I'm trying to find out as much about her as I can."

"Horrible?" asked Venetia, who was an attractive redhead in her early fifties. She was heavily made up, and her strong, baby-powder scent was a definite presence in the small office. "Of course, all murders are horrible."

Lucy decided to share the details of Darleen's death in hopes that it might encourage Venetia to open up. "Well, the truth is, Darleen was dismembered. They've found a few body parts, notably two feet and an arm, but that's all so far."

Venetia's hand flew to her mouth, and her eyes widened. "How was she identified?"

"DNA. Her mom lives in town."

"Oh. My goodness."

"Yes. As you can imagine, people are wondering if there was something in Darleen's past that might have led to her death."

"I can't think of anything. Like I told you yesterday, all her clients adored her. She was absolutely reliable, worked here for fifteen years, rarely took a sick day."

"Did she talk about the job she was taking in Tinker's Cove?" prompted Lucy.

"No. I assumed it was something similar. There's a huge demand for home health aides."

"She actually took a job as director at our newly built community center."

Venetia considered this. "A good fit, I think. She had excellent organizational skills. She'd often call in with suggestions for improving a client's care. A change in schedule, adjusting meds, things like that."

Lucy was jotting it all down in her reporter's notebook. "Do you know anything about her previous employer? Maybe her references when she applied here?"

Venetia began to hedge. "You know, these things are confidential. I've probably said too much already."

"Well, I'll consider anything you might say about Darleen as off the record," said Lucy. "Background can be so helpful in reconstructing a victim's life."

Venetia wasn't convinced. "I'm sure that's true, but I have to abide by state laws concerning employers and employees."

"I understand," said Lucy. "I don't suppose there's any law against telling me the average wage for home health aides?"

"No. No law at all. And the going rate ought to be much higher. We usually start at ten dollars an hour and go up to fifteen."

A far cry from the salary Darleen had negotiated at the community center, thought Lucy. Maybe that's all there was to it. Darleen had worked hard for low wages all her life and decided to get what she believed she was worth, no matter what it took.

"Well, thanks so much for your time. I appreciate it." She paused. "You wouldn't happen to have any photos of Darleen at work?"

"Actually," said Venetia, brightening up, "she's pictured on the very front of our brochure."

"May I have one?"

"Sure. Take a bunch." She plucked one from the cardboard holder on her desk and stared at the photo of Darleen offering a beverage to an elderly woman with freshly styled white hair who was wearing a blue twin set that matched her bright eyes. "I think we're going to have to design some new ones, with a different photo," she finally said, with a sad sigh.

Lucy smiled sympathetically and thanked her, leaving with a handful of brochures featuring Darleen.

Checking her watch, she saw it was getting on to noon and decided to call Zoe, who worked in Portland, and invite her to lunch. Zoe accepted eagerly; as a recent grad working at her first job, she was always grateful for a free meal. They agreed that Lucy would pick her up outside Hadlock Field, the Sea Dogs stadium, where the management offices were also located.

Lucy wasn't all that familiar with Portland, so she followed Waze into town and soon spotted the banks of lights high above the stadium, which was conveniently located by the highway. As promised, Zoe was standing right in front of the main entrance, looking every bit the rising young PR professional in a sleeveless linen dress that flattered but didn't reveal too much of her shapely figure and conservative heels.

"Hi, Mom," she said, reaching for the door. "This is a nice surprise."

"I'm working on a story." Lucy waited for Zoe to buckle her seat belt, then began rolling down the street. "Any ideas where to eat?"

"Umm, what are you in the mood for?"

"Not fast food, not fish."

"Sandwich?"

"Too many carbs."

"I know a Thai place . . ."

"Great. Lead on, MacDuff."

Zoe laughed. "Turn right at the corner, and we'll be there."

"Very convenient. Do you eat here much?"

"No. I'm a brown bagger. This is a treat."

The Thai restaurant was small, but attractively decorated in a minimalist, modern Asian style. The booths were inviting, and Zoe and Lucy slid into one. A server presented them with menus, and Lucy ordered beef salad, while Zoe went for a hearty bowl of pad thai. That bit of business settled, Zoe asked her mother about the story she was covering.

"Darleen Busby-Pratt, the director of the new community center, has been turning up in bits and pieces all around town," began Lucy, taking a sip of water.

"What do you mean?" Zoe was withdrawing her cutlery from the paper napkin it was wrapped in and arranging it on the table.

"Exactly what I said. Somebody killed her and cut her up. They've only found her two feet and part of an arm so far."

"Whoa, Mom. Hold on," sputtered Zoe, flabbergasted. "I need a minute to process this. Is this actually true? And this all happened in Tinker's Cove?"

"Crazy, huh? We've never had anything like this before." Lucy began unwrapping her cutlery. "And it gets weirder. That's why I'm here. It seems that the victim, Darleen, submitted a completely made-up résumé when she applied for the community center job. She claimed to be CEO of a United Fund when she was actually only a home health aide working here in Portland."

"Sounds like she was trying to create a new identity. Escape from her past," speculated Zoe, "but it caught up with her."

"Well, if she wanted to do that, she should have changed her name and gone someplace where she wasn't known, where her family hasn't lived for a couple of centuries."

"There must be a reason," insisted Zoe. "It sounds like somebody went to a lot of trouble to get rid of her."

"That's what I'm trying to figure out," said Lucy. The server was approaching with their meals, and Lucy and Zoe suspended their conversation to sample their dishes. "I love Thai beef," said Lucy, savoring the spicy hot flavors.

"They have huge servings here," observed Zoe. "I'll probably have enough to take home for dinner."

Lucy smiled approvingly at her daughter's budding thriftiness and changed the subject. Darleen's gruesome death wasn't exactly mealtime conversation, and she really wanted to get Zoe's take on a different subject. "You know Tim is still AWOL," she began.

"Since that day at the Point?"

"No. About a week later. About the same time, actually, that Darleen disappeared."

"Well, surely a coincidence," Zoe was quick to say. "Tim wouldn't harm a fly."

"That's my impression, too. I've been wondering if there were signs of depression when he was a kid. I seem to remember he was concerned about the environment back then. He was in that Earth Day Club at high school, wasn't he? Do you remember what that was all about?"

"Well, he was always kind of odd, but everybody thought it was just because he was so smart. Tinker's Cove is a small town, and by the time we got to high school, everybody knew everybody really well. Tim was weird, sure, but that was just the way he was. He was accepted; there wasn't any bullying or anything." Zoe was ripping up a sprig of basil and sprinkling it into her dish. "The environment was beginning to be a big deal back then. Bottle recycling was supposed to save the planet, and I was eager to get involved. I joined the club when I was a freshman, so he must've been a senior. There was a group of guys who wanted to stage some, well, not violent exactly, but sort of extreme protests. The town was planning to cut down some trees on the common, said they were unhealthy and dangerous, and these guys were going to chain themselves to the trees in order to save them. In the end, we voted them down and raised money to buy some young trees to replace the old ones."

"Do you remember who these guys were?" asked Lucy.

"Well, Tim, of course. He was kind of the leader, the instigator. He always wanted to push boundaries. I dropped out; it all seemed kind of stupid to me. Like this little club could really make a difference against Mobil and Chevron and all those big companies." Zoe was picking up steam, remembering how frustrating she'd found the club. "I mean, look at China and India, and all that pollution. Not that we're so great, everybody driving huge SUVs to go around the corner. And the tree thing was stupid; those trees were actually real old and diseased. What if they fell on a car? Or a person?"

Lucy tried to get her daughter back on track. "It's complicated, I know. But do you remember any of the other members besides Tim?"

Zoe shook her head. "Honestly, I think I only went to a couple of meetings. Field hockey started up, and the meetings conflicted with practices." She slurped up some noodles. "Why do you want to know? They couldn't be connected with this murder, could they?"

"I don't think so. I sure hope not, but Tim had a motive for killing Darleen," admitted Lucy. "I don't want it to be him. I'm trying to think of other reasons why he might have dropped out of sight."

"Like some undercover radical environmental group?" Zoe's tone of voice indicated she thought this was a ridiculous idea.

"Don't scoff," said Lucy, spearing her last piece of delicious beef. "There's folks who are really worried about climate change; they're stocking up on supplies and weapons so they can survive whatever disasters may come our way. They're worried about civilization collapsing, diseases, roving bands of migrants, food shortages, no electricity, you name it."

Zoe scoffed. "Well, if civilization collapses, it isn't going to be like a hurricane when you stock up on batteries and canned goods and everything goes back to normal in a couple of days. It's going to be forever, so good luck to them."

"I'm afraid you're right," said Lucy, signaling for the check.

Chapter Nineteen

Back at the office on Tuesday morning, Lucy was surprised to see Ted crouched over the antique rolltop desk he'd inherited from his grandfather, a noted local journalist. She quickly decided to take advantage of this rare sight and proudly presented him with one of the brochures picturing Darleen as a smiling, helpful home health aide.

He looked up from his computer, where the single sentence on his screen seemed to indicate he was having trouble getting started on his weekly editorial column. Taking the proffered brochure, he examined the picture, then tossed it on his desk. "Good work, Lucy," he said, somewhat grudgingly. "Did you get anything more on Darleen's past?"

"Mostly just confirmation that she truly was a home health aide making fifteen dollars an hour, tops, not a CEO. But her boss said she thought the community center job was a good fit for Darleen; it seems she was really underemployed. She was smart, had good organizational skills, and often made suggestions that improved patient care."

"Well," said Phyllis, chiming in from her corner, "it

seems she also had plenty of imagination." She was beaming with pride, peering over the bright pink cheaters perked on her nose. "I called each of the organizations she listed on her résumé, and the numbers she gave were all disconnected. Then I used directory assistance to get the correct numbers, and none of them ever heard of her. It was all phony. Darleen was a big fake."

Lucy looked at Ted, waiting for instructions as to how she should proceed. "You've got to get reaction from somebody on the Personnel Committee," he said, saying what Lucy already knew. "But you've got to be careful; they're going to be defensive. This is going to make them look pretty bad, especially since they gave her such a big salary." He chewed his lip. "Got any ideas on an angle?"

"Darleen was no fool," began Lucy. "I definitely got that from the director. And she must have carefully developed this scheme in order to get the job and the money she wanted. She was a cool customer, a gifted con artist."

"And the committee did their due diligence," offered Ted.

"But she was way ahead of them," added Phyllis. "She'd covered all the bases, right down to providing fake references."

Lucy took a deep breath. "Okay, here goes. I'm going to call Lydia Volpe and wreck her day."

"Day?" scoffed Ted. "No way. It's going to take months, maybe years, for the committee to live this down."

But when she answered the call, Lydia said she was just about to give a statement. "After you called me last week with the information you'd discovered about Darleen, I knew we had to get to the bottom of this. We needed to discuss the situation and figure out where we went wrong. I called an emergency meeting on Sunday. Everything completely aboveboard, of course, and we immediately we went into executive session."

"That was fast," said Lucy, who was surprised by the committee's quick reaction.

"Well, we want to get ahead of this thing. So we went over the résumé and the interview notes very carefully. Darleen's interview was perfect; she had all the right answers, and she projected a warm, competent attitude that stood out in stark contrast to the other candidates."

"Are you getting blowback from any of them?" asked Lucy. "The candidates?"

"Not yet," said Lydia. "But once it goes public, I expect that we will. We're aware that we might be sued by one or more of them, and we're preparing for that eventuality. This is off the record, of course; we don't want to give anybody any ideas."

"I understand."

"Good. So after we assured ourselves that everything was okay with the interview, we reviewed how we verified Darleen's claims of employment and the references. Harmony Cooper checked her education, called the University of Connecticut and got confirmation of her degree. Phil Kwan did the same with her previous employers, and I called each of her personal references. They all checked out. I actually remember thinking maybe it was too good to be true; she seemed almost too perfect, but the truth is we were all terribly excited to have such an excellent candidate. In fact, we apologized for only being able to offer her $105,000, which was quite a lot less than the $160,000 she claimed she was getting from the United Fund." There was a pause as Lydia collected herself. "We did everything by the book, but it apparently wasn't enough. She must have been laughing at us the whole time."

"I doubt it; she was probably fearing discovery."

"I just can't believe we fell for it," confessed Lydia. "But this is our official statement. Are you ready?

"I'm all ears."

"Here goes: 'After a thorough review of the Personnel Committee's search process to fill the new position of community center director, I am confident that the committee conducted a thorough and exhaustive examination of all the candidates and took all the proper steps to verify the information provided by each and every candidate. Committee members soon agreed that one candidate stood out due to her superior qualifications, and Darleen Busby-Pratt was chosen by a unanimous vote. It now appears that Darleen Busby-Pratt falsified her qualifications and perpetrated a fraud on the committee and the town of Tinker's Cove. The committee wishes to reassure citizens that the members sincerely regret this unfortunate development and are considering changes in policy that will prevent any similar occurrence in the future.' "

"That's good," said Lucy, approvingly. "I know you did everything you could. Phyllis has been digging around and discovered her whole résumé was fake; she was working as a home health aide. Those charities never heard of her; neither did the University of Connecticut."

"How did she do it? How did she fool us?"

"She was a skilled con artist; she took advantage of the fact that people tend to trust one another. She figured out a way to sell you guys what you wanted. She provided the fake phone numbers and figured you'd use them."

"That's for sure. We all thought she was the right person for the job. She was the ideal candidate."

"Any ideas how she managed the phone business?" asked Lucy.

"I don't know. We thought we were speaking to creditable references. I myself thought I was speaking to a gentleman with a British accent, and two women, one of whom had a slight New York accent. I guess she recruited a bunch of friends. But that doesn't seem realistic. We asked each individual a lot of detailed questions. I don't think casual acquaintances, or even old friends, would have been able to give such thorough answers. And I'd like to think most people are too honest to get involved in something like that."

"It seems awfully complicated. There were a lot of different numbers."

"The voices were all different, too. Male, female, ethnic-sounding . . . she must have constructed various personalities, too. It was quite a show. It's too bad she's dead; I would love to be able to ask her how she did it."

"Do you think she tried it somewhere else, previously, and that's what got her killed? Somebody she tricked?"

"It's possible, Lucy. I wouldn't be surprised. There have been times in the past day or two that I would have gladly strangled her."

"I'm sure you want that off the record," teased Lucy.

"Absolutely!"

Ted, who had been listening in, perked up. As soon as Lucy ended the call, he didn't hesitate to voice his displeasure. "Don't encourage people to go off the record, Lucy. What were you thinking?"

Lucy bristled, quick to defend herself. "It was a joke, Ted."

"Joking's not a good idea, either, when you're interviewing a source."

Lucy glanced at Phyllis, as if to ask *What's with him?* She got a shrug in response.

"I'll bear that in mind, Ted," she said, picking up her phone and checking in with the other members of the committee who had been involved in vetting Darleen's résumé, and they all confirmed what Lydia had said. There was nothing for it now but to write the story, and she got right to work. Ted managed a few more pecks on his keyboard, then announced he was going out for a walk to clear his head. Phyllis, who was working on the events roundup column, took a few calls. It was so quiet in the office that Lucy could hear the Willard clock on the wall ticking away the minutes. She was struggling to find a synonym for *con artist*, realizing she'd used the word about a dozen times in her story, when her phone rang. Checking the screen, she saw it was her daughter-in-law, Molly, calling from Alaska.

"Hi, Molly. Thanks for calling."

"No problem. Toby says you want some information about the Earth Day Club in high school. I'm not sure I can be very helpful. It was such a long time ago."

Lucy smiled, thinking that she had been out of high school a lot longer than Molly. "Oh, come now, it hasn't been all that long. And face it, good or bad, you never forget high school."

Molly laughed. "I guess you're right about that. I do remember some pretty contentious meetings of our little club. The guys all wanted to be like Greenpeace, chain themselves to trees, sabotage bulldozers; one guy even converted his car to run on used cooking grease. Extreme recycling. It was awful; it just made you hungry, smelling that cooking smell. We called it the Frialator."

"I remember that car!" exclaimed Lucy. "You could smell it coming a mile away!"

"Hard to forget," agreed Molly. "It was the girls, you know, who did all the real work. We were the ones who raised the money to buy the replacement trees for the common. We made the posters to encourage recycling, we canvassed for the plastic-bag ban and the water-bottle ban.

The guys mostly clowned around, suggesting all sorts of crazy stuff." She paused. "If I remember right, some of them did get arrested, but I forget the details."

"Are you still in touch with any of the members?"

"Only Jason Babcock. He and his wife just had a baby, the cutest little baby girl. He put photos on Facebook."

"Give you any ideas?" suggested Lucy. "A little sister for Patrick?"

"Sorry, Lucy. One's enough. I'm done. You've got three daughters to give you more grandchildren."

"You're right. They're definitely shirking their responsibility."

Molly laughed. "They've got plenty of time."

"Clock's ticking," said Lucy, glancing up at the Willard. "Is there any way I can contact Jason?"

"Well, you can friend him on Facebook."

"Um, I was thinking of a phone number . . ."

"Old school, Lucy. But you can probably find him on Google. He's an environmental lawyer in Washington, DC. The firm's probably got a website . . ."

"Websites I can manage," said Lucy. "So when are you coming to visit?"

"Right back at you, Lucy. Alaska is lovely in autumn."

"Touché. Love to all."

Lucy got right on Google and easily found Jason Babcock, a junior partner in a DC law firm, just as Molly had said. She called and left a message; Mr. Babcock was home on paternity leave. Her next call was to DA Phil Aucoin. Lucy was eager to share the information she'd gathered about Darleen and get his reaction to her startling discovery. But when he took her call, she learned he was way ahead of her.

"State police investigators are working on the case," he

told her, "and have discovered much of the same information."

This was news to Lucy, who truly thought she'd broken the case open. Lydia hadn't mentioned talking to investigators, and neither had Venetia. "Who did you talk to?" she asked.

Aucoin hesitated. Lucy knew full well that he rarely, if ever, commented on an ongoing investigation. Finally, he spoke. "Okay, Lucy, what I'm going to tell you is absolutely off the record, and I'm only sharing it because you're in pretty deep and you probably know it already. You can take this as confirmation from a source, but you didn't get it from me. Okay?"

"Absolutely," said Lucy, somewhat amazed.

"For starters, cousin Cassie was very helpful; she was there with her grandma when we approached Millicent about giving a DNA sample. Once we made the ID and knew Darleen was the victim, we checked the résumé and realized it didn't jibe with what Cassie had told us."

"You're way ahead of me," admitted Lucy. "I had to go all the way to Portland."

"Hey! What about me?" demanded Phyllis, from her corner across the room. "I made those calls."

"And," continued Lucy, heeding her protest, "Phyllis discovered she'd never worked for the United Fund or any of the others."

"Well, we have ample resources, and our experienced investigators know what they're doing," said Aucoin, implying that Lucy and Phyllis were in above their heads.

"We certainly don't have your resources," said Lucy, bristling. "So what theory have your expert investigators come up with? Any ideas how she fooled the Personnel Committee?"

"Uh, yeah. After the DNA came through and we had her ID, we searched her car and found a briefcase with six cheap cell phones, a device that altered her voice, and several outlines giving speaking points for her various fake references."

"Wow," said Lucy. "Quite the con artist. Do you have any evidence that connects her fake identity to her murder?"

"It seems likely," he said. "Right now, we're trying to figure out if she'd done anything like this before."

"Like another con?"

"Yeah. It was real professional, very thorough, not like a first attempt. She even got the correct area codes on the phones. She didn't make any mistakes, which is what usually trips these actors up. They're living two lives, after all, and keeping them straight can get very complicated. She was living with her mother, for instance, at the same time she was getting calls and answering them in phony voices. It's like a guy having an affair; sooner or later he slips up and wifey finds the lipstick stain or the hotel on the AmEx bill. But Mom insists she didn't know anything; neither did the cousin. Darleen was real smooth, and that makes us think that she'd been involved in this sort of thing before, maybe at a low level in some sort of scam operation." He paused. "She might well have been involved with some heavy hitters, some pretty nasty types. If she had something on one of them—say she tried to blackmail somebody—well, that would have been a very foolish thing to do."

"Have you checked her bank account?"

"Nothing out of line there, but the cousin, Cassie, pointed out that Darleen had some very nice stuff. An Audi car, some jewelry, nice clothes."

"Hold on, Phil. What about the car?"

"Still in the garage. Mom said she had arranged to take a limo to the airport. So whoever killed her probably picked her up; Darleen thought it was her ride to the airport. Thanks to the stuff in the car, we're firing on all pistons now, digging deeper, looking for other accounts. This is a big investigation, Lucy, and it could lead to organized crime."

"Organized crime?"

"It's everywhere, Lucy. And it's not just drugs and sex trafficking; it's scams, too. They pop up constantly: investment frauds, fake charities, a friend is in trouble in Mexico and needs money, send a gift card." He paused. "My point is, there are some very bad actors involved in these schemes. I think, in future, for your own safety, you should leave this investigation to us."

Lucy didn't like what she was hearing, but she didn't like to back away from a story, either. "You've given me fair warning," she said, unwilling to drop the story. "So when is the press conference?"

Aucoin laughed. "You'll be the first to know."

As soon as Lucy was off the phone, Phyllis demanded to know what she'd learned. Lucy gave her an update, then asked the question that had been nagging at her. "Tell me the truth. Did you suspect Darleen was a fake?"

Phyllis shook her head. "No. In fact, I was a bit jealous. We had similar backgrounds; we grew up in the same town. How come she was so successful, and I'm plugging away here?"

"She was so successful she got herself killed . . ."

"And cut up in small pieces," added Phyllis, with a shudder.

Chapter Twenty

L ucy was looking over the written statement from the Personnel Committee that had landed in her email file, making sure she'd gotten it right when Lydia gave it to her over the phone, when Jason Babcock returned her call. "Hi, Lucy," he began, sounding quite chipper, "I never thought I'd be getting a call from Tinker's Cove's top reporter. What can I do for you?"

Oh, boy, thought Lucy. Where to begin? "I just want to ask you a few questions about the Earth Day Club at the high school. You were a member, right?"

"Golly. That was a long time ago. I'm a new dad now. Did you see the pictures I posted of little Lindsey Cora Babcock?"

"Congratulations! I haven't actually seen them, but my daughter-in-law, Molly, has and said little Lindsey is adorable. Molly and Toby are living in Alaska now; they have a son, Patrick."

"You're taking me right down memory lane. So Molly married Toby. I remember her; all the boys were in love with her."

"She said she was a freshman when you were a senior," chided Lucy.

"Yeah. Back then, seniors dating freshman girls was definitely discouraged, but we all noticed her, for sure."

"Well, Molly says that some of the guys in the club wanted to do more than make posters and collect bottles. Do you remember that? Something about chaining yourselves to trees?"

"Oh, yeah, I sure do," admitted Jason, in a rueful tone of voice. "I got arrested at a Save the Earth rally when I was in college; we threw red paint all over a gas station. My folks got me a good lawyer, and I got off with probation and community service . . ."

"That was lucky," said Lucy.

"Yeah. Some of the others weren't so lucky, got hit with fines, and one guy did get a year in jail. The whole experience made me decide to study law so I could fight for the environment in court. I figured I could be a lot more effective in court than in jail."

"Good decision," said Lucy. "Do you remember any of the other more radical club members?"

"Let me think. There was Tim, for sure, a guy named Mike Something. Mike, Mike, Mike Morrison. That was it. And Rob Jackson. We sort of spun off from the club; we thought of ourselves like we were Greenpeace or something. Gonna change the world and save the planet."

"Were you really prepared to break the law?"

"We talked about it a lot," laughed Jason. "We had kind of a guru, an older guy who had a lot of ideas about getting in tune with nature, like the Native Americans. He was all about magic mushrooms and trances as a way to discover what he called 'the place just right.' But we never actually did much. For me, that came later, in college."

"Do you remember his name?"

"Will. We called him Wild Willy."

"Wow," said Lucy. "He's still around. In fact, until recently, he was living the natural life in a shack he built in the woods. It seems some kids torched it, but there's no actual proof."

"Gee, that's too bad. Willy was a cool guy."

"Still is, in fact; he's staying with Rob Jackson, who's now our building inspector. Do you think Tim stayed in contact with him?"

"I dunno. People change. My life is sure different these days."

"New babies will do that," said Lucy, remembering the confusing mix of emotions that accompanied her babies' arrivals: joy and relief right along with fear and panic as she acknowledged it was up to her and Bill to make sure this tiny little being grew and thrived. "Well, thanks for your time. And good luck with little Lindsey."

Jason was right, she thought, that people do indeed change. But old loyalties often lingered, especially among comrades in arms. The Amvets club in town was always busy, the Nam Vets lobbied for better benefits, the diminishing group of World War II and Korean War vets reunited and marched in every Fourth of July parade. Even moms, like her Thursday-morning breakfast pals, were comrades of sorts, having successfully raised reckless toddlers and resentful teens. It seemed to her that the fire at Willy's shack might well have rekindled those old friendships. Rob had reached out to Willy in his hour of need, and maybe he was helping Tim, too. Maybe the three were actually plotting some sort of retaliation for the fire.

Lucy was thinking along these lines, staring out the window at the town hall across the street. Rob Jackson's office was in that building, and he was just passing by in his SUV, turning into the drive that led to the rear parking area. Most likely, she decided, returning from an inspection. Maybe she should pay him a visit.

"I can hear the wheels turning, Lucy," said Phyllis.

Lucy stood up and grabbed her bag. "I want to check something out," she said.

Phyllis smiled. "Go on. Let me know what you find out."

When she reached his office, Rob was just settling in at his desk, opening a file folder. He was a big guy and seemed a bit out of place in an office; his face was sunburned, and his muscular build indicated he worked out regularly. She could easily imagine him stalking game, though probably with a camera rather than a gun. She was startled out of this train of thought when he looked up and greeted her. "What can I do for you?"

"I'm just following up on the fire out at Wild Willy's shack. Have you heard anything?"

"Me? Shouldn't you be checking with the fire department?"

Good question, thought Lucy, reaching for a credible answer. "Um, well, I was thinking more along the lines of it being a nonconforming structure that didn't meet the building code? Is that sort of thing allowed?"

Rob shifted a bit uncomfortably in his desk chair. "Um, well, it wouldn't be allowed if it was discovered. But Willy was kind of operating under the radar."

"He was there for a long time, pretty well-established. And I believe you and he are friends?"

Rob was quick to correct her. "Acquaintances. And if you're trying to imply that I was negligent or ignored a dangerous habitation, you would be dead wrong."

Something in the way he emphasized the word *dead* gave Lucy pause. "Not at all. I didn't mean to imply anything like that." She smiled. "I'm glad you've come back to Tinker's Cove. I remember you back when you were in high school, with my kids. You were all in the Earth Day Club together, right? And Tim Stillings, too."

"That was a long time ago . . ."

"Not so long, really," said Lucy, interrupting him. She decided it was time to take a load off and sat down, uninvited, in his spare chair. "And it's hard to imagine that someone who was so committed to environmental action just gave up, especially when climate change is more of a threat than ever."

"I've always been a committed environmentalist," he admitted. "I'm working on some changes to the building code that will make new construction more environmentally friendly. Heat pumps, for example, stuff like that."

Lucy nodded approvingly. "A far cry from the antics you used to get into with Jason and Tim."

"Like I said, that was all a long time ago. I'm a lot older and wiser now."

"Have you been in contact with Tim?" she asked, getting straight to the point. "You know he's struggling emotionally; he's left home and his parents are terribly worried about him. They haven't had a word from him for weeks."

Rob took his time to answer and finally decided to share what he knew. "You can tell them that Tim is fine," he said. "He's actually helping Willy get back on his feet."

Lucy's heart leaped at this news. "That's such a relief!" She couldn't wait to tell Pam and Ted, but she needed more information. "Do you know where they are?"

"I do, but I'm not gonna tell you. Willy was attacked once; I'm not gonna let it happen again."

Lucy didn't like it, but she could see his point. "But they're both safe?"

"For the moment," answered Rob, "and I'm going to make sure they stay that way."

"You know," began Lucy, "they're both loosely tethered

to reality, and they both have a history of getting themselves in trouble."

Rob smiled and shook his head. "You're telling me?"

"Well, thanks for sharing." She thought of Ted's warning and dismissed it. "You can trust me; all this is off the record."

"Don't make me regret I told you," he warned. "And keep my name out of it. I don't know what's going on with Tim, but I've got to respect his boundaries, and he's pretty paranoid at the moment. He doesn't want anyone, not even his folks, to know where he is."

Lucy nodded, wondering what had spooked Tim. Was it the fire? Or something else? She considered pressing Rob about it, but sensed there was no point in antagonizing him. He was fingering a folder, clearly eager to be rid of her. "Thanks," she said, leaving him to the files and building plans that were covering his desk.

Stepping out of the town hall, Lucy paused on the shady front steps and looked up at the huge maple tree, where a breeze off the cove was lifting the leaves. A scattered few, she noticed, were already beginning to turn. Now in mid-September, summer was winding down in Tinker's Cove, and October, with its special town meeting, was just around the corner. Shrugging off that discouraging thought, she reached for her phone and called Pam.

"Okay," she began, "I can't tell you who, what, or where, but I have heard from a reliable source that Tim is okay."

"Who told you? How do you know?"

"I can't tell you, but it seems he's with a friend."

"Why can't you tell me?"

"I had to promise I wouldn't say anything except that he's okay and safe."

"Well, that stinks," grumbled Pam. "I don't know if I can even believe this mystery person."

"Yeah," agreed Lucy. "I tried to get more info but no cigar. This person is trustworthy, I think, and it must be kind of a relief that Tim's not alone and he's okay, right?"

"It's complicated," confessed Pam. "I'm done with grief, now I'm into anger. To tell the truth, I'm really pissed at Tim. Why is he treating us, treating me like this?"

Lucy leaned her fanny against the wrought-iron railing. "I don't know. I don't think he understands how upset you are. He's caught up in his own head."

"I know, but it doesn't make it any easier," admitted Pam. "I've been trying to keep busy, keep my mind off it. I'm back teaching yoga, in fact."

"That's great!"

"It's good for me, but it's only temporary. Ananda Johnson broke her ankle and asked me to take her classes at the community center. You should come, Lucy. Seven a.m. every weekday."

"Uh, I'm usually on my first cup of coffee around then."

"Yoga's better than coffee! It'll wake you up . . ."

"Getting to sleep is more my problem," confessed Lucy.

"It helps with that, too. Relieves stress."

Lucy was suddenly eager to end the call. "Well, I'll think about it. Take care."

"You too, Lucy. And thanks for the Tim update."

Lucy started down the steps and, noticing that traffic was unusually heavy, decided to follow Ted's lead and take a walk to clear her head before attempting to cross and go back to the office. Main Street was togged out for the shoulder season, and planters filled with chrysanthemums had been placed along the sidewalk by the Chamber of Commerce. Flags flapped gaily in front of many stores, and end-of-season sales were offering tempting bargains, often spilling out of the stores and displayed on the sidewalk. As she walked along, Lucy noticed the tourists who were perusing the sales, licking ice cream cones, even resting at the outdoor tables at the Queen Victoria Inn and sipping iced tea or afternoon cocktails. The shoulder-season tourists were an upscale crowd, she decided, judging from the designer logos on their polo shirts, and they were free-spending, if the large number of shopping bags hanging from their arms were any indication.

Folks in Tinker's Cove often complained about the tourists, but, in truth, their spending was vital to the town's economy. It provided jobs, enhanced cash flow, and even contributed to tax revenues, thanks to levies collected from hotels and restaurants. And, thought Lucy, the lucky residents got to enjoy clean air and water, quaint towns, and scenic views all year long; their enjoyment wasn't limited to a couple of days or even a week.

She knew she was one of the fortunate few to live in a town like Tinker's Cove. It was a privileged existence, she realized, that avoided many of the problems of modern life. The town still operated under the town-meeting form of government, so citizens got direct control of their town government. In Tinker's Cove, whatever the majority wanted, the majority got. National politics, with all its fire and fury, seemed rather remote. The region was also less affected by climate change than other parts of the country. True, the lobsters were crawling north to cooler Canadian waters, but the region had mostly been spared the forest fires, floods, and tornadoes that were occurring with greater frequency in the South and West.

Reaching the end of the shopping district, Lucy spotted a gap in the traffic and dashed across to the other side of the street. Heading back to the office, her thoughts turned to Darleen. Her discontent with the modest lifestyle afforded her in Maine had, according to Aucoin, led her to become involved with what he called "very nasty types." Lucy wondered about that. If anything, she thought, Darleen had practiced her deceptions among upstanding, decent folk. That, to her, seemed to be the secret to her success: she appeared to be a devoted daughter caring for her fragile, aged mother. The Personnel Committee, for example, had been easily fooled by her fake references; they'd never dreamed she could be lying. As far as anyone knew, until she embarked on this massive fraud, she'd been a model employee at Silver Linings, where she gave satisfaction for a rather small reward.

Glancing in the window at the Trading Company, a boutique that offered high-priced designer clothing to the local gentry, Lucy remembered seeing Darleen at a library Christmas party. It was several years ago, she recalled, and she'd noticed that Darleen was wearing a quilted Burberry jacket that was quite the rage that year. She'd even tried one on herself and discovered that, while it was expensive, it wasn't outrageously so, and she'd secretly hoped Santa, aka Bill, might splurge on one for her. She chuckled to herself, recalling that he'd splurged, instead, on a new toaster oven.

The annual party had been fancier than usual that year because the library had been celebrating a set of original Tasha Tudor Christmas drawings that had been donated by the local antiques dealers, Hayden Northcross and Wayne Love. The pictures were lovely watercolors of old-fashioned family gatherings, and Lucy, who had long been a Tasha Tudor fan, had been quite enchanted. She had hoped to catch the donors for a quick interview, but Darleen had dashed in front of her and grabbed the couple before she got a chance. The three had left together soon afterward, she remembered, but not before Darleen paused to fill her pockets with a handful of Sue Finch's peanut butter buckeyes wrapped in a holiday paper napkin.

Now that she knew more about Darleen's circumstances at the time, that Burberry jacket seemed a bit suspicious. Perhaps she was already supplementing her income with some ill-gotten gains. Maybe stealing from her clients? That didn't seem likely since she was so highly regarded at Silver Linings. Then Lucy remembered the fake Nantucket lightship basket that Millicent had been so eager to show her. Stealing from her mother would have been a lot safer than helping herself to her clients' cash, and it was easier to rationalize, too. Mom's stuff would eventually become her stuff, so why not get what she could for it sooner, rather than later?

Lucy realized she was actually now standing in front of Northcross and Love, the town's premier antiques shop, which was located next door to the Trading Company. Acting on impulse, she went in and was warmly greeted by one of the owners, Hayden Northcross. He was a trim-looking man in his late fifties with a bit of gray in his full head of hair, dressed in coastal casual khakis, a blue button-down shirt, and tasseled loafers.

"Lovely to see you, Lucy. Are you shopping for antiques or covering a story?"

"A bit of both," she said, picking up a Rose Medallion china plate and wincing at the price. "I haven't written about antiques in a while, and I was wondering, especially considering rising inflation, if locals are selling off their antiques. A lot of folks around here are sitting on small fortunes, stuff that's been stored in their attics and barns."

"We get our stock from a lot of sources, Lucy. Estate

sales, other dealers, and, like you say, regular folks who've discovered that old kitchen chair is an antique Windsor." He paused, scratching his chin. "I can't say there's been an uptick in folks looking to sell Grandma's rocking chair."

"I suppose you do have regular sellers, don't you? Folks who show up with a Nantucket basket one week and, a few weeks later, maybe a bit of Paul Revere silver?"

Hayden gave a rather fake laugh. "And do you have anyone in particular in mind?"

"Uh, no. Do you?" Lucy gave him her most winning smile. "Someone I could interview for a feature? Maybe someone who's downsizing?"

"Ah, Lucy. My sources appreciate my strict policy of confidentiality. People don't usually want to advertise the fact that they have valuable things, and they most especially don't want to have it known that they need to sell off their valuables."

"I understand," said Lucy, screwing up her mouth. "But is there a way to trace the sale of an especially valuable piece? Like a genuine Nantucket lightship basket?"

"Do you know of a lightship basket, Lucy? I'd be interested if you've got a lead on one. They're quite rare, and I can't remember the last time I saw one."

"Me, too. I'd love to have one, but no such luck. I'm just using it as an example. I'm working on a piece about how prices for antiques are established. How can people figure out how much Grandma's rocker is worth?"

"Your best bet would be some recent auction catalogs. They're mostly online now. I know that Burke's in Portland has a big summer sale every year."

"That's a great idea! Thanks!" exclaimed Lucy.

"You're welcome," said Hayden. "Sure I can't interest you in something? These hurricane lamps just came in . . ."

He pointed to a pair of gleaming brass candlesticks,

each supporting a hand-blown glass shade. They were gorgeous, and they'd look perfect on her living room mantel. "How much?"

"A steal at five hundred, for the pair."

Lucy laughed. "The only way I can afford them is if I steal them!"

Hayden shrugged. "Too bad. Have a nice day."

She gave him a little wave and continued on her way, back to the office. "I owe, I owe, it's off to work I go," she hummed to herself, in a popular parody of the Disney dwarves' song.

Chapter Twenty-one

That evening, after she'd cleaned up the kitchen and Bill had settled in the family room to watch the Red Sox lose once again to the Yankees, Lucy set her laptop on the round golden-oak table in the kitchen and fired it up, entering *Nantucket lightship basket* in the search field. While there were plenty of listings, the information was too broad to be useful for her. She was looking for recent sales, so she decided to try a different approach. Following Hayden's advice, she found recent catalogs from Burke's and impatiently flipped through the pages. She found fabulous tallboys, grandfather clocks, Windsor chairs, endless pages of oil paintings by obscure artists, some sea chests that caught her eye, but no Nantucket lightship baskets. Realizing it was well past ten, she admitted she wasn't getting anywhere and logged off. It was when she was soaking in her bath that she decided to have a little talk with cousin Cassie, who she remembered had been quite chatty, recalling happier days as a young girl getting into all sorts of mischief with Darleen. Maybe Cassie had some thoughts about Darleen's more recent escapades.

Next morning, she decided to swing by Millicent's house

on the off chance that Cassie was home with Aunt Millie. She figured a casual approach would be best, rather than phoning and setting up an interview. As she'd hoped, Cassie was still staying with her aunt and was outside in the yard hanging up the wash when Lucy drove by. Making a quick turn and parking in the driveway, she hailed Cassie. "Hi! Have you got a minute?"

Cassie paused, holding a pair of rather large white jersey underpants. "A minute? I've got hours and hours," she declared, rolling her eyes.

"Elder care getting you down?" asked Lucy, offering a sympathetic smile.

Cassie sighed. "I know I'm being petty. It's terrible for Aunt Millie: children aren't supposed to die before their parents. She keeps saying that over and over. She can't seem to think about anything else, and, well, there can't be any closure until they find the rest of poor Darleen. It's so awful, it's almost funny," she concluded, with a little giggle.

"How's she taking the news that Darleen faked her résumé to get the community center job?"

"Not well. Complete denial. Simply doesn't compute in her mind." Cassie was clipping a series of enormous cotton jersey underpants to the line in a neat row. "Of course, I wasn't surprised, not when I got over the shock and really thought about it. Darleen was always a little cheat as a kid. The amazing thing was that she pulled the wool over everyone's eyes for such a long time. If she hadn't been killed, nobody would've been the wiser, right?"

"Right," admitted Lucy, in a thoughtful tone. "Everyone thought she was doing a good job at the center."

Cassie produced a very substantial white broadcloth bra from the basket at her feet and shared an amazed look with Lucy before clipping it to the line. "I haven't wanted to say anything to Aunt Millie," she began, in a confidential tone, "but I suspect Darleen was selling off some of Aunt Millie's antiques."

"Really?" asked Lucy, feigning astonishment. "How could she do that?"

"I'm not sure, but I was dusting the dining room yesterday—Aunt Millie's a fiend about dusting and vacuuming, and having to empty the kettle every time and heating up fresh water, and never having tea in a mug, has to be made in a teapot and served in a cup and saucer, oh, and we can't put the Canton in the dishwasher, it has to be done by hand, and the bedsheets have to be ironed . . ."

Fascinating as all this was, and despite feeling enormous sympathy for Cassie, Lucy felt it was time to get back on track. "You were dusting the dining room?"

"Oh, sorry. I was dusting and noticed that the Paul Revere teapot was a reproduction, silver plate actually. Said so right on the bottom. And when I looked closer, I realized it wasn't dented, like the real one was."

"Anything else?" prompted Lucy.

Cassie nodded. "That fabulous Canton that can't go in the dishwasher? Well, quite a bit of it is repro, too. Dishwasher and microwave safe, in fact. Says so right on the bottom."

"It must have taken some planning," said Lucy. "Darleen had to research the antiques and find substitutions, acquire them, switch them out, and then find buyers for the genuine ones. It must have been a long-term project. Hard to carry out right under Millicent's nose . . ."

Lucy looked at Cassie, and Cassie looked at Lucy; the air seemed charged between them as they had the same thought.

"Do you?" began Lucy.

"She must've . . ." said Cassie.

"You think she knew?"

"Absolutely." Cassie gave a sharp nod. "She can tell if I skipped dusting the baseboards."

Lucy took a deep breath, then exhaled slowly. "Aunt Millie doesn't, by any chance, happen to have . . ."

"A very large freezer?"

Lucy nodded.

"She does indeed. In the cellar. But she doesn't like me to go down there. She thinks there are rats."

"What's she doing now?" asked Lucy.

"Watching Kelly and Mark; she adores them."

"It's probably crazy, but I think we have to take a look."

Cassie pulled herself up to her full five feet two inches and straightened her shoulders. "Not that we expect to find poor Darleen."

"Of course not," agreed Lucy, following as Cassie went up the steps to the back porch and into the kitchen. The sound of laughter filtered in from the TV in the room Aunt Mille most certainly referred to as the parlor. They made their way across the linoleum floor to the cellar door, which was fastened with a sliding bolt. Cassie slipped it across, and the door swung open with a creak.

"It's like a horror movie," said Lucy, staring down the wooden steps into the darkness. She didn't really think they'd find Darleen in the freezer; she certainly hoped not. But there was a slim chance, a very slim chance that Millicent had run out of patience with her daughter and taken steps. Irretrievable steps.

Cassie flipped a switch. "Better?"

They descended slowly, dreading what came next. Frozen peas and ice cream, or . . .

"I can't believe she would . . ."

"How could she manage it? She's old."

"I can't imagine. Darleen was pretty big."

There, against the stone wall, sat the freezer. A big, white, rectangular box. It hummed quietly. "There's probably nothing in there but a frozen turkey and some of Darleen's Lean Cuisines," said Cassie.

"I'm sure you're right," agreed Lucy, hoping against hope that they would find an assortment of frozen foods. "So, together?"

Cassie nodded and the two women stood side by side, in front of the freezer. They each placed their hands on the lid and lifted, peered in, and slammed the lid down.

"That's definitely Darleen," said Cassie, collapsing forward and pressing her hand on her chest.

"What's left of her," said Lucy, who had closed her eyes in hopes of unseeing what she had seen. And then it happened.

"Yoohoo," came a voice from the top of the stairs. "Anybody down there?"

"I thought you said she was watching Kelly and Mark," hissed Lucy, wide-eyed.

"She was," whispered Cassie. She walked over to the bottom of the stairs. "I thought I heard something, maybe a mouse," she said, calling up the stairs.

"Oh, no. I warned you about the rats. Did you see one?" asked Millicent.

"No. Nothing. Everything's under control."

Not really, thought Lucy, wondering how exactly one should deal with an octogenarian murderer. It was a situation she'd never confronted, until now.

"Are you alone?" asked Millicent. "I thought I saw Lucy Stone coming up the walk."

Cassie looked at Lucy, who shrugged, leaving the ball in

her court. "Um, that's right. Lucy's here. She wanted to see the cellar; she's interested in antique houses."

"That's nice. As it happens," began Millicent, beginning to descend the wooden staircase, "you girls can help me with a, well, a rather nasty job." Reaching the bottom of the stairs she trotted right over to the freezer, where she paused and thoughtfully fingered her pearl necklace. "You see, I need to empty the freezer for Mr. Delaney. He hunts, you know, and he'll soon need a place to store his venison and bear meat. I don't mind because he lets me take as much as I want." She paused. "Personally, I don't care for bear but a nice bit of venison, properly stewed, you know, is very tasty." She flipped open the lid of the freezer, and Lucy and Cassie both looked away. "I need to finish the job," she said, shaking her head sadly. "It started out all right but soon got to be rather too much for me. But you girls are young and strong; I don't think it will take very long if I tell you exactly what to do." She gave a little smile, as if remembering something pleasant. "My pa was a butcher, you know, and he taught me all about joints and tendons and things, so I could help him in the shop. He used to deliver in a horse and wagon to all the fancy summer people, and he even had a boat to get to the ones on the islands."

Lucy was speechless, actually thinking this must be some sort of surreal nightmare or something. She couldn't actually be seeing and hearing what she was seeing and hearing, could she?

"Now what did I do with that carving knife?" Millicent looked around the cellar, trying to recall where she'd stashed it.

Cassie very gently closed the freezer and took her aunt's hand. "Auntie, how did Darleen end up in the freezer?"

"I put her there," she said, as if it was the most natural thing in the world to store one's adult child in a freezer. "It was quite a job, as you can imagine. But fortunately for me she was in the cellar when she collapsed . . ."

"So she fell ill? Had a heart attack? A stroke?"

"Not exactly," admitted Millicent, eager to set things straight. "I'm sure it was the tea."

"Earl Gray?" asked Cassie.

"With a little something extra. Foxglove. It grows right outside the door. Lovely flowers."

Foxglove, otherwise known as digitalis, thought Lucy.

"Why did you give her foxglove?" asked Cassie. "It's poison, you know."

"I know." Aunt Millicent's eyes glinted mischievously. "You might not be aware of this, but Darleen had become very annoying, barging around the house, slamming doors and wrestling with the windows. She was so noisy. But the thing that really got my goat was the way she was stealing my things. She thought I was some sort of idiot and didn't notice, but I did. She took the Revere teapot, quite a lot of my Canton, even the pewter porringers. Substituted cheap modern stuff. It made me so angry." She paused, still fuming at the memory. Then, giving a little shrug, she continued. "So I decided to, well, make her stop. And when I remembered she was taking digoxin for her heart, I thought I'd give her a bit more and see what happened."

"Quite understandable," said Cassie, humoring her aunt and patting her hand. "But you certainly didn't intend to kill her, did you?"

"What she did was wrong, and I wanted to punish her," she admitted, "but the foxglove worked faster than I expected. She'd barely finished her tea when she got up and said she needed to go down cellar to move the wash into the dryer. It seemed to be taking rather a long time, and I didn't hear the dryer start, so I came down to see what was the matter, and there she was. On the floor."

"I see," said Cassie. "Why didn't you call 911?"

"It was too late for that, dear. Darleen was definitely dead, and, well, I guess I panicked. I decided putting her in the freezer would give me some time to figure things out."

"Understandable," said Lucy, both horrified and fascinated. "But Darleen was a big woman. How did you get her in the freezer?"

Aunt Millicent, rather surprisingly, was quite eager to explain. "Well, you know I lived alone for quite some time before Darleen came back home, and with no man in the house to do the heavy lifting, I had to work out some techniques on my own. For one thing, I'm not in any rush. I've got lots of time to think things through, and I use gravity to my advantage. A push here, a shove there, inch by inch, I can move very large objects." She held up a cautionary hand, knobby and misshapen by arthritis. "This, however, was a new challenge for me, because I had to lift her body up from the floor. Usually I can just slide things around."

"That would be especially challenging," said Cassie, agreeing with her. "How did you do it?"

"See that big piece of plywood, over there?" She pointed it out. "It was left over from when Mr. Winkle's son repaired the shed for me. I propped it on the freezer and rolled Darleen across the floor and onto the wood. I thought I might be able to lift it up and roll her into the freezer, but I couldn't manage it; she was too heavy. But I remembered about levers and had a little think about what might work and remembered the jacks in the cars. If they could lift a car, I figured they could manage Darleen. So I got the jacks out of the cars—two cars, hers and mine, and two jacks. Bit by bit, I got the plywood up, and when it was high enough, I tucked some concrete blocks under the wood. I dragged them, you know. So that was about halfway. Then I remembered about pulleys. My late husband was a well-digger, you know, and he often needed to use a pulley to raise rocks and dirt when he was digging. So I rigged a pulley and some rope over that beam . . ." Lucy and Cassie followed her pointing finger. "That one right up there. Quite handy. Then I spotted an old life jacket, that one over there." Once again, they followed her pointing finger, which indicated a bright orange life jacket hanging on a nail, which was a match to the one they'd glimpsed in the freezer, "and got it on Darleen, looped the rope through it and, alley-oop, in she went. Nice and tidy."

"That is absolutely amazing," said Cassie, in what Lucy thought was a giant understatement. "But now I think we need to go upstairs and get some helpers." She gave Lucy a meaningful glance. "I think, um the next step, is much too big a job for us."

"Really?" Millicent was clearly disappointed. "You seem quite fit, both of you, and much younger than me. I can give you instructions. It's really not that difficult, not with the electric carving knife." She clucked her tongue. "What did I do with it?"

"I'm sure you're right, but Lucy has a bad back, and I just got a new manicure. See?"

Millicent glanced at Cassie's hands, which she waved in front of her aunt. "Lovely shade, my dear. I don't much like those garish black and green polishes girls wear these days. I much prefer pink."

"Me, too," added Lucy, pulling her cell phone out of her back jeans pocket. "So let's all go upstairs. and I'll call for the helpers." She watched as Cassie helped Aunt Millie climb the stairs and dialed 911.

"You're not going to believe this," began Lucy, after identifying herself to the dispatcher, "but we've found Darleen Busby-Pratt's body in her mother's freezer."

There was a rather long silence. "Is this some sort of joke?" the dispatcher asked.

"No. I'm dead serious. Millicent Busby has confessed to murdering her own daughter. She poisoned her tea."

"And got her in the freezer?"

"Yes."

"How did she manage that? She's eighty if she's a day."

"I'm sure she'll be only too happy to tell you all about it."

"Okay. I'm sending a car over."

"Good. I think we'll have a refreshing drink while we wait." *But definitely not tea*, thought Lucy, starting up the stairs.

That evening, Lucy watched the local news, which showed video of Aunt Millie being escorted, ever so politely, into the police station. She'd made it very clear from the outset that she didn't require handcuffs and seemed to enjoy the attention from the hastily assembled news crews. In fact, thought Lucy, she reminded her a bit of the late Queen Elizabeth II, when she paused on the police station steps and gave everyone a smile and a lightbulb wave.

The story was huge; it was on all the national news and cable channels. The video went viral, and folks in Tinker's Cove couldn't poke their noses out of their houses without being asked by some eager reporter if they'd suspected what was going on in the Busby home. Nobody did, not a one.

Town business proceeded, however, and when citizens gathered at the high school auditorium on the first Tuesday in October for the special town meeting, it seemed that more people than usual had showed up. In fact, thought Lucy, surveying the crowd, select-board chairman Franny Small's fears that they might not achieve a quorum had been unfounded. Everybody had an idea about the murder and was eager to share it with their friends and acquaintances.

"I heard she's hired Gerald Fogarty, and he's going for an insanity plea," said one lady, who could have been one of Millicent's Garden Club friends.

"I warned her about those homemade herb teas," confided her friend. "I told her they could be dangerous."

"Oh, no. She knew the properties of all the local flora. Claimed she was descended from some shaman or something."

The gentleman seated on Lucy's other side had a different take. "Cunning as a fox, and if you know what you're doing is wrong, pleading insanity won't work. She hid the body, that's proof of consciousness of guilt."

"I dunno," mumbled his pal. "Sounds like dementia to me."

Lucy had raised that very question with Miss Tilley, who had relished hearing every gory detail when Lucy visited her at her little Cape Cod house to get her reaction. "Was Millicent quite right in her head?" she'd asked, posing the question to her aged friend as delicately as she could.

Miss Tilley paused, a Pepperidge Farm Milano cookie in her hand, and took a moment to think. "Depends on what you call right," she answered, biting into the cookie.

"Alzheimer's? Dementia?" pressed Lucy.

"No, none of that," she insisted, finishing off the cookie. "She was sort of warped, I guess. Mentally warped. Even as a child, she had odd reactions to things. Little things, like dropping worms into a pail of water to see if they could swim."

"Could they?" asked Lucy.

"For a while," remembered Miss Tilley. "I dumped the bucket out on the dahlias when they started sinking."

"Seems the humane thing to do," observed Lucy.

"Don't accuse me of going soft, Lucy. I did it because it had been a lot of trouble digging them up, and I knew they were good for the garden soil."

Sitting there, lost in thought while she waited for the meeting to begin, Lucy jumped when the PA system let out a shriek, prompting a collective groan of protest from the assembled voters. The town moderator responded by banging his gavel, calling the meeting to order and asking the town clerk to determine if there was a quorum. That bit of business settled, he turned to the single article on the warrant: "To see if the town will vote to approve a bond issue to fund additional costs related to the construction of the community center."

Such a request, even though recommended by both the finance committee and the select board, would normally have prompted much discussion. Some would argue that increased debt would inevitably require a tax increase, which would be a hardship for retirees living on fixed incomes; others would argue for fiscal responsibility and that default would be worse than death; others would beg for the question to be called so they could go home. But tonight, there was little discussion; the article passed almost unanimously. The town moderator had called for a motion to adjourn when, suddenly, the lights went out.

Power outages were not infrequent in town, and people knew the drill; after sighing in frustration, they waited for the emergency lights to turn on. That didn't happen, however. Instead, the curtains on the stage opened, a movie screen was lowered, and the gathered citizens became a captive audience.

Mournful cello music filled the room, accompanying a photo montage of ecological disasters. There was footage of flooded fields in Pakistan, a gigantic island of trash floating in the Pacific Ocean, frogs with two heads, and mass die-offs of fish; even the migration of Maine lobsters into Canadian waters was chronicled. When it was all over, the lights went on, and Rob Jackson took the mic.

"Thank you for your attention. I promise this will only take a moment," he promised, noticing that some people were starting to stand up, intending to leave. Somewhat grudgingly, they sat back down. "As you can clearly see, our planet is in trouble. We need to take action now if we are going to preserve life as we know it for our children and grandchildren. The dinosaurs didn't have the brain power they needed to cope with cataclysmic change, but we do. We have to take action now before it's too late. Keep that thought in mind as you safely exit the hall. My colleagues are posted at the doors and will be distributing invitations to a countywide Climate Action Summit scheduled to take place in the coming weeks. We hope to see you there."

Getting to her feet, Lucy was shocked to see Wild Willy standing in one of the exits and Tim Stillings in the other. She grabbed Pam's hand and pointed. Seeing her son, Pam did a double take, then reached for Ted's arm, grabbing his wrist and attempting to pull him along as she began running to her son. He resisted, wrapping his arm around her waist and holding her, bending down and whispering in her ear, apparently cautioning her to restrain herself. Pam nodded, and the couple stood, watching and waiting as Tim passed out the invitations. He appeared stressed and anxious, focusing on the task at hand; but occasionally he managed a smile or a nod. When the crowd finally thinned, his parents approached.

"So this is what you've been doing!" exclaimed Pam, hugging her son.

"Couldn't you have bothered to give us a phone call?" demanded Ted, losing his previous restraint. "Your mother's been frantic."

Tim seemed surprised by his parents' reaction. "Um, I guess I just forgot. I was busy with this project."

Glancing at Ted, Lucy saw an expression on his face that she knew only too well. He was beet red, his eyes were bulging, and she could practically see steam exploding from his ears. "You whuh . . ." he began, but Pam took his hand and squeezed it.

"We're really proud of you," she told Tim. "And we're going to do whatever we can to support your Climate Action Summit." She turned to Ted. "Right?"

Ted gritted his teeth. "Right," he said, pulling Tim into an awkward embrace.

Chapter Twenty-two

It was a few days later, on the weekend, when Pam's friends gathered for a quilting bee to finally assemble her crazy quilt. Lucy, Sue, and Rachel were there, as well as Miss Tilley, Franny Small, and Lydia Volpe. The women gathered around Pam's dining room table, where the quilt top was laid out over the fluffy white batting and the backing fabric, a simple blue-and-white-check gingham.

The first order of business, once everyone was seated, was to decide on a plan of action. After some discussion, they decided to adopt Miss Tilley's suggestion and work from the center outward, stitching the classic tufts of thread that would hold the three layers together. Once that was done, they would fold the backing around the edges and stitch it in place, creating a neat border.

"I must say, Pam," ventured Miss Tilley, "you have created a very artistic design." Spry as ever, Miss Tilley's curly white hair created a sort of halo around her rosy cheeks and bright blue eyes, but her friends knew that angelic appearance was quite deceiving. Miss Tilley was sharp as a tack and didn't hesitate to say exactly what she thought.

"I love the way you've worked the bits and pieces together. It's got all these lovely reminders of Tim's life, but the shapes you've used and the colors make it more than a simple trip down memory lane," said Franny. Franny dressed to unimpress, and no one would suspect she had a keen eye for design, unless they had followed her career creating and marketing unique jewelry. She was also a shrewd investor, having increased the profits from the sale of her company many times over by buying low and selling high.

"It's a work of art," said Sue, agreeing with Franny, "it really is."

"I've been telling her she should enter it in a contest," added Lucy.

"Look," crowed Lydia, pointing to one of the photos that Pam had printed on fabric, "that's one of my kindergarten classes. There's Tim and Eddie Culpepper, and little Rosie Tighe. I think that was one of my favorite classes."

"What about my kids?" asked Lucy, feigning insult.

Franny, known for her empathy and her huge brown eyes, was quick to reassure her. "They were favorites, too, Lucy."

"And Sidra?" prompted Sue, naming her daughter.

"Sidra Finch, Richie Goodman, Tim Stillings, and all the little Stones, I loved them all," claimed Lydia, laughing.

"Well, that's nice to hear, but I'm not sure I believe it," said Rachel. "Richie, I remember, could be quite a handful. I was often called into school for a little chat with the principal."

"And Sidra got in trouble for bullying that little Wilcox girl . . ." remembered Sue.

"And Toby," recalled Lucy. "He organized a massive snowball fight that got the whole school in trouble."

"It would have been okay if it was just the kids, but they went too far when they all started throwing them at the principal. Mr. Wood at the time, I believe," said Lydia. "He was not known for his sense of humor."

"Such good times," offered Lucy, sarcastically. "But what's going on with Tim?"

Pam looked up from the needle she was attempting to thread. "So far, so good. Rob Jackson has an apartment over his garage that he's been loaning to Tim and Willy; the idea is that he could keep an eye on them. They're all working hard on this Climate Action Summit, and he's also back at the community center, where Sheri is running things . . ."

"Is she temporary?" asked Lucy.

Franny and Lydia shared a glance. "Well," began Lydia, "we'd love to have her . . ."

"But she wants the same salary that Darleen was getting," said Franny.

"And it just doesn't seem that the Finance Committee . . ."

"They're getting a lot of input from voters . . ."

"I will have a word with Sheri," said Miss Tilley, tying her thread in a neat knot. "I'm sure she will see reason. That whole Darleen incident was terribly unfortunate. An example of what happens when a person tries to take advantage of others."

"She really did push her mother too far," suggested Lydia. "And the town, too."

"Her mother was loony, cuckoo!" protested Lucy. "If you'd heard her describe how she did it, how proud she was of herself, you'd be horrified. No sign of motherly love at all, not even a shred of remorse. It was shocking."

"Millicent always was greedy," observed Miss Tilley. "She had to have her own way. Poor Winslow Busby, she actually trapped him into marriage claiming she was pregnant when she wasn't. That was back in the day when a fellow who got his girlfriend in trouble was expected to do the right thing. She absolutely dominated him, and he died young, which . . ." She fell silent, no doubt weighing Millicent's probable guilt in Winslow's death. "It certainly makes you wonder in light of recent developments. The sad truth is she didn't love any person, not living people, anyway, only her ancestors, and her antiques. Her heritage was everything to her, but she really had no achievements of her own, except producing Darleen, who arrived years after her marriage."

"And when she had to decide between Darleen or her antiques, Darleen lost," said Lucy.

"Absolutely disgusting," said Franny, with a sniff. "And I don't know why she thought so highly of that dirty old quilt."

They all laughed. "It was from the Civil War," said Pam. "There's only a handful left, from the hundreds of thousands that were made."

Miss Tilley rolled her eyes. "If you believe her."

"Well, what's going to happen to Millicent?" asked Lydia, those big brown eyes full of concern.

"She has Gerald Fogarty for a lawyer," observed Rachel. "He'll probably go for an insanity plea."

"That would mean she'll spend the rest of her life in a mental hospital," said Pam.

Miss Tilley disagreed. "Wouldn't surprise me," she said, snipping her thread with her teeth, "if she manages to convince a jury it was justifiable homicide."

Chapter Twenty-three

Millicent became something of a media sensation, and for weeks on end, Tinker's Cove was filled with white TV trucks with satellite dishes on top, and folks had to dodge reporters' questions about the Ghoulish Granny, also known as the Q-Tip Killer thanks to her snow-white head of hair. Gerald Fogarty was a constant presence on news shows, arguing for Millicent's innocence and insisting that she was far too old and frail to have done the dreadful things she was charged with. On the other side, DA Aucoin, who had become a shameless publicity hound, was suspiciously absent from the airwaves, and Lucy began to wonder if the case had stalled. Other stories broke, and the TV crews vanished; life returned to normal, and Gerald Fogarty succeeded in getting bail for his elderly client, arguing she was not a threat to the community and there was no risk that she would flee. Millicent was placed under house arrest at her home on Aunt Lydia's Path, where she was attended by her niece Cassie and lived quietly, only allowed to leave the house once a week, to attend services at the Community Church.

One Monday morning, when Ted turned the calendar to

November, he turned to Lucy. "You know, it's been almost two months since Millicent's arrest, and nothing's happened. What do you think is going on?"

Lucy shrugged. "I've been wondering about it myself. The case seems pretty straightforward; there's all that evidence in the freezer, not to mention Millicent's confession. I've been asking around at the police station and the courthouse, and everybody seems to be wondering what's going on."

"Have you called Fogarty?"

"Multiple times," said Lucy, rolling her eyes. "He seems perfectly happy with the delay . . ."

"Of course he is," volunteered Phyllis. "He doesn't want to go to trial in a supercharged emotional atmosphere. Better to let everybody calm down; let her plead guilty and hopefully get some sort of plea deal from the DA. I don't think anybody in town wants to see Millicent Busby go the state pen."

"Point taken," said Ted. "I guess we don't really want to stir the waters and make trouble for Millicent."

Lucy was wondering what had come over Ted when she checked her emails and found one from the DA's office. "Whoa, the universe has answered your prayers, Ted. Aucoin's holding a press conference tomorrow morning."

"What's it about?"

"Doesn't say, but it's gotta be Millicent, right?" said Lucy. "Nothing else is going on."

"Tim's climate summit is coming up," offered Phyllis. "Something to do with that?"

"No, the police department will organize parking, arrange special details, all that stuff. Unless," she turned to Ted, "there's been some threat from counterprotesters; that's the only way the DA would be involved."

"Tim hasn't said anything, not that he would," admitted Ted.

"Well, the only way I'm going to find out is to go," said Lucy. "You'll know as soon as I do."

The next morning, Lucy went to the press conference, which was taking place in a basement meeting room in the County Courthouse in Gilead. The first thing she noticed was that, although Aucoin had booked the large room, it was far from full. The cable stations and the national news hadn't shown up; it was mostly local reporters and stringers, along with one TV crew from NECN.

"Where is everybody?" Lucy asked Deb, the stringer for the *Boston Globe*.

"Bigger fish to fry, I guess," she answered. "I hope Aucoin's got something worth my time. I could be working on a preview of the Turkey Trot."

"Maybe it is about the Turkey Trot," said Lucy, realizing she'd forgotten about the annual 5K race on Thanksgiving that raised money for the food pantry. The race had grown in popularity through the years and was now a major event that required extensive planning from safety officials.

But when Aucoin finally entered the room, accompanied by the medical examiner, she figured it wasn't anything to do with road closings and emergency services for the Turkey Trot.

"Thanks for coming," Aucoin began, looking rather disappointed at the turnout. "I've called this press conference to announce that all charges against Millicent Busby are being dropped, except for a single count of mishandling a dead body."

There was a stir among the gathered reporters, and Aucoin continued. "Our medical examiner, Dr. Sharon Oliver, will explain the basis for this decision."

Sharon had dressed for success in a flattering yet professional pantsuit and had added a jaunty little scarf around her neck and a pair of substantial gold hoop earrings. Her hair had been recently styled and colored, and she was camera-ready, clearly anticipating more cameras.

"She's got something big," murmured Deb. "She was planning on seeing herself on a lot of screens."

"Thank you, DA Aucoin," began Sharon, stepping up to the mic. "As you know, the partially dissected body of Darleen Busby-Pratt was found on August 23 of this year in a freezer in the basement of a house owned by her mother, Millicent Busby. Subsequent to this discovery, Millicent Busby confessed to killing her daughter by administering a tea she concocted from foxglove leaves, otherwise known as digitalis. She also admitted partially dissecting Darleen Busby-Pratt's body in an attempt to dispose of the body.

"Because the body was frozen, and the dissected parts, two feet and an arm, were found promptly, I was able to perform an extremely thorough forensic examination. This examination included a survey of the body and dissected parts, an autopsy, and the collection of samples for laboratory examination. As a result of this process, I can state with complete certainty that Millicent Busby did not kill Darleen Busby-Pratt."

This announcement landed in the room like a meteorite from space or the pallet of shingles that had recently broken through the roof of an apartment building, plummeted through four stories, and landed in the basement, harming no one but destroying several apartments. It was a shocking development that took some time to process.

Finally, hands were raised and questions were called

out: "Who did it?" "How do you know it wasn't Millicent?" "Why would she lie about it? Is she protecting someone?"

Sharon held up her hand. "I will explain. My first indication that Millicent Busby did not commit the murder was from the initial survey of the body. There were clear indications that Darleen Busby-Pratt was strangled. These indications included bruising around the neck, facial distortions, and burst blood vessels. Because the body was so well preserved, I was able to measure the bruising and determine the size of the killer's hands. I compared that measurement with Millicent Busby's hands and determined that her hands were much smaller than the killer's. In her confession, Ms. Busby claimed she had poisoned her daughter with digitalis, so I sent tissue and blood samples to the state lab to test for digitalis, and while some digitalis was found, it was consistent with the prescribed dose of digoxin she regularly took. The lab did, however, find rosmarinic acid, allantoin, and pyrrolizidine alkaloids, which are found in the common herb comfrey. I thereby concluded that while Ms. Busby may have thought she was poisoning her daughter with foxglove tea, she was actually giving her an infusion of comfrey, which can be harmful but not in the amounts discovered."

"So she thought she was poisoning her with foxglove but actually gave her comfrey tea?" asked Lucy.

"So it seems," said Sharon.

"However," said Aucoin, stepping forward, "we are taking the matter of the dissection very seriously and will prosecute to the full extent of the law."

"What does that mean?" asked the cub reporter from the *Portland Press Herald*.

"Probably a fine," admitted Aucoin. "The case has been

referred to family court, where there will be a competency hearing. We are asking the court to appoint a guardian for Ms. Busby, who is clearly unable to manage her affairs due to her advanced age and mental condition." He looked around at the handful of gathered reporters. "Any questions?"

There were plenty, and when Aucoin and the medical examiner finally declined to answer any more questions and the conference was over, Lucy found Gerald Fogarty waiting outside on the courthouse steps. He was clearly eager to make a statement, and the little knot of reporters gathered around him.

"As you have heard, all charges of murder have been dropped against my client, Millicent Busby, and she plans to plead not guilty to the charge of mishandling a body. A competency hearing is planned, and I believe that will render the remaining charge moot. Family members are making arrangements to transfer Ms. Busby to the memory care unit at Heritage House, a senior-living facility, and if the court approves, she will be confined there for the remainder of her life."

Fogarty was happy to stand on the courthouse steps all day answering questions, but Lucy had all she needed and hurried back to her car, calling Ted as she jogged through the parking lot and giving him the story.

"Good news for Millicent," he said, but Lucy sensed he'd left something unsaid. Good news for Millicent was potentially bad news for Tim. It was no secret at the community center that Darleen had had it out for Tim, frequently scolding and berating him for poor work. Even more damning was the fact of Tim's mental problems and his propensity for spending long periods of time roaming through town, especially at night.

Pam admitted as much when the friends gathered for breakfast on Thursday morning. "Tim's been called in for questioning a couple of times," she said, looking worried and poking her spoon into her yogurt parfait but not actually eating any.

"I know Darleen was pretty mean to him," said Lucy, preparing to dive into her eggs and hash, "but do they have anything more substantial?"

"That's a pretty weak motive," said Sue, with a shrug, pausing to take a sip of coffee. "We've all had to put up with a mean boss at some point in our lives."

"Have you?" asked Lucy, puzzled. "When have you ever had a job?"

"For your information, Lucy, I worked in a dress shop when I was in high school, and the pay was so low that I couldn't afford anything there even with the employee discount, and the owner was so nasty that I've never been able to work again," said Sue, with an injured sniff. "I get all anxious and PTSD just thinking about it."

"Honestly, Sue," said Rachel, looking dubious, "I can't tell if you're pulling our legs or if this is actually true." She plucked a chunk off the top of her Sunshine Muffin. "Maybe it's some sort of fantasy? Possibly a false memory?"

Somewhat affronted, Sue raised her right hand, as if taking an oath. "Absolutely true. It was the Bon Ton in Morristown, New Jersey, where I grew up. And the owner, who deserves to burn in hell or at least be audited by the IRS, was a certain Ms. Eleanor Froelich."

"Well, I guess we have to take your word for it," admitted Lucy, "but I think we're getting off track here." She turned to Pam. "Has Tim said anything about the police interviews?"

Pam shook her head. "No, but I am worried. What was

he up to all that time he was missing from home? I know he was at Rob Jackson's, working on that video, but I also know he spends a lot of time walking, working out his emotions with restless roaming. I believe him, but I'm afraid the cops won't. It's certainly not normal behavior."

"Well, nowadays a lot of people have those doorbell cameras," suggested Sue. "I suppose there's video of him walking by."

"That's what I'm afraid of," confessed Pam. "What if he wasn't just walking, but peeking in windows, spying on people . . ."

"Or, worse, spying on Darleen," said Lucy.

Back in the office that afternoon, Lucy learned that the case against Tim seemed to be gathering speed. Ted was on the phone with Rachel's attorney husband, Bob Goodman, asking him about the limits of search and seizure. "Can the cops just take somebody's phone?" he was asking, indignantly.

Lucy couldn't hear Bob's answer, but she knew that investigators could seize a cell phone if they could convince a judge they had probable cause. When Ted slammed his phone down on his desk, she asked if Tim's phone had actually been seized.

"Afraid so," he admitted, looking dejected. "It doesn't look good for Tim; he told me he did snap some photos of Darleen, from outside, through the window."

"Why on earth would he do that?" asked Phyllis, shocked.

"He says he was curious about her, thought something fishy was going on; she didn't seem like the professionals he'd worked with at the museum."

"Well, he was right," said Lucy, "but it's not going to look good for him."

"Tell me about it," said Ted, with a big, discouraged sigh. "Honestly, that kid. It's hard to believe he could be so dumb."

"Naïve, more like," offered Phyllis. "Look at my Elfrida. She's no dummy, but she makes the same mistake over and over. All a guy has to say is that his wife doesn't understand him and . . . well, you know the rest."

"How's Tim coping with being a suspect?" asked Lucy, aware that his mental health was still fragile.

"You can ask him yourself," said Ted. "He's coming by today to drop off information about the Climate Change Summit." Ted made a few stabs at his keyboard. "If he remembers, that is."

Tim did remember and wandered into the *Courier* office just as Lucy was getting ready to call it a day. She'd just shut down her computer and was gathering up her bag when the bell on the door gave a jangle, and there he was, clutching an armful of papers that kept slipping out of his grasp.

"Hi, Tim," said Phyllis, jumping to her feet. "Let me help you with those."

"I've got them, I've got them," he said, as the sheets cascaded to the floor.

Lucy bent to help him gather them up, and Phyllis produced a folder to contain them, and soon Tim was seated in Lucy's visitor's chair, provided with a cold glass of water, and waiting for Lucy's PC to come back to life. While they waited, Lucy sorted through the folder of papers and attempted to pull out the useful ones from the irrelevant ones.

"There's a lot of information here, Tim," said Lucy. "Maybe you should tell me in your own words what you've got planned . . ."

"Umm, okay," he began, somewhat uncertainly. "Well, you know, it's gonna take place in two weeks at the high school. It's two days, Saturday and Sunday, and we need a lot of publicity so people will come."

Lucy suppressed a smile. "That's where I come in, Tim, and I'm happy to help. I know this is an important issue that faces us all. Is it a series of talks and panels, like a conference?"

Tim chewed his lip and squeezed his hands together. Lucy noticed, with dismay, that his hands were indeed large, and might well match the bruises on Darleen's neck. He was big and loose-limbed, and his shambling walk made him look weak and out of shape, but Lucy knew he was much stronger than he looked. His appearance was deceptive; she'd seen him splitting firewood in Rob Jackson's yard, wielding that heavy maul with ease and accuracy.

"There'll be speakers, yeah," he said, breaking into her unpleasant train of thought. "We managed to get some big names, folks who are well known in the environmental justice movement—scientists, activists, they're all on one of these papers . . ." he added, with a wave of one of those enormous hands.

"I've got it here," said Lucy, casting her eyes on the roster and seeing a number of names she recognized. "This is impressive," she said.

"Yeah," he said, shrugging those square shoulders. "Well, Willy knows a lot of people."

"I saw something about a Global Responsibility Fair," prompted Lucy.

Tim's face brightened up. "Yeah! This is kinda cool. It'll be like an old-fashioned Christmas fair. We're gonna have a solar-powered merry-go-round, there'll be live music, refreshments like hot cider, and booths offering information about stuff like nitrogen loading and upcycling textiles." He snapped to attention. "Do you know that discarded textiles are a huge landfill problem? Almost as bad as plastics."

Lucy thought guiltily of the old clothes she'd purged from her closet. Some went to the thrift shop, but others, the ones that she'd decided were too far gone, got thrown into the trash. "I didn't know," she admitted.

"Well, they are." He shuffled through the papers. "Here, look at this picture." The picture showed an immense collection of discarded textiles covering miles and miles. "Underdeveloped countries accept this stuff; this is in Chile. All those synthetics are full of poison that leaches into the desert; it's a blight on the earth. You can see it from space."

"Wow, this is definitely going to open a lot of eyes to what's going on," said Lucy. Tim was up on his feet, clearly eager to flee, when she asked one last question. "I heard the police have been questioning you. Are you worried that you'll be arrested before the summit?"

He looked at her startled and wide-eyed. "No way," he said. "They don't arrest innocent people."

"Right," she said, nodding. Looking across the office, she locked eyes with Phyllis, who was silently mouthing a word. Even from fifteen feet, she got the message: "Naïve."

Chapter Twenty-four

After Tim shuffled out of the office, Lucy decided she'd better double-check her facts and called Rob Jackson, who she considered the most reliable of the summit planners. Rob confirmed everything Tim had told her and added that he'd just finished speaking with Jane Goodall, who was currently on a US book tour, and she was seriously considering participating.

"Jane Goodall? That's amazing," said Lucy. Across the room, Phyllis had raised her eyebrows in surprise. She knew, like almost everyone on earth, that Jane Goodall was a big advocate for climate action.

"Yeah," agreed Rob. "But if she does agree, I think we're going to need a bigger venue."

"That's a problem," said Lucy. "The high school auditorium is the biggest space around. You'll have to get a tent."

"This is both exciting and terrifying," said Rob.

Lucy sympathized and, without thinking, said, "And you've got to worry about Tim, too."

"Tim? He's been great."

"He's made big progress, for sure, but you must be aware that he's the prime suspect for Darleen's murder."

This was news to Rob. "Tim? Really?"

"The police have questioned him several times."

"I didn't know that," admitted Rob, sounding shocked.

"He's innocent, of course," said Lucy, hoping it was true. "But that doesn't mean he won't be charged."

"That is not what I need right now," said Rob.

"No, I suppose not." Lucy wasn't convinced she'd done the right thing, but Rob really needed to know, didn't he? "I thought you knew," she added.

"Well, thanks for telling me. Forewarned is forearmed, right?"

"That's the spirit." She made a quick decision. "I won't mention Jane Goodall until you get a definite confirmation, right?"

"Absolutely. But you'll be the first to know."

"Thanks," she said, ending the call.

Turning back to the task at hand, writing a preview of the summit, she wasn't sure what to do about including Tim's name. "What am I going to do?" she asked Phyllis. "I don't want to link Jane Goodall with an accused murderer."

"She's not definite, right?"

"But what if she does come? Tim could be arrested any day now. The timing is really bad for the summit."

"You could leave Tim's name out . . ."

"Ted would kill me."

"Okay. Mention all three organizers in a dense, packed sort of paragraph, the sort of thing readers skim. After that, refer to all three as 'organizers.'"

"You're brilliant," crowed Lucy, picking up her ringing phone and identifying herself.

"You sound happy," said Cassie, who was the caller.

"For the moment," admitted Lucy. "It doesn't usually last."

"Too true," offered Cassie. "I'm kind of underwater here myself, sorting out Aunt Millie's stuff and packing things up. We're going to have to sell the house, you know, in order to pay for Heritage House."

"That's a big job. Are you holding an estate sale? Or putting things up for auction?"

"I'd like to, but the rest of the family aren't on board. I'm the one who got stuck with all this stuff, and to tell the truth, I'm not at all clear on what's genuine and what's not, thanks to Darleen." She sighed. "In fact, I have some doubts about the Civil War quilt. Do you have some photos I could look at?"

"Photos of the quilt?"

"Yeah. You took some at the quilt show, right?"

"I did. I'm on deadline, and I'll need some time to pull them up and print them out for you . . ."

"That's fine, Lucy. Just give me a call when you're ready."

Lucy was thoughtful as she ended the call, finding it hard to believe that Darleen would have sold her family's most important treasure. The woman had been a liar and a cheat; she'd lied to get the job at the community center, and she had sold things she had no right to sell, but she surely knew that her mother absolutely cherished the ratty old thing, deeming it proof positive of her family's importance. It was more than fabric; it was the Busby family heritage in material form.

She'd know the truth soon enough, she decided, shelving thoughts of the quilt and turning to the preview that Ted expected her to send him shortly. She fretted that

Ted would expect her to give Tim major credit for participating in the Climate Action Summit and was well aware
that he was terribly proud of Tim's recent progress. He
viewed the police investigators' interest in Tim as an intru-
sion into his family's privacy and dismissed Tim's suspicious behavior as part and parcel of his mental instability,
not as indicative of guilt. And that behavior was all in the
past; Tim was recovering and deserved all the credit he
was due.

Feeling a bit as if she were between the devil and the
deep blue sea, worried that Tim's arrest was imminent and
that it would cast a definite shadow on the summit, she
decided to try to discover what Tim's status was. Was he
actually suspect number one, or simply someone who'd
behaved foolishly and was in the wrong place at the wrong
time? She picked up her phone and dialed Officer Sally's
personal number.

"I've been expecting your call," said Sally.

"Oh, no," said Lucy, with a terrible sense of foreboding.
"Is it that bad?"

"I'm sorry to say it doesn't look good for Tim."

"Really?"

"Yeah, Lucy. The evidence just keeps piling up. And
there's nobody else in the picture. He was stalking her; he
took photos. He was there that night." She paused. "I'm
really sorry."

"So, off the record, any idea when he'll be charged?"

"Soon. Aucoin is wrapping up a few details; could be
any day now."

"Damn."

"You said it, Lucy."

Her decision made, Lucy finished up the preview, taking

Phyllis's advice and burying Tim's name at the bottom of a rather wordy third paragraph, which she hoped and prayed would be continued in the "Read More" section of the online post. That job done, she turned to the photo folder and found the pics she'd taken at the quilt show, an event that now seemed to have taken place in the distant, almost prehistoric, past. But there it was, clear as day, with a beaming Millicent standing front and center. Maybe not so good for Cassie's purposes, so she clicked on a few more images, which showed Millicent first on one side and then on the other. Taken together, she had pictures showing the complete quilt. She sent them to the printer and, gathering the pages up, headed over to the Busby homestead.

She decided to walk, calling Cassie as she went, to let her know she was on her way. It was late afternoon; the days were ending earlier now, and the trees had mostly dropped their leaves. She thought about sweaters and open fires and mulled cider; she noticed the blowsy look of the gardens she passed, where the lawns were dotted with colorful leaves, and decided that fall was her favorite season. And then she turned the corner onto Aunt Lydia's Path and saw Cassie standing on the porch, waiting for her.

"That was quick," said Cassie, smiling at her.

"Computers have changed everything. It's hard to believe I used to have to study contact sheets full of teeny black-and-whites with a jeweler's loupe to choose photos for the paper. Now I use my phone, upload the pics to the cloud, and they pop up supersized in glorious technicolor on my monitor. Crazy."

"What's crazy is that I really think the quilt's not genuine; it seems different."

"You really think Darleen sold it?"

Cassie shrugged, yanking open the screen door and holding it for Lucy. "I don't know what I think anymore. The real estate agent is all over me, wants to clear the house out and stage it, whatever that means. I'm getting constant calls and even unannounced visits from antiques dealers, and I'm getting no help at all from my relations. They all expect to get a little something to remember Auntie by, but that is the only thing they all agree on. Auction? Estate sale? Donations? Uncle Harold wants one thing, Cousin Betty another, but nobody wants to mow the lawn, or take the garbage to the dump, or help me pack up the books for the library, or take the sheets and towels to the thrift shop."

"Sounds pretty typical," said Lucy, with a sympathetic smile.

"Well, at least I don't have to stay here nights, now that Auntie's over at Heritage. I've made it clear, I'm working at the house nine to five, like a job. Then I go home to my hubby and my kids." She sighed. "Which is a mixed blessing."

"Good for you," said Lucy, hoping to avoid further disclosures about hubby and kids. "So where's this dubious quilt?"

"I spread it out on the dining table, in here," said Cassie, leading the way through the hall and living room, where Cassie had attempted to sort the various bits and pieces into categories. Lamps were gathered on one table, colored pieces of glassware on another, a pile of neatly folded throws sat on an armchair. "Should I pack it all up and store it?" asked Cassie, waving an arm at the orderly disorder. "Should I get the estate sale people in? We've got to decide; the house goes on the market in three weeks, and all this stuff, everything, has to be gone."

"I guess you have to do what Millicent wants," suggested Lucy. "She should decide what to do with her stuff."

"Aunt Millie wants to come home; she's in complete denial," countered Cassie.

"Hire a lawyer; the hourly fees alone will scare the family into action."

"Good idea." They stepped into the dining room, where the quilt was draped on the table, like a tablecloth after a particularly messy dinner.

Lucy pulled the photos from her bag and spread them out on top of the quilt. It was immediately apparent that the quilt on the table did not match the one in the photos.

"Oh, my," murmured Lucy, "the stains don't match."

"They sure don't," agreed Cassie. "I knew it was fake; it didn't smell right, for one thing."

"It's good, it's pretty close; it would fool a casual observer."

"Or an old woman with failing eyesight."

"What are you going to do? Report it to the police?"

Cassie had settled into one of the chairs and was slumped over the table, leaning her head on her hand. "I don't know, Lucy, I don't know."

Lucy was thoughtful, fingering the fake quilt. "This took a lot of effort from somebody," she said. "It's hand-sewn, made with potholder squares, just like the original was. And it didn't happen overnight; it's been aged, maybe buried or something. Somehow it doesn't seem like something Darleen would do."

"She did all that fake identity stuff," said Cassie.

"Yeah, but that was technical, if you know what I mean, what with the phones and all. It took a lot of mental work. This quilt was finicky, hands-on. There's a difference."

Cassie chuckled. "Techie, finicky, what's the difference? Besides, she could have paid somebody to duplicate the quilt."

"That would have been dangerous. It would mean letting the secret out. It would require a very high level of trust. And contacts with certain skills."

Cassie was studying the photos, which she suddenly tossed onto the table. "Look, those stains on the original quilt," she said, stabbing at the photos, "they're blood stains. Some Union soldier's actual blood, maybe even George Busby's. Auntie's quilt represented sacrifice and suffering; people sacrificed time and labor to make it, and it warmed and comforted men who had offered up their lives for a cause greater than themselves. Darleen knew that. I have to believe it was real to her in a way that the other stuff wasn't. She used to complain about polishing the silver, and how Auntie wouldn't let her put the china in the dishwasher, and the certain way she had to buff the furniture with beeswax, but I never heard her complain about the quilt. It was too fragile to wash, for one thing, and she appreciated that. She used to say it was the one thing of Auntie's that had true meaning for her; the rest was nothing but trouble." She began folding up the fake quilt. "It's kind of ironic, I guess, but Auntie said she found the quilt stuffed in the dryer, where she said it had no business being, when she discovered Darleen's body."

"That's interesting," said Lucy, filing that thought away for future reference. "Are you going to go public about the quilt?"

Cassie shook her head. "No. It would kill Auntie."

"How is Millicent doing?" asked Lucy.

"You can see for yourself. She's allowed to have visitors, but her old friends have been avoiding her."

"That's a shame. I'll recruit Miss Tilley. It will be a mission of mercy."

"First time ever for that old biddy," said Cassie, laughing so heartily that Lucy found herself joining in. The two women laughed until their stomachs hurt and they had to stop.

Chapter Twenty-five

M iss Tilley was pleased as punch to accept Lucy's invitation to pay a visit to her old friend. When she was settled in Lucy's SUV, however, for the short drive to Heritage House, she had something else on her mind.

"Lucy, have you heard that Jane Goodall is coming to the Climate Action Summit?"

Lucy jammed the key into the ignition and let out a groan. "That's supposed to be a secret. It's not definite. Where'd you hear that?"

"I think I saw it on Facebook."

Lucy shifted into drive and pulled out into the road. "You follow Facebook?"

"Of course. And Twitter, too. It's interesting to see how people can mangle the English language."

"I'm surprised you approve," said Lucy, understating her reaction to this news, which she found absolutely mind-boggling.

"I don't approve. I enjoy disapproving."

"That's more like it," said Lucy, somewhat relieved that Miss Tilley was still her cantankerous self.

"I also enjoy disapproving of Heritage House," she added.

"They took good care of you when you were sick," Lucy reminded her old friend. "And the new management has made a lot of changes." A large corporation had recently bought the facility, promising to improve care and transparency.

"Promises, promises," scoffed Miss Tilley, rolling her eyes. "They're all in it for the money." She turned to Lucy and asked pointedly, "Who's paying for Millicent's incarceration?"

"It's hardly jail, and she's not costing the taxpayers a penny. The family agreed, as part of the plea deal, to shoulder the cost. They're going to sell her house to raise the money."

"Could go for as high as a million," speculated Miss Tilley, who had also been watching the rising property values in Tinker's Cove. "Not to mention all those antiques. If there's a sale, I wouldn't mind picking up a bit of Canton."

Lucy bit her tongue. "Here we are," she declared, pulling up to the front door. "Shall I let you out here so you can wait inside while I park the car?"

Miss Tilley gave her a disdainful look. "I am fit as a fiddle," she proclaimed. "In fact, Rachel and I take a constitutional every day." Lucy knew that Rachel Goodman was Miss Tilley's part-time caregiver, providing light housekeeping and meals as well as companionship.

"Okay, then." Lucy drove on to the parking lot, and the two women walked past the flower beds to the door. "Why do they use that awful bark mulch everywhere?" demanded Miss Tilley. "It's not good for the soil, or the plants."

"Keeps down the weeds," offered Lucy, "and looks neat."

"It's a cover-up," snapped Miss Tilley. "Who knows what's lurking underneath?"

Lucy smiled in agreement. These days, it seemed a lot of covering up was going on. The question was what to continue to conceal and what to reveal, always bearing in mind that she was covering real people with real problems. When they reached Millicent's room, however, it appeared that the woman with the most problems swirling around her was doing just fine.

"Did you come to visit me?" she asked coyly, responding to their knock. "How lovely! Do come in. I'll give you a tour, and then we can go down to the café. It's almost like being in Paris."

Lucy indeed remembered the basement café, which featured bistro chairs and tables and had a mural depicting a Parisian scene. "That would be lovely," she murmured, stepping inside Millicent's room, which was filled to bursting with her precious treasures.

"As you can see, it's much smaller than my house, but I've managed to bring quite a bit with me. And now," she added, with a wave of her hand, "I don't have to clean or worry about what I'm going to eat; it's all taken care of. It's like living in a fancy hotel."

Miss Tilley plunked herself down in a rocking chair, and Lucy perched herself on a needlepoint hassock, while Millicent pointed out the treasures she'd been allowed to bring with her. "They wouldn't let me bring my bed, my four-poster," she complained, indicating the hospital bed. "But I have my candlewick spread, and the patchwork shams, so I've managed to make it look homey." She paused, then narrowed her eyes suspiciously. "Cassie says she'll bring over the Civil War quilt, but I'm starting to think she has other plans for it . . ."

"I see you have your *Mayflower* chest," offered Lucy, as a distraction.

"Ah, yes." Millicent pressed her lips together. "The staff

here, well, they're not quite up to snuff, they've been using that spray furniture polish . . ."

"Oh, no!" exclaimed Miss Tilley.

"I'm afraid so," confirmed Millicent, with a knowing nod. "They insist it won't do any harm but . . ."

"Well, that's flat-out wrong," said Miss Tilley.

"There's nothing I can do about it," said Millicent, expressing defeat, and Lucy got the sense she knew more about her situation than she let on. "But they have been quite good about the things in the cabinet." She indicated a glass-fronted curio cabinet that was filled with colorful Sandwich glass, a scrimshaw whale's tooth, the silver "Revere" teapot, and a large tree fungus carved with the initials MB and WB enclosed in a heart. "I've asked them not to touch them and they haven't."

"If you ask me, that's because they're lazy," observed Miss Tilley.

Millicent seated herself in the other chair in the room, a Windsor armchair, and sighed. "I suppose you're right," she admitted, going on to add, "My Darleen, now, she complained and grumbled, but she did take cleaning seriously. She did know how to make a bed properly and wouldn't dream of washing a pot before the glassware. It was glasses, silver, china, and then the pots."

"But you were quite angry with her, weren't you? You admitted that you were trying to poison her."

Millicent looked at her with tired eyes; her smile was gone, her face had fallen, and she looked every bit of her eighty-plus years. "I did give her the tea, but I only wanted her to be sick, and in pain. She was so big and healthy, and I thought if I could weaken her, then I could get her to stop taking my things."

Lucy wondered if that was true or if Millicent had actually paid attention to her lawyer and was following his advice. "It must have been a shock when you found her dead," prompted Lucy.

"Oh, my, it certainly was. I had dozed off; I do that now and then, and when I woke up, there was no sign of her, you know, only a half-drunk cup of tea by the recliner she used to sit in to watch TV. I heard some noises from the cellar, so I figured she was down there doing laundry. I went into the kitchen to wash the teacups, and I noticed the cellar door was open. I thought she was going to start the dryer, which makes an annoying sound, so I went to close it. I do hate an unlatched door, don't you? So I was closing the door, and I saw that she was lying there on the floor at the bottom of the cellar steps. At first, I thought she had fallen down the stairs, and I hurried down, and that's when I realized she was gone and that the tea had killed her. What a problem! Then I remembered the freezer, and well, you know the rest."

"But now we know your tea was harmless. Someone else killed her." Lucy reached out and patted Millicent's hand. "Did she often have visitors?"

"You're a sharp one, Lucy Stone," said Millicent, with a smirk. "She had plenty of men friends; they'd come in the evening, after I went to bed. I used to hear them, grunting and groaning..." She paused to sniff in disapproval. "They sounded like pigs, like the pigs on my grandpapa's farm." She shook her head. "No better than pigs. She thought she was fooling me, but I knew what she was up to." She gave a righteous little nod. "That's another reason why I gave her the tea. I thought it would slow her down in the man department."

"Do you know who these men were?" asked Lucy, thinking one of them must have been the killer.

Millicent raised her eyebrows in indignation. "Of course not!" she declared. "I would never! What an idea!"

Lucy assumed from her response that she had indeed spied on Darleen, but would probably never admit it even under pain of torture. Nevertheless, she thought it was worth a try. "Perhaps inadvertently, without meaning to," began Lucy. "Perhaps if you couldn't sleep and came down to the kitchen for some warm milk."

"I have never had any trouble sleeping," insisted Millicent. "I have a clear conscience."

Lucy found this statement rather shocking and glanced at Miss Tilley, who gave the tiniest shrug.

"In our day," Miss Tilley said by way of explanation, with a tilt of her head that included Millicent, "sex without marriage was an absolute taboo. My father considered my honor his greatest treasure."

"My father, too," added Millicent, in a wistful tone. "What he would have made of Darleen I simply don't know."

Lucy noticed that Millicent seemed to be running out of steam; it was time for her and Miss Tilley to say their goodbyes.

"I do hope you'll come again," she pleaded, taking Miss Tilley's hand and looking at her old friend with watery eyes.

"Of course, I will," promised Miss Tilley, shocking Lucy by giving her old friend a hug. It was likely the first, and probably the last time, she'd ever done such a thing.

Out in the hall, Lucy teased her. "I never knew you to be all touchy-feely."

"I do feel badly for Millicent, such a muddle she's made for herself." She was thoughtful as they walked toward the elevator. "She was living in the past, and suddenly she's been yanked into the present, and now she's struggling like a fish out of water."

A fish out of water, thought Lucy, as they got in the elevator. Tim could be described like that, too. He had been trapped in his own reality and had attempted to escape his demons by constant walking and marching. He was always on the move, night and day, she remembered, as the elevator doors opened and they stepped into the sun-filled lobby. What had he seen as he roamed through the night? He had been peeking at Darleen, and she wondered if he'd observed any of Darleen's nocturnal callers?

When Lucy delivered Miss Tilley to her little gray-shingled Cape-style house, she found Rachel had invited Pam to join them for lunch. They were soon gathered at the table and enjoying Rachel's homemade fish chowder. Lucy sprinkled in a handful of oyster crackers and asked Pam about Tim. "How's he doing?"

"He's putting all his energy into the summit," offered Pam. "I think it's a good thing. He seems much better."

"Would it be okay for me to interview him?" asked Lucy, angling for an opportunity to question him about Darleen. "Get an update about the summit?"

"Sure," said Pam. "You can find him at the house. He's turned the basement into summit headquarters."

"Is Jane Goodall really coming?" asked Miss Tilley, in a hopeful tone.

Pam laughed. "Tim is very persistent," she said. "I think she'll have to come simply to get him to stop pestering her."

"I'd love to see her in person," admitted Miss Tilley, somewhat starry-eyed. "I remember reading about her and Doctor Leakey in *National Geographic*. She was such an inspiration, studying chimpanzees in the African jungle. Girls—and she was really just a girl back then—didn't do things like that. She was such an inspiration to a little librarian like myself."

"Librarians can be inspirational, too," said Rachel. "You gave quite a few girls the encouragement they needed to pursue their dreams."

"Oh, bosh," sniffed Miss Tilley dismissively, but her cheeks had grown rather rosy.

Full of chowder and cranberry muffins, Lucy gave Pam a ride home, where she hoped to find Tim. Stepping inside, they were blasted with loud rock music. Pam shrugged and covered her ears, pointing to the cellar door. There was no point trying to call Tim's name—he'd never hear her—so Lucy went on down. He looked up from his computer with a curious expression. "Can I help you?"

"I hope so," said Lucy, patting her ears. "Do you mind turning down the music?"

"Okay, Mrs. Stone," he said, and the noise dropped about fifty decibels. "I'm kind of busy," he said, turning back to his computer.

"I understand. In fact, that's why I'm here. I just want to get an update on the climate summit."

"I, um, gave you all the information when I came to the office," he said.

"Right," agreed Lucy. "But I have a few questions." Glancing about, she took in a scene of absolute chaos. Papers and books were strewn everywhere in the finished basement; several computer monitors were set up, and a whiteboard listed "things to do." "Wow, you've really got a lot going on."

"Yeah. I'm kinda busy, so . . ."

"Okay, Tim," began Lucy, deciding there was no point pretending she was there to ask about the summit, "I've got some questions about the night Darleen was killed, and I hope you can help me."

Tim gave her a guarded look. "I don't know anything about that."

Seeing no possibility of sitting on a chair, as they were all covered with mountains of papers, Lucy sat down on a step that was one up from the bottom. "I know you spent a lot of time walking through town, and I wonder if you saw anybody visiting Darleen, that's all."

"There's a lot to do; we've got bands coming, maybe Jane Goodall. It's really important, you know."

"I know, but if you're arrested, you won't be able to work on the summit, right?"

"I've been trying to get the tent people to donate the tent, or at least give us a break on the price, and the parking is going to be a problem. We'll need volunteers to show people where to park. Do you think Mr. Stone would help with that?"

"Probably," said Lucy, hoping to steer him back to the night in question. "He can also do construction stuff if you need it."

"That'd be great. We're gonna need a platform or something. And what about a PA system? Do you know anybody who could do that?"

"I think Sid Finch used to be a roadie for a band."

"Really? Mr. Finch?"

"Yeah. Oyster Outlaws, I think."

"Never heard of them."

"Anyway, he knows about sound systems, and he'd probably help. But, Tim, I need you to focus. Darleen's mother says she had a lot of visitors at night, and you might've seen a car or seen somebody going in her house. Do you remember anything like that?"

Tim was pacing nervously back and forth. "What? You think I'm some sort of peeping Tom?"

"Not at all. But it's normal to be curious about people.

Especially if you know who lives in a house, you might pay a bit of attention if you happen to be passing by. Something might catch your interest, no?"

"It might," admitted Tim, hanging his head.

"So you did notice something?" Lucy's voice was gentle, coaxing.

His eyes went off to the side. "Maybe."

"It's nothing to be ashamed of. Golly, I'm fascinated by lighted windows at night. I'm always trying to catch a glimpse of people's rooms when we're driving through town at night. Pictures on the wall, paint colors, sometimes I see people gathered around a table, there's always that blue light from the TV . . ."

"There was a van," said Tim. "It was parked on the street a few houses over; that's why it caught my eye. Everybody else was parked in their garage or their driveway, but it was parked on the street."

Now that made sense, thought Lucy, with growing excitement. A buyer for the antiques Darleen was hawking might well have a van. "Was it the night she was killed? Are you sure about that?"

"I don't know when she was killed, but I know it was the night after, the night after she, um"—he paused, taking a deep breath—"I was in the lunchroom at the center, and she, um, she was yelling at me . . ."

"Got it, Tim," said Lucy, cutting him off. "That would be the night she died."

"So you think the van belonged to the person who killed her?"

"It could. Do you remember anything distinguishing about the van? The color? Make?"

"It was night, kinda hard to tell. Not black, I know that. And there was a logo on the door. Some letters."

"Like a name?"

"No. Just letters."

"Do you remember which letters?"

"No." He shook his head. "But they were big."

"You've been a big help, Tim," said Lucy, standing up and intending to give him a hug.

Tim neatly evaded the hug, but did allow her to shake his hand.

"Thanks, Tim, and good luck with the summit."

But Tim was already back at one of the computers and had turned up the music. Shaking her head, Lucy climbed back up the stairs, intending to go to the office. But when she stepped out of the house, she encountered Officers Barney Culpepper and Todd Kirwan marching purposefully up the walk. Their cruiser was parked in front of the house.

"Oh, no," she said, standing in the doorway.

"Step aside, Lucy," advised Barney. "We've got an arrest warrant for Tim Stillings. Is he home?"

Lucy nodded, feeling her heart plummet to some interior space where it didn't belong.

Todd was ringing the bell and, predictably, getting no answer. He began pounding on the doorjamb, calling Tim's name. It was only after Barney bellowed, "*Police! We're coming in*!" that Pam appeared.

"Can I help you?" she asked, looking puzzled.

"We're here for Tim," said Barney, holding his hat in his hand and looking miserable.

Pam seemed to go all wobbly for a moment, and Lucy started to reach for her, when Pam straightened her shoulders. "I'll get him," she said. Minutes later, she appeared with a confused-looking Tim.

"Timothy Stillings, I'm arresting you on the charge of

murder. You have the right to remain silent..." began Todd, producing a pair of handcuffs.

Lucy was focused on supporting Pam, reassuring her that everything would be okay, when she remembered she was a reporter and this was news. She had a job to do, so she pulled her phone from her pocket and snapped a photo of the two officers leading Tim to the patrol car. Tears blurred her vision as she tapped the little button, and she brushed them away, catching one final image of Barney gently placing his hand on Tim's head as they got him into the back seat.

"Ohmigod," moaned Pam, watching them go and brushing away tears. "I better tell Ted."

"I'd start with Bob," advised Lucy. "He'll make sure Tim doesn't say anything he shouldn't when they question him."

Pam squeezed Lucy's arm. "Thanks, Lucy." She pulled her cell phone out of her back pocket. "I can't believe this is happening," she said, as she scrolled down her contacts and hit Bob's name. "Just when I thought things were getting better ... oh, hi, this is Pam Stillings. I need to speak to Bob." Lucy heard Bob's receptionist ask what this was in relation to and Pam employed her Mama Bear tone of voice, saying, "This is urgent. I need to speak to him right away."

Lucy was impressed and reassured; it seemed Tim's prosecutors were going to have a fight on their hands.

Chapter Twenty-six

Lucy was thoughtful when she walked to her car, intending to go back to the office to write up her account of Tim's arrest. As she walked, she decided she'd better check in with Ted.

"We were expecting this," he admitted, sounding defeated. "Pam's already got Bob on board. He's on his way to the police station."

"That's good," said Lucy. "He'll make sure Tim's rights are protected." He quickly ended the call, and she started the car, driving slowly through town. Reaching Main Street, she spotted a free parking spot and flicked her blinker on, stopping to back in. Climbing out and preparing to cross the street to the office, she noticed a white van parked in front of the Trading Company. A van with two black letters and an ampersand on the door in a lightly embellished, classy font. N&L, which she knew represented Northcross and Love, the upscale antiques shop next to the Trading Company.

Lucy parked and took a moment to gather her thoughts. Her mind went back to the day she'd dropped into the shop and spoken to Hayden Northcross, asking him about

Nantucket lightship baskets. He'd pleaded ignorance to any recent sales of such a basket but sent her to the local auction houses, which had turned into a bit of a wild goose chase. Had he purposely misdirected her? Had Hayden and his partner, Wayne, the ultrarespectable and highly regarded antiques dealers, been flogging Darleen's family treasures for her?

Instead of going into the office, Lucy crossed the street and strolled past the storefronts, pausing to study the cashmere sweaters in harvest tones that had just gone on display in the Trading Company's windows, along with a scattering of fake pumpkins and colorful autumn leaves. Moving on to the antiques shop, she noticed that the display hadn't changed in months. The same pine candlestand and battered sea chest sporting rope handles and blue milk paint that had been there for as long as she could remember were now actually gathering dust. Weird, she thought, aware that the business had a reputation for a brisk turnover. "If you see something you want," she remembered Sue counseling her, "you've got to grab it because it won't be there tomorrow." Lucy hadn't bothered to mention that she couldn't possibly afford anything that Northcross and Love were selling because Sue was defending her impulsive purchase of a set of utterly charming, and very expensive, French plates depicting the four seasons. "If I'd waited, hoping the price would drop, I would've lost them," Sue said, proudly displaying the bucolic scenes featuring beautiful people gathering apples, ice skating, picnicking, and boating.

Perhaps prompted by the memory of the plates, with their old-fashioned country images, she thought of the Tasha Tudor watercolors that were on display in the town library. She remembered the party proudly celebrating their presentation by Hayden Northcross and Wayne Love, and how Darleen had frustrated her attempt to interview the two. As she recalled, Darleen had rudely thrust herself between Lucy and the antiques dealers and had dragged them away from the party celebrating their generosity. What had been so urgent that she had to talk to them? It was well known that the two men loved a party, especially one in their honor, so it must have been something very important, meaning most likely something very profitable, that would have caused them to agree to the early departure.

She was now passing the police station, where she paused yet again and thought of poor Tim, probably undergoing questioning in an interview room. Or perhaps already confined in a cell, having been photographed and fingerprinted. What a terrible turn of events, especially considering his fragile mental status. Pam and Ted would certainly be beside themselves with worry, terrified for Tim and what his future might hold. She was standing there, fretting, when a voice broke into her thoughts. "Lucy! Is everything okay?"

Snapping to attention, Lucy saw Officer Sally looking at her with an anxious expression on her face. "Just worried about Tim."

"Yeah. What a shame. But don't worry, he's well-represented. Bob Goodman's with him." Lucy noticed Sally was out of uniform, dressed in jeans and a pink hoodie.

"Will they hold him?" she asked.

Sally shrugged. "I don't know." She bit her lip. "From what I've heard, it's a pretty shaky case, but Aucoin is determined to wrap this thing up. Dismemberment and an old lady don't look good; he wants it over."

"Who can blame him?" She gave a weak smile. "The Chamber of Commerce must be all over him."

"Oh, yeah," agreed Sally.

"You know," began Lucy, somewhat tentatively, "I've been thinking . . ."

"Oh, no," moaned Sally, in mock horror.

"Have you got a minute? We could get some coffee . . ."

"A glass of wine?" suggested Sally. "I'm off duty."

It was a bit early for her, but Lucy quickly agreed. "My treat."

Together they walked down to Sea Street and the harbor, where Cali Kitchen was perched on one side of the parking lot. Upon entering, they were greeted with a big welcoming smile by the proprietor, Matt Rodriguez, and shown to a quiet table in the bar. While they waited for their wine to be served, Lucy dove right in, speaking her thoughts as she struggled to make sense of the memories and impressions that had been flooding into her mind.

"It's like this. Millicent says Darleen had lots of gentlemen callers, and she thought it was sex, lots of groaning and moaning, but I just don't see it."

"Why? Darleen was human; humans have sex."

"But Tim saw the Northcross and Love van parked outside. They could've been moving furniture around, digging out Millicent's valuable stuff."

Sally laughed, and Lucy blushed, realizing she sounded rather ridiculous. "Sex? Moving furniture?" She paused, while the server set two glasses of chilled sauvignon blanc on the table, then raised her glass in a toast. "I think there's quite a difference, Lucy, but here's to whatever turns you on."

Lucy clinked her glass against Sally's. "Well, trust me, money seems to have been a lot more exciting to Darleen than sex." She took that first delicious sip. "And we know she was stealing her mother's treasures and selling them to somebody . . ."

"And why not somebody local, like Northcross and Love," offered Sally. "But it's a far cry from swindling an old lady to murder."

"Crooks fall out all the time," said Lucy.

"In the movies," said Sally.

"Yeah. Well, cousin Cassie has discovered that Millicent's very valuable Civil War quilt has been replaced with a fake." Lucy took another sip of wine. "And Cassie also says that Darleen would have drawn the line at stealing the quilt. What if . . ."

"Her fence, in this case Northcross or Love or both of them," began Sally, growing somewhat animated under the influence of the wine, which she'd drunk rather rapidly, and now signaling for a refill, "wanted the quilt, and she refused, and a fight ensued and she got killed?"

"Well," suggested Lucy, somewhat defensively, "it's not as farfetched as it sounds. Especially if they'd invested time and money in a fairly decent facsimile. They'd want their money back." She took another sip of wine.

"Oh, yes, it is. Extremely farfetched," said Sally, as the server arrived with her wine and removed the empty glass.

In response to the server's offer of another glass, Lucy shook her head. "Okay, forget about the possibility of murder. What about the quilt? I did some research, and it's worth hundreds of thousands of dollars. There are only fifteen of these quilts in existence, and that makes it really valuable. And Millicent found the fake quilt stuffed in the dryer when she discovered Darleen's body."

"Hundreds of thousands of dollars?" Sally was well into her second glass. "It may be the wine talking," she admitted, "but you're starting to make sense. I suppose there could have been a struggle over the quilt." She leaned across the table. "So what do you suggest?"

"We need to get into that shop and look around."

"For that, my dear, we'd need a search warrant, and no judge is going to agree just because somebody's got a hunch. We'd need probable cause."

"Well, then," said Lucy, undaunted, "we'll need Plan B."

The next morning, Lucy took special care with her appearance, applying an extra-generous dollop of moisturizer to her face and dressing in her good slacks, a silk blouse, and a nubby tweed cardigan Sue had insisted she buy when she spotted it on sale at the outlet mall. Feeling a bit as if she were preparing for battle, she added the pearl necklace and chunky gold bracelet she'd inherited from her mother. She fumbled a bit with the safety clasp on the bracelet, remembering how her mother always wore a spritz of Arpège and popped a Chiclet in her mouth before going out for an afternoon matinee or lunch with friends. Repeating the ritual, Lucy squirted some Lauren fragrance on her neck and, transferring her wallet, phone, and lipstick from her everyday bag to her best purse, she discovered a crumpled tube of Mentos. She popped a few in her mouth in memory of Mom as she descended the stairs.

She felt nervous as she drove to town and rehearsed the plan she and Sally had worked out in her mind. Were they crazy? Was Sally going to get in trouble for . . . for what? It would be best, she thought, if it all came to nothing, if Northcross and Love had not risen to the bait and had left the shop no poorer and no wiser and had gone on about their day. That was what she hoped would be the case, sort of. On the other hand, if her hunch proved to be true, Tim would be free and clear.

Her spirits rose as she proceeded along Main Street and

spotted Sally's cruiser parked in front of the store. Most likely scenario, she'd go in, she'd come out, she'd signal Sally with a shake of her head, and Sally would drive off to catch speeders on Route 1. In the other scenario, the one that kept her awake all last night, she'd text Sally, who would back her up, drawing her gun, if necessary. Buoyed somewhat by the thought that help was nearby, that she was not venturing into the dragon's cave alone, she parked behind the cruiser. Climbing out, she straightened her shoulders, gave Sally a little wave, and crossed the sidewalk. She took a deep breath and pulled the door open, not sure what she would find in the shop.

What she found was Hayden Northcross, a blue linen apron over his usual button-down shirt and chinos, polishing a huge silver ladle while standing behind the old general-store counter that had been buffed to a shine and repurposed. "Hi, Lucy, you look very nice today," he said, appraising her outfit. "Something special going on?"

"Actually," said Lucy, attempting a confidential attitude, "as it happens, I came into a little inheritance."

Hayden licked his lips. "Just the sort of thing I love to hear." He paused and appraised her pearls with his glance. "That is a lovely necklace."

"This old thing," said Lucy, dismissively. "The money, well, just between you and me, it's quite a windfall, came out of the blue. So my husband, bless him, said I should use it to buy something special. Something to remember Aunt Helen by."

"Bill is a true gentleman," said Hayden. "What a lovely thought. Did Aunt Helen have any special interests?"

"As a matter of fact, she did," said Lucy. "She was very interested in what she called 'the unappreciated artistry of women who practiced traditional crafts.' You know, samplers and hooked rugs and all the homely arts. She used to say knitting a pair of argyle socks was every bit as challenging as sculpting a nude."

"I think I would have liked Aunt Helen," said Hayden. "Can you give me an idea of how large a splurge you have in mind? You don't have to be specific, but a ballpark figure would be helpful."

Lucy paused, attempting to appear reluctant to discuss anything as crass as a dollar figure. "Well," she drawled out the word, "a bit over a hundred."

"Dollars?" asked Hayden, somewhat discouraged.

"Oh, no. Thousands."

His eyebrows rose, and he gave a nod. "A significant amount," he said, impressed. "As it happens, I don't have any argyles, but I do have something that might appeal; it's a rather nice hooked rug. It's a primitive, with some very charming cows and sheep, also a rabbit. Would you like to see it?"

"Yes, I would," said Lucy, hoping he might lead her into the back room, where who knew what she might find.

"I'll be right back," said Hayden, dashing her hopes and disappearing through the door, which he closed carefully behind him. In a moment, he was back, with the rug, which he laid out lovingly on the counter. The door to the back room, she noticed, had now been left ajar.

Lucy reached out to finger the wool and smiled at the cow, which smiled back. "It's lovely," she began, "but rather, um, well, it would be very nice in a child's room, but I'd like something a bit more meaningful, more historical."

"But this is the very definition of historical. Look at the colors. These are all natural dyes. The maker gathered pokeberries and goldenrod and such and brewed up her own dyes, which she used to color the wool she spun, shorn from her own sheep. Sheep like these," he said, stabbing at the small flock in the upper-right corner. "It's a record of her world, the world around her." He paused. "And I can give you a very good price." Lucy smiled indulgently. "I do appreciate that. I do. But it just doesn't speak to me. And honestly, I can pick up something similar at an estate sale for much less money. I'm looking for something significant connected to our nation's history. Something that will be a good investment and will grow in value."

"Ah, I couldn't help overhearing," said Wayne Love, Northcross's partner, coming out from the back room and joining them. Like his partner, he was a pleasant-looking middle-aged man who took good care of his appearance and dressed in preppy styles. He was less conservative than Hayden, however, choosing Nantucket red slacks and socks featuring whales or lobsters. "I think we may have just the thing for you, Lucy." Pulling Hayden aside, he murmured something in his ear, something which made Hayden react negatively, shaking his head. It looked to Lucy that this might just be the opening she needed.

"You've got something special back there, don't you?" teased Lucy. "Can't I take a peek?"

Wayne gave her a wink and disappeared through the doorway, followed at top speed by a flustered and agitated Hayden. Deciding it was better to be safe than sorry, Lucy reached for her phone and dialed Sally, speaking in a whisper. "Something's going down, I think. You better come in."

A sudden thud confirmed her suspicion that something was indeed going down in that back room. Cautiously, she stepped around the counter to the door, still ajar, and peeked inside. The two partners were clearly arguing, although keeping their voices low. Hayden was glaring at Wayne, shaking his head and waving his arms. Wayne's posture was defensive, but he seemed to be arguing, insisting that he was right.

Realizing the cell phone was still in her hand, Lucy activated the video app.

"Not a good idea . . ." Hayden hissed.

"She said she's got a hundred thousand."

"Not enough, trust me. We can get more."

"But it's risky. This is the bird in the hand. We get rid of it, and we get a good price."

"She's bluffing. If she does have that money, trust me, she's not going to spend it on that." Northcross tilted his head toward the storage drawers and shelves that stood against the back wall. "She'll tell her husband; he'll stop payment on the check, and Lucy's inheritance will end up in a Seamen's Bank CD."

"She wants to invest in a significant antique; that's what she said, and that's what we've got. They're probably much richer than you think. Like Franny Small. You'd never guess she's got millions and millions tucked away. It's the Yankee way. They don't flaunt their wealth. He's a contractor; they've got that big house, and they strike me as people who've been socking their money away." Wayne let out a frustrated sigh. "They're empty nesters, and now she's got an inheritance. And the, you know, is exactly what she's looking for."

"Exactly!" proclaimed Hayden. "A little too perfect, if you ask me. Don't forget, she's a reporter. An investigator. This might be a trap."

"Don't be idiotic," scoffed Wayne. "Like she's got the brains . . ."

"Did you call me an idiot?" demanded Hayden, eyes blazing.

"Well, turning down the possibility of a big sale is kind of idiotic," insisted Wayne, with a dismissive shrug. He turned to pull open one of the storage drawers ranged along the back wall, and Hayden grabbed his arm, just below the shoulder. "Let go!" Wayne snarled, angrily, yanking his arm free.

The two were at a standoff, glaring at each other, until Wayne bent down and pulled a quilt from the drawer. A sad and tired old thing that Lucy recognized, with a jolt, as the genuine Civil War quilt. She felt a tap on her shoulder and turned, seeing Sally had arrived, and put a finger to her lips. Together, they watched and listened through the crack.

"Drop it!" warned Hayden, attempting to grab the quilt.

"No! I'm not going to lose this sale," snarled Wayne. "This is our chance to get rid of the damn thing. It's evidence, you know. It could be used against you."

"That's why I want to wait," said Hayden, hissing. "Let the kid take the rap for killing that bitch. Once he's convicted, I'll be safe. That's when we can approach buyers. Discreet buyers who don't go boasting about their acquisitions to their girlfriends."

The two women's eyes locked. Sally started to draw her gun, but Lucy restrained her, indicating her cell phone, which she was using to record the incriminating scene.

"We can't wait, Hayden. We need the money now," said Wayne. Hayden shook his head but didn't offer any resistance. Wayne took this as assent and turned toward the door, quilt in hand, only to be grabbed from behind by Hayden, who had him by the neck. The quilt dropped to the floor as Wayne struggled to loosen his partner's grip. Lucy watched, horrified, as Hayden's grip grew stronger and Wayne seemed to weaken. She was about to attempt to intervene when Sally pushed her aside, yanked the door open wide, and drew her gun. "Police, hands up!" she yelled, legs apart, raising the gun with outstretched arms, ready to fire. "I said hands up," she ordered. "Don't make me shoot."

"That won't be necessary," said Hayden, releasing his partner, who fell to the floor, clutching his neck, and chest heaving as he struggled to breathe.

A commotion in the front of the store signaled the arrival of Officers Todd Kirwan and Barney Culpepper. "What's going on here?" demanded Barney, taking in the scene. Hayden was standing with his hands over his head; Wayne was still prone and gasping for breath, atop the crumpled quilt.

"I'm arresting Hayden Northcross for assault, we need an ambulance for Wayne Love, and we've got to collect that quilt for evidence," said Sally.

"Okay," said Todd, clearly amused by his younger cousin's command of the situation.

"I've got it all on my cell phone, including Hayden's confession," said Lucy. "He killed Darleen."

"I'm innocent!" declared Hayden, as Todd snapped the handcuffs on his wrists. "You'll never convict me!"

Wayne was sitting up now, glaring at his partner. "You tried to kill me. I'm not going down for any of this, not after what you did to me," he said, gathering up the quilt and turning to the officers. "I'm ready to talk."

Later that afternoon, when Lucy was writing up the arrest in the *Courier* office, she got a call from Pam. "Tim's been released," she crowed. "No charges."

"That's great," said Lucy, feeling a great load had suddenly been lifted from her shoulders. "What a relief."

"Bob said somebody else is being investigated for the murder . . ."

"Did he say who?"

"I didn't think to ask," said Pam. "I was just so happy that Tim's been cleared."

"How's he doing?" asked Lucy, worried that the experience might have triggered an emotional relapse. "Is he okay?"

"Oh, he went out for a walk," said Pam, with a sigh. "That's Tim being Tim."

"Well, that's all right then," said Lucy, ending the call with the feeling that, for a brief while, anyway, all was well.

Epilogue

It was the day before Thanksgiving, and Lucy was distracted, trying to finish up her stories so she could get home to prepare for the holiday. Sara and Zoe were both coming home, and Zoe was bringing someone she wanted her parents to meet. Lucy was juggling a number of emotions: anticipation and high hopes that this someone was the one for Zoe, a desire to put the family's best face forward to this person, and anxiety that the dinner she was cooking would be extra-specially delicious. Plus, she thought it would be a good idea to whisk around the already clean house once again with a vacuum and to give the bathrooms a quick lick and a polish.

But, first, she had to finish her account of the select board's last meeting, and she was struggling to decipher her own handwriting in the notes she'd scrawled in her notepad when the bell on the door jangled and Cassie came breezing in. "Hi, ladies, are you ready for Thanksgiving? Pies baked? Turkey stuffed?"

Phyllis, dressed in her favorite Thanksgiving sweater, the one boasting a colorful sequined turkey with a rainbow-colored tail, moaned. "Wilf wants to deep-fry the turkey; he's got a special fryer ready to go in the driveway."

"A lot of people swear by that," said Cassie.

"I have my doubts," confessed Phyllis, looking worried. "And Elfrida's coming with the gang, so we're going to have five hungry kids if it doesn't work."

"If I were you, I'd stock up on some frozen pizzas," advised Lucy, who had decided that loop was indeed a *y* and was clicking away on her keyboard. "What brings you in, Cassie?"

"Oh, just a classified ad. We sold Auntie's house, and now we're having an estate sale."

This caught Lucy's interest. "All those antiques?"

"A few, but the really good stuff that Darleen hadn't got around to selling will be auctioned. The sale is mostly household stuff, useful things like linens and kitchen items."

"What about the Civil War quilt?" asked Lucy.

"Auntie's donating it to the Tinker's Cove Historical Society. She said that's the best thing."

"I have to say I'm a little bit surprised . . ." said Lucy, who was peering at her screen, cleaning up some typos.

"It was Miss Tilley who convinced her." Cassie pulled a sheet of folded paper from her purse and handed it to Phyllis. "Here's the ad. How much do I owe you?"

Phyllis counted the words and gave her a price, which Cassie promptly paid. "Well, I'm off. I've got a turkey to cook . . . have a Happy Thanksgiving."

"You, too," said Lucy, giving Cassie a little goodbye wave before turning back to her computer and hitting send. "One down, one to go, and then I'm out of here," she declared. "I've just got the climate action shindig."

"Bit of a bust, if you ask me," complained Phyllis. "I went to see Jane Goodall, and maybe one of her chimps, and all I got was a Zoom."

"They had a giant screen," said Lucy. "And there was footage of the chimps . . ."

"Old footage, in Africa."

"What did you expect? They're not pets; they're wild creatures. Her work was to learn about them and, now, protect them. And the planet. I thought she was great."

"I wonder what she uses on her skin," mused Phyllis. "She's no spring chicken, and she looks really good."

"Probably good, clean living," observed Lucy, chuckling. "You gotta admit, the fair was a big success. They had an overflow crowd, and people really got motivated. The select boards in both the Cove and Gilead have passed resolutions calling for solar panels on town buildings and replacing aged vehicles with electric models. It makes sense; those vehicles can charge overnight, when they're not used."

"All that's gonna cost a mint. Taxes are gonna go up."

"Maybe, maybe not. The town committees are pressing our state and national reps to take action, including funding for projects that reduce carbon emissions."

"I'll believe it when I see it," grumbled Phyllis, turning to see whose arrival the jangling bell was announcing.

"Sounds like too much gabbing and not enough working," declared Ted, marching directly to his desk and firing up his PC. "It's a deadline, not a guideline. I don't want any delays; we've got a ton of holiday ads in this issue."

"I'm on it, Ted. I've just got the Climate Action Summit story to do."

"Be sure to give Tim plenty of credit," he advised, shrugging out of his jacket and clicking his mouse, opening a file for editing.

"How's he doing? Resting on his laurels?" asked Phyllis.

"Not Tim. He's back home and doing great. We finally got him a new therapist, who says he's on the Autism spectrum, which explains a lot. She's changed his meds, got him working on social skills, and it's made a huge difference. He's interviewing for a couple of jobs; the art museum in Portland has asked him back for a second interview. They were real impressed with his work on the Climate Action Summit."

"Wow, Ted, that's great," said Lucy, who was clicking away on her computer. "How many inches do you want? I've got company coming . . ."

"Twenty ought to do it," he said. "And I want a fresh perspective, since we've already posted Pete's story online."

"Aye, aye, captain," she replied, glancing at the clock and sighing. Maybe Zoe and her special someone would be late . . .

Thanksgiving Day dawned bright and crisp, perfect weather for the annual Turkey Trot. Lucy was covering the 5K race, having left the turkey cooking in the oven. Bill and the others were at the high school football game, rooting for Tinker's Cove against their traditional Thanksgiving rivals, Gilead.

The starter's gun fired, and the runners surged forward; Lucy snapped a couple of photos before moving on to the finish line. Pam was already there, ringing a cow bell and waving a pom-pom she'd saved from her days as a high school cheerleader.

"Hi, Lucy!" she exclaimed. "Tim's running."

"Wow, that's amazing."

"I know. I can hardly believe it." She paused to rattle her cow bell. "This new therapist is fabulous. Tim's finally on the right track."

"Ted says he's interviewing for jobs . . ."

"Oh, yeah, but what's this I hear? Zoe brought home a boyfriend? It must be serious."

"Maybe," admitted Lucy, spotting the pack of runners approaching the finish line.

"Do you like him?" demanded Pam.

"He seems okay," said Lucy, determined to be noncommittal. "But you know Zoe. He could be here today, gone tomorrow."

"But she brought him home to meet you and Bill. That's big, Lucy." Spotting her son, she paused to yell, "C'mon, Tim! You can do it!" Turning back to Lucy, she asked, "What do you think of him? Do you like him?"

"He's big and has a big appetite," said Lucy. "He sure seems to like Zoe . . ."

"Tim! It's Tim! He's in the lead!" screamed Pam, jumping up and down and waving her pom-pom furiously. "C'mon! C'mon!"

Lucy watched, openmouthed, as Tim neared the ribbon across the finish line.

"Get the photo!" yelled Pam, whacking her on the back. "He's gonna win!"

Lucy raised her camera and snapped the picture, catching a smiling Tim Stillings, chest forward, breaking the ribbon, a big smile on his face. She hoped it was a good photo; she had a feeling it was going to be above the fold on the front page of the *Courier*.